THE
CRIME
REPORTER

STEPHEN
KNIGHT

 www.trafford.com
North America & international
toll-free: 1 888 232 4444 (USA & Canada)
fax: 812 355 4082

Dedicated to my children Alison,
Bradley and Michael

"Every great fortune begins with a crime."
— Honoré de Balzac

"Law without reason is criminal."
— Criss Jami

"Never open you mouth unless you're in the dentist chair."
— Sammy Gravano

"The police can be more corrupt than the criminals."
— Steven Magee

"If there is no law there is no crime."
— Gerald Visperas

"Obviously crime pays or there'd be no crime."
— G. Gordon Liddy

"The triumph of anything is a matter of organization."
— Kurt Vonnegut

A dark pick-up truck slowly makes it's way down a dimly lit pot-holed street in the gathering dusk. In the back are several threatening looking young men wearing bandanas and back-to-front baseball caps. They are wielding an assortment of scary looking weapons.

It looks like the latest news footage from Somalia or some other hot spot on the other side of the world. But in fact it is actually a narrow street in south central Los Angeles. A rag tag, Hispanic-Latino gang of young adolescents of Puerto Rican and Mexican parentage are patrolling the streets to see if they can find anyone to intimidate or even maim to emphasize their unfounded claim to the run-down neighbourhood.

These days' criminal activities in America have become so widespread and so far reaching it is unlikely they will ever be reeled in. The only difference between here and the most dangerous places in the world is that the under privileged still have some dignity and the vast majority of them continue to respect the rule of law. However, pressure is mounting and it may well be only a matter of time until the situation gets out of control and anarchy becomes a reality.

SAT JUL 22

There was an assortment of empty bottles and an overflowing ashtray on the coffee table in front of the couch I was dozing on at my Ex's apartment in North Redondo Beach.

She occasionally enjoyed my company while she continued to search for 'The One'.

I was woken by the apartment door squeaking open and could see a shaft of light gradually getting wider, shadows appearing and disappearing in the doorway. I checked my watch and it was just before midnight.

Knowing what could well be happening. I slipped my loafers on, grabbed my backpack with my stuff in it and stealthily made my way through the kitchen and out of the door. I figured the assailants had likely picked the lock and were making their way over to where I'd been snoozing, likely with their weapons out.

I started to tremble with fear as I raced down the brightly lit hallway and upon reaching the stairs flew down them two at a time. No one seemed to be following me as I made my way out of the building to where my trusty old Buick was parked.

I dumped my backpack on the passenger seat and gunned it out of the parking lot.

I hoped Sally my ex would be alright because it was me they were after, not her.

It was a mystery how these killers had found me again so soon but why they were looking to kill me wasn't. I was thinking *it looks like I continue to be a target since I'd stuck my nose in where it wasn't wanted.*

* * * *

What had happened was. As I was leaving Jules, my favourite bar, in the early hours of a Sunday morning. I noticed an unmarked cube van across the road in the parking lot of a bar called Ernie's.

I quickly got my car and parked so I had a good view of the parking lot. I didn't have to wait long before I saw two men and a young woman come out and get into the van. Several men who'd been waiting outside quickly piled in as it drove off.

I began to follow it knowing what I was doing could be dangerous.

I followed it along several downtown streets past Echo Park onto Highway 101 North. Through the Hollywood Hills onto Highway 170 passing through Universal City and the San Fernando Valley.

After travelling for quite a distance it turned off onto Highway 118 heading towards Simi Valley. Eventually turning south into Topanga Canyon until it reached the Chatsworth Reservoir northwest of Los Angeles.

Undoubtably on the way the men in the van had viciously raped and murdered the young woman I'd seen leaving Ernie's.

If I kept following them I was going to be front and centre when they dumped the dead body. I just hoped I had kept far enough back surrounded by other cars that the driver of the van wouldn't have noticed me.

However here beside the reservoir it was going to be difficult to conceal myself even though I'd turned my car lights off.

It was very dark the only light coming from the van's taillights. I could occasionally see them being obscured by someone walking in front of them.

The van hadn't been parked long when it suddenly turned and headed back towards where I was parked, it's high beams turned on.

I was no longer in my car having crawled out as soon as I saw the van turn around. The van didn't wait long before navigating around my car and continuing along the trail leaving me lying in the grass in complete darkness.

Using my mobile phone which I was fortunately able to get a signal on. I called 911 and gave them details of where I was and what was going on, before getting back into my car and waiting.

Not long after a police patrol car with flashing lights and it's siren blaring pulled up beside me.

I rolled the window down and after turning his siren off the police officer asked me if I had made the call. I said I had and told him he should proceed further up the trail where he would likely find the dead body of a young woman.

His patrol car followed by two other newly arrived police cruisers with their flashing lights on, but sirens off, headed further up the trail. I really didn't want to see the body so stayed where I was and noticed it was almost three o'clock by the clock on the dash. Several more police cruisers with flashing lights passed by and an ambulance.

I figured I should stay where I was, until someone talked to me and not long after I could see a police car returning down the trail, it's flashing lights turned off. It stopped in front of my car. I got out and walked over to speak to the police officer who was getting out.

"Could I have your license and registration please?" he asked as if this was a routine traffic stop.

I said "I can give you them but do you need to be so formal? Can I just tell you why I'm out here in the middle of nowhere at this ungodly hour!"

"You can. But first I need to see your papers" replied the officer.

I went back to my car and fumbled around in the glove box and found the small folder that contained my so called 'papers' and went back over and handed them to the officer.

He looked at them, jotted a few things down and said "So Mr. Walsh please tell me why you are parked out here by the Chatsworth Reservoir in the middle of the night?"

He obviously didn't know who I was so I wasn't sure how to play this. Get into the full scenario of what had been going on since the beginning of the year or just tell him what had happened during the last few hours. I decided to keep it simple.

I said "I saw an abduction in progress downtown and followed their van out here. That's why I'm here. I assume you've found the dead body of a young woman?"

"Yes we have but this has been a body dumping ground for years. Do you have any information that might be useful to us?" the officer asked.

"I know there is usually five of them. Unfortunately, because I kept my distance and my eyes aren't that good at night anymore, I was unable to make out their license plate number. By the way did you see a white cube van on your way here?" I asked.

"No" said the police officer handing my papers back to me and asking me for my phone number.

I thought about telling him everything but given I'd decided to keep it simple thought better of it and asked him if I could go?

"Yes" he said while opening the door to his patrol car no doubt mystified as to why I was out here and how I'd known it was an abduction.

As I started to drive off I was thinking I hope the police don't consider me as a suspect.

That night it would seem even though I didn't get the killer's license plate number they got mine and from it have identified me and have been trying to shut me up ever since.

*   *   *   *

After negotiating several local streets. I took the southbound on ramp onto the Pacific Coast Highway not knowing where I was going and once I was sure I wasn't being followed, not wanting to draw attention to myself, I slowed to a steady pace.

I took a cigarette out of a soft pack in my shirt pocket and lit it up once the car cigarette lighter heated up sufficiently and it immediately began to calm me.

Being a crime reporter had it's moments and this was yet another.

I was thinking *that it was only a week ago when I'd been staying at a beach house in Venice Beach owned by my editor and these same killers had caught up with me there too.*

Because I figured this was always a possibility, I'd grabbed my backpack with my stuff in it and made my way along the beach to the very busy boardwalk where I'd quickly melted in with the throng of people enjoying a sunny Saturday afternoon.

The killers would have seen me heading away from them along the beach close to the water, in a tee shirt and shorts. But in their dark suits with automatic weapons slung over their shoulders, would have looked much too conspicuous if they'd followed me.

I figured the killers had picked that day and time to come after me because of the crush of people that were enjoying loud music and making all kinds of noise. Taking me out would have had a very good chance of going unnoticed. Venice Beach being the second largest tourist attraction in California after Disneyland.

I'd spent the afternoon in a quiet bar enjoying a cold beer, while I composed my column. Once it started to get dark I'd doubled back to where my car was parked. In a public parking lot just off the beach, a few blocks from where I'd been staying, for just this eventuality.

That night I was so scared I'd almost driven all the way to the Mexican border before turning back and finding a Starbucks with Wi-fi to e-mail my column in.

*　　*　　*　　*

Since the start of the year young women have been being brutally raped and murdered at an alarming rate. From the information I've been able to glean it seems that they are mainly being snatched downtown and dumped on the outskirts of the city.

Without exception the murdered women when found are naked with no identification or personal belongings and there is very little incentive for the police to spend any time investigating these Jane Doe murders.

No notoriety, fame or publicity can be gained by solving any of them and unless anyone else shows they care by filling out a missing person report. The police are taking the stance why should they and they are quickly becoming unsolved cold cases, sparsely filled evidence boxes, gathering dust in police stations all across Los Angeles County.

The murders are still continuing one every week.

Every weekend for centuries. It has been the custom in the western world for young people to go out and have fun on a Saturday night, frequently ending up with them having too much to drink.

Those responsible for the brutal rapes and murders are taking full advantage of this and have established their own communication network which allows them to pick their victims at random based on the circumstances at the time.

The killers operate in such a way that there is something in it for all of them. A vicious gang bang which seems to make it worthwhile.

They work in five man teams, two of them usually going into the seediest bar they can find that Saturday night, while the remaining team members wait outside next to their white unmarked cube van. They identify a suitable victim, who without exception, is on her own and after quickly assessing the situation phone their boss to get the go ahead.

Whether they get it normally depends upon whether a victim has already been selected that night. If they get the green light they start plying the chosen victim with free drinks and being as complimentary and friendly as they can.

It's always near closing time so they wait until she is ready to leave and offer her a ride and before she knows what's hit her she's bundled into the back of their van.

After speaking to those involved in the recovery of the naked lifeless bodies they say it's usually very clear what has happened to the victims prior to their deaths.

I am a well-known crime reporter, even if I do say so myself, working for the Los Angeles Times. I can only do so much, even though I've been reporting on these murders since they began.

My name is Harry Walsh divorced and happy. I've just had my fifty second birthday. Am in reasonably good shape, try not to drink too much and eat healthy whenever I can.

I have been described as a disheveled George Clooney but personally think I resemble Harrison Ford, when he was younger circa. Indiana Jones and the Temple of Doom. Anyway how I look hasn't got me too far but my ability to write has.

Lately I've been moving around a lot, since I have also become a target of those carrying out the murders. At least with the Internet I can send my column in using Wi-fi.

* * * *

As I continued to drive south I was thinking about *the great afternoon and evening I'd just spent with Sally.*

We'd started out at Naja's famous bar a cobbled together collection of buildings along the Redondo Beach boardwalk, which offered an amazing selection of beer. I'd stuck with a few cans of my regular brew low calorie Michelob Ultra while Sally was much more adventurous trying a selection of weird named beers. The most memorable being Moose Drool and Turbo Dog.

From Najas where we'd spent most the afternoon we'd moved on to Charlie's, a restaurant on the beach that offers complimentary mussels during happy hour.

After getting our fill of mussels, we'd moved on to have a sit-down dinner at a newly opened restaurant called Surf's Up, that Sally had been wanting to try.

We'd both had the seafood grill which was excellent and had shared a bottle of Chianti to wash it down with. We sat overlooking the Pacific Ocean as the sun was setting. It was the end to a perfect day which had been truly wonderful.

It had been an all round fun day so we'd kept it going when we got back to Sally's. I polished off a few more beers and she drank whatever wine she could find chilling in her fridge. An hour or so later when she'd just about passed out I helped her to bed.

*   *   *   *

After thinking about what I'd been doing that afternoon and evening. I realized I'd probably had way too much to drink to be driving around, so took the next off ramp to find a place to crash for what remained of the night.

I'd e-mailed tomorrow's column in earlier in the day using Sally's Wi-fi. A recap of the young women murders to try and keep the heat on those doing the killing.

It didn't take me long until I found what I figured should be an inexpensively priced motel. Got a room and feeling dog tired had my last smoke of the day before crawling into bed.

Not long after falling asleep at the Shamrock Motel near the harbour in San Pedro I was woken by a police siren and my immediate thought was *surely not another young woman murder?*

As I lay there trying to get back to sleep I was thinking *how Los Angeles was a long way from Platteville, Wisconsin where I'd grown up being tutored by my mother. My father was an English teacher so I had no choice but to be good at English.*

Taking great inspiration from authors like Dylan Thomas "… the sun declared war on the butter and the butter ran …" my English essays received high marks so a career involved with writing was always in the cards.

Having got the necessary grades my parents dispatched me off to Greenlee College in Iowa where I obtained a Bachelor of Journalism degree.

My first job after graduation was at the Platteville Journal where I was about as junior as you could get. Working the night shift tasked mainly with ordering supplies for the stationary cupboard and ensuring hot coffee was always available in the lunchroom.

Occasionally I was asked to write a brief report or small story on local petty crimes, which sometimes made it into the seldom read middle pages of the newspaper.

I moved on to better reporting jobs at the Dubuque Telegraph Herald and the prestigious Chicago Tribune. Where I honed my crime reporting skills until at a company Christmas party one year.

I got into a group conversation with some people from the parent company Tribune Publishing and asked tongue in cheek if there were any vacancies at the Orlando Sentinel, another of their newspapers. I said I would love to work in a city with palm trees and a warm climate.

One of them upon hearing this suggested that if I was serious there was currently an opening for a crime reporter at the Los Angeles Times, another newspaper in the Tribune chain. He said he had heard a crime reporter had recently retired and the climate there was perhaps the best in the country.

The rest as they say is history.

SUN JUL 23

It was not until after ten the next morning that I awoke. I brewed some coffee using the in room plastic coffee maker. I lit up a cigarette and opened up my laptop and began to scroll through my contacts to see who I hadn't imposed on yet.

Even though seedy motel rooms are usually quite reasonably priced they are a waste of money if you know someone you can stay with for free. That's the way I looked at it anyway.

There was currently no way I could go back to where I lived at the moment, as those trying to shut me up would likely be watching it.

Unfortunately after going through my contacts and phoning around I'd struck out. So for now I would have to stay here at the Shamrock Motel.

* * * *

Martin Nelson was drinking coffee in the family kitchen of his spacious mansion, in the Pacific Palisades highlands, west of Los Angeles, when to his surprise his mobile phone began to ring.

He rarely received calls on it and was curious to know who was calling.

He picked it up and sheepishly said "Hello"

"Marty, it's Joe" answered the caller.

It was Joe Salvatore, Nelson's Head of Murder Teams.

"This better be good Joe. You know this number is for emergencies only" Nelson replied rather angrily.

"Sorry but one of my murder teams had a problem with the police last night" Joe was saying as Nelson cut him short.

"Stop right there. We need to discuss this in person" Nelson replied still sounding angry.

"But I thought you should know as soon as possible" whispered Joe quietly.

"Enough" Nelson said "I'm hanging up."

After hanging up Nelson immediately called his lawyer Ronald Wells, his eyes and ears, for all matters pertaining to the criminal justice system.

"Ron we need to talk. Can you come over right away?" Nelson asked.

"Yes sure. I'll see you soon" replied Wells.

Ron Wells had been his lawyer since getting him off a promoting prostitution charge back when he was running his escort business in his early days in Los Angeles.

Ron was a fiftyish, confident, rotund, jovial partner in a well-known and respected Los Angeles law firm whose association gave a little more credence to Nelson being an upstanding citizen.

He also phoned Brian, his right hand man and asked him if he could come over right away, to meet with him and Ron, because he was most unhappy with a call he'd just received.

Nelson never liked discussing anything to do with his businesses over the phone. His number one rule being never do anything that might draw attention to his organization.

He prided himself in running a tight ship and couldn't tolerate incompetence. He was constantly preaching doing what had to be done, but if you couldn't, postpone it until you could.

While waiting for Ron and Brian to arrive he was sitting out by his pool, the Pacific Ocean off in the distance. He was wearing a white sleeveless tee shirt showing off two uncharacteristically celebratory tattoos on the outside of each bicep. Likenesses of the two women he was pimping as high priced escorts during his first successful business venture.

He was thinking *about the so-called 'beach house' his parents had in the Hampton's. He had spent most summers there with his mother and sister Millicent. His father joining them on weekends and during the month of August.*

The "beach house" which was more of a lavish mansion was on the south finger of Long Island near East Hampton across the road from the beach and the Atlantic Ocean.

He had spent the summer surfing, playing football and baseball with his sister and their friends. It brought back fond memories of a privileged up bringing in a warm and loving family.

Ron Wells arrived interrupting Nelson's train of thought. He told him that he'd found out that two members of one of Joe Salvatore's murder teams, had been arrested last night and charged with assaulting a police officer, during an abduction that had gone wrong.

Ron indicated the situation had been mishandled due to the fact it turned out the selected victim wasn't alone, as first thought and a struggle had ensued.

Nelson was most upset about this because an opportunity to murder another young woman had been missed and much worse, attention had potentially been drawn to his organization.

This was unacceptable as far as Nelson was concerned. He said he couldn't tolerate such incompetence and those responsible would need to be dealt with.

Brian arrived and joined in the discussion.

Brian James who has only ever been known as Brian, was without doubt Nelson's most loyal friend. He was medium height, tanned with a slim build and had short blonde curly hair. He had a kind of young Mike Love of the Beach Boys, without the beard look.

Brian had met Nelson playing squash, in the recreation center at the apartment complex where they both lived, soon after Nelson arrived in Los Angeles.

One thing that had always stood out about Nelson was how immaculately dressed he always was. Even his squash outfits were ironed to perfection.

Brian had grown up in Santa Monica and knew Los Angeles like the back of his hand, from Malibu to Newport Beach. Since they'd met he'd been like a brother to Nelson and had been very instrumental in getting him settled.

Brian's parents had been 'old money' wealthy. So he'd spent most of his adolescent years in private schools and although they had stretched his intellect they had been very damaging to his soul. Essentially leaving him to endure a family devoid upbringing.

His father seemed to be at work all the time and his mother was a member of so many clubs, she almost forgot she had a husband and an only son.

He had inherited his parent's wealth and their Santa Monica mansion when they had recently passed away just weeks apart and now lived there on his own.

It was only after Brian met Nelson his life had really begun. He was now so dedicated to taking care of him and his businesses that nothing else mattered.

Nelson was like a father figure to him even though they were about the same age. He also knew he was in much too deep now to ever think of doing anything else but why would he when he was enjoying life so much.

He was in his early forties and had the world by the balls, figuratively speaking and 'Bring It On' was his favourite expression.

Nelson asked Brian if he would bail out the two guys who had been arrested early this morning, sometime tomorrow. He suggested he take them and the rest of their murder team out to eat and then have them all killed.

"I hope the pigs are hungry" quipped Brian.

A number of years back when Nelson was getting his organization off the ground, Brian had introduced him to a struggling anti-establishment pig farmer. Brian said he thought they should employ him given the businesses they were getting into.

Nelson knew exactly what he meant and ever since had been paying the pig farmer to be ready at any time day or night to feed his pigs with whatever was dropped off.

The pig farmer explained that pigs are omnivorous and will feast on pretty much anything which Nelson said was perfect.

The arrangement had been working very well so far. Nelson disposing of anybody who was causing problems, hadn't worked out, had screwed up or had potentially damaging evidence against his organization, while at the same time supplementing the pig farmer's income.

As Brian and Ron left Nelson started to swim laps.

A bit about Nelson and his home.

He has always been attuned and alert to potential opportunities and craves challenges even though his golden rule is 'Never rock the boat'.

He tackles problems head-on until they are expeditiously resolved. Never defers anything and is never too busy to listen to anyone who comes to him with a suggestion or problem and in fact encourages it.

On the surface he has no flaws. He keeps his body at it's optimum weight, has never smoked and rarely drinks alcohol, except on celebratory occasions, when he usually only takes a sip or two.

He tries to swim as many robust lengths as he can in his pool every day. He often spends time in his gym doing aerobic exercises or lifting weights. If he has time he walks the perimeter of his significant property and is almost robotic in the way he maintains his healthy eating habits.

He has simple meals.

For breakfast he usually has several coffees and buttered toast which he makes in his family kitchen.

Most days lunch consists of a chicken Caesar or Greek salad.

He likes fish and his dinner frequently consists of a wild salmon plate. Even when he eats out, which is quite rare, he usually orders the fish entre.

He drinks Perrier on ice with most of his meals and on special occasions has a small glass of red wine.

He is suave looking, in his early forties with dark hair and a face that looks like it hasn't been lived in. He has a pale complexion, a slim build and always looks good in whatever he's wearing, especially his tailored suits. He is fastidious about many things including his casual dress clothes and can often be found wearing silk pyjamas late in the day ala Hugh Hefner.

He dresses casually most of the time only dressing up on formal occasions such as fund raising dinners. His casual slacks are tailored, just like his formal suits and every pair has to fit him like a glove or they're soon discarded.

He spends most days working in the office in his home and rarely leaves the premises.

As for his home.

His mansion is built on several acres of prime real estate halfway up the bluffs overlooking the Pacific Ocean. It is a natural plateau with stunning vistas.

The main house is over eight thousand square feet and is adjacent to a number of other buildings including a guest house, living quarters for his support staff and several other structures, including a number of garages.

There is a pool between the main and guest house on the west or Pacific Ocean side of the property. There are various fountains, waterfalls and ponds, interspersed throughout the impressive gardens and a driveway snakes around the front and back of the main house.

There are also expansive lawns and walking paths throughout the property. Rose gardens, flowerbeds and vegetable patches, along with several greenhouses under the imposing bluffs.

Growing up in a Manhattan apartment and spending the summers out at the Long Island 'beach house'. Nelson had always longed for a nice garden and now he had one many times over.

The property was built with the profits from his early illegal ventures and during it's construction, he'd met Rocco Gazzaro, still his Head of Construction to this day.

The flat land to build on the bluffs overlooking the Pacific Ocean in the Pacific Palisades highlands is limited. In order to overcome this during the construction the flat land was significantly increased, by illegally bulldozing behind the property right up against the bluffs.

The officials of Los Angeles County were most perturbed about this at the time. But couldn't do much about it except fine him a sizeable sum which Nelson gladly paid.

With this illegal construction Nelson had fully closed off the back of his property eliminating a dirt track that was planned to become a paved road in the near future.

With the front being a sheer drop from the natural landscape, fences and gates were only needed on the north and south sides of the property, as a result.

It is almost castle like the way it's perched high up on the bluffs providing Nelson with both privacy and protection.

He has a full-time support staff of around twenty. A chef and server who work in the under utilized commercial catering kitchen at the back of the house which boasts industrial style ovens, refrigerators, a walk in freezer and adjoining pantry.

Meals for Nelson, guests and staff are prepared in the commercial kitchen. As well as food for occasional get togethers and other social events.

There are two housekeepers, a handyman, three gardeners, one of whom also takes care of the pool and twelve bodyguards who work in shifts. So there is always at least four of them very close to Nelson at all times. In addition, he has a contract with a security company, to provide at least three guys at all times, at each of the two entrances to his property, all year, around the clock.

The support staff, except for the bodyguards and the guys on the gates, all live on the property. With the exception of one of the housekeepers, some of the bodyguards and the gardeners. The support staff all travel with him whenever he has an extended stay on one of his two luxury yachts, complementing the crew.

He lives on his own. Has never been married. But can often be seen with a stunningly good-looking woman on his arm.

While swimming Nelson was mulling over *why he was purposely targeting the lowest level of society to create a diversion to take the heat off his illicit undertakings, primarily drug trafficking and prostitution.*

He felt strongly that murder was a necessary part of his criminal enterprises because even though the Los Angeles Police Department was a huge organization homicide investigations always took precedence over everything else.

He knew that the people he depended on and trusted the most disagreed with him on the need for these murders. Brian and Ron had both told him to his face on several occasions that he was misguided in his thinking regarding the effect the murders were having.

He, Brian and Ron had discussed the need for the murders at length following the Monday meetings. Both of them telling him that the Los Angeles Police Department were already turning a blind eye to his illicit activities so the murders were unnecessary.

He had suggested that he was doing the community a service by removing a blight on the land getting rid of these homeless and derelict young women. They had responded telling him that this was not always the case.

He had told them that his murder teams were a necessary part of his organization and these murders kept them fresh for when they were needed to deal with people who he needed to get rid of and also to occasionally send his enemies a message not to mention protecting the two of them and himself.

Brian and Ron kind of understood this.

Despite their protestations that they didn't think the murders were necessary he seemed fixated on murdering these hapless unsuspecting young women.

Brian especially thought it was irrational but hadn't been able to change his mind.

Although he was undeniably loyal to him on all other matters he was most uneasy about the murders because it seemed so out of character for Nelson based on the way he had run his affairs over the years and wondered if he was becoming unhinged. It was as if it had become an unthinking obsession that only made sense to him.

The murder teams never argued and were of no help in dissuading him because they were all career criminals who were being well paid to do the one thing they did well and knew what fate awaited them if they ever objected.

Brian did understand that they were a deterrent to everyone in his organization who were not meeting his expectations and although he had looked at the murders from every possible angle he still didn't see a need for them and felt he was being illogical when considering their worth and necessity.

Nelson's perspective was that his murder teams in most cases had proven to be most efficient and effective and having them as part of his organization was an important deterrent to those thinking of ripping him off or bringing attention to his organization.

Whether it had a positive effect on the community as a whole he didn't really know but hoped there were less homeless and hapless young women out on the streets as a result.

He also didn't have any proof that it had taken police focus off his illegal activities but there certainly hadn't been any police interference in any of his businesses since the beginning of the year.

He knew he could trust Brian to do whatever he asked and he would expeditiously have those killed in the murder team in question but the Head of Murder Teams, Joe Salvatore, also had to go.

He had obviously not clearly communicated Nelson's number one message about not drawing attention to the organization to his murder team members or this would never have happened and as he was one of his Heads it was only fair that he should deal with the matter himself.

Brian had already agreed to take care of the murder team who in Nelson's eyes had screwed up but this was something Brian didn't like about working for him. His need to eliminate anyone who might have brought attention to his organization even if as in this case it seems it was unavoidable.

The situation had been out of the murder team's control that resulted in two of them being arrested. It was nothing they had intentionally done or could have undone.

However it was the way Nelson had always operated. He was always the judge and jury deciding on the verdict and sentence.

Joe Salvatore had been a notorious killer in his own right for several decades before joining Nelson's organization.

Regardless of the facts in Nelson's opinion he had screwed up and would have to pay the price.

The question was how?

Nelson was not a killer himself and in fact had never killed anyone but felt he had to take care of this because Salvatore was someone he had personally selected and who reported directly to him.

He certainly didn't want to burden Brian with it. He would however ask Brian to take care of the removal and disposal of the body afterwards.

Nelson had previously done research into different poisons that were unnoticeable in alcoholic drinks usually resulting in the victim collapsing within minutes after it had been consumed.

He still had several of them readily available to him so called Joe Salvatore and asked him to come over and meet with him to discuss the incident last night.

Upon Joe's arrival Nelson invited him into his office and as he sat down asked him somewhat off handily "What his poison was?"

"Bourbon on ice. Thanks" responded Salvatore getting comfortable in one of Nelson's oversized padded leather easy chairs.

"I just need to get some ice" commented Nelson making his way over to the bar and grabbing a bottle of Jack Daniels before leaving his office.

Once he got into his kitchen he quickly found the small bottle of liquid poison that was clearly marked with a cautionary skull and crossbones which from the research he'd done previously knew it was supposed to mix well with alcohol and be completely undetectable to the taste.

He filled two tumblers with ice, poured a generous amount of bourbon into each one pouring some of the poison into the one on the right, gently stirring it to mix it in.

As Joe sat waiting for Nelson to return he was looking around at the opulent surroundings thinking *it was amazing what dirty money could buy and doubted if even the wealthiest people anywhere had such a lavishly furnished office.*

Nelson had previously described his office furniture to Joe so he knew the panelling was mahogany, the bookcases were rosewood and the desk was antique Victorian oak. He also knew the sofa and chairs were Chippendale style upholstered in dark brown strong smelling leather.

Obviously no expense had been spared.

As Joe was continuing to take it all in Nelson returned carrying the drinks.

"Here you go Joe" said Nelson handing Salvatore the glass in his right hand.

"Thank you" responded Salvatore leaning forward and taking the drink from Nelson.

Nelson rarely drank alcohol but realized in this situation he was obliged to at least take a few sips of his uncontaminated drink.

His father had been a big drinker, which along with chain smoking cigars had probably led to his early demise. During the time Nelson had spent out in the Hamptons with his family it seemed like his father drank Scotch whisky and smoked large smelly cigars morning, noon and night. He didn't know how he maintained some semblance of sobriety but it was at that time he decided he wouldn't take up either habit.

"Saluti. Cheers or whatever you say Joe" said Nelson reaching and clinking his glass with his.

They both took a sip of their drinks Nelson watching Salvatore very closely to see if there was any reaction.

"So tell me what happened last night?" asked Nelson.

"What would you like to know?" asked Salvatore taking a swig of his drink "Before I get into the details

I would like to say I'm very sorry about what happened and phoning you this morning."

"How did the police get involved?" asked Nelson.

"Let me see. Two of my guys were making their way out of the bar with a young woman when her boyfriend and his friends showed up and ...."

Salvatore suddenly slumped falling head first banging his head on the edge of Nelson's desk before dropping to the floor in a crumpled heap.

Nelson quickly got up and went around to where Salvatore was lying and checked his neck for a pulse even though it was obvious he was dead. His eyes were wide open and his tongue was slightly protruding from the side of his mouth.

Nelson didn't feel very good about what he'd just done but had felt compelled to do it.

He called Brian's mobile and ironically soon after members of one of Salvatore's murder teams were rolling his body up in one of Nelson's expensive Persian rugs and wrapping it with duct tape. The rug with Joe in it was carried out and dumped into the back of the team's van and it drove off heading for the pig farm.

Still in his office Nelson picked up Salvatore's glass off the floor, it hadn't smashed. He took it and his own glass to the kitchen, emptied his glass into the sink and put them both in the dishwasher with several other dirty dishes, loaded the soap and turned it on.

Nelson got some strips of paper towel and a bottle of cleaning spray and went back to his office and cleaned a few drops of blood off the edge of his desk. The hardwood floor where the rug had been, showed no traces of blood and not that he was expecting a police forensics team to suddenly burst in, Nelson wiped the floor around his desk.

Anyway, his office would be thoroughly cleaned tomorrow morning as it always was by one of the housekeepers.

He had already asked Brian to get another similar rug and within half an hour for a generous fee Salvatore's car was towed away to be scrapped even though it was almost brand new.

Nelson already had a replacement in mind. A guy that went by the nickname of Jimmy the Fixer who had been mentioned to him on several occasions if things went wrong with Joe.

Nelson figured he would need to quickly setup an interview with Jimmy, hopefully tonight, providing he was available.

Nelson would see if he thought he would make a good Head of Murder Teams and was someone he could depend on to deliver a clear message about what was expected of them within his organization.

Nelson hired Jimmy later that night.

*   *   *   *

I made my way downtown to my office at around three o'clock.

When I got there my editor Mike Simmons told me there was a young lady in the lobby waiting to speak with me. I immediately went down and found a pretty blonde in a shiny pink jacket with a long fluffy purple scarf around her neck sitting waiting.

I walked over and introduced myself "I understand you would like to speak to me?" I asked.

"Yes. If that's okay?" she asked as she stood up.

"Sure. Let's go upstairs and we can talk" I replied.

We got out of the elevator and I led the way ushering her into an empty meeting room where we began to chat.

"I guess you know who I am. Could you tell me something about yourself?" I asked.

"Yes. I'm Cynthia Samuels but everyone calls me Cindy. I'm originally from Sacramento, California where I grew up but I now live here in Whittier" she responded.

"So Cindy what do you want to speak to me about?" I asked.

"You know how you are always writing about young women getting murdered? Well I think I nearly became a victim myself last night" she said.

"Oh really what happened?" I asked.

Cindy began "After my shift ended, being a Saturday night I'd gone out with some of the people I work with. We'd had something to eat in the food court in the mall and gone on to a bar called Uncle's where my boyfriend said he and his friends would meet up with me later.

Towards the end of the night I got into a big argument with everyone at the table and was surprised when they all got up and stormed out even though we had just paid for another round of drinks.

You know people are so sensitive these days although I think alcohol might have had a lot to do with it because we were all pretty drunk by then. If I remember I think all I'd said was I'd never really liked the place very much and for some reason they all took huge offence to this as if I was being all high and mighty.

I wasn't going to let the drinks go to waste knowing my boyfriend and his friends were on their way so I stayed there on my own.

Not long after two good looking guys came into the bar and seemed to be checking the place out and soon left. A few minutes later they returned and came right over to where I was sitting and asked me if I would mind if they joined me. Somewhat surprised I said no and they sat down and began to chat me up saying all the things a girl who's had a few too many likes to hear.

Even though there were still a lot of drinks on the table when last orders were called they bought more drinks. I told them my boyfriend and his friends were meeting me but whenever I called him I kept getting his voice mail.

When we were almost the last ones left in the place they asked me if I needed a ride home. Even if my boyfriend didn't show up I could have paid for a cab but why waste money when I had the offer of a ride. Also by this time I was quite drunk and not thinking too straight and also very upset with my boyfriend who as it turned out finally showed up with his friends just as we were leaving the bar.

The two guys who were going to give me a ride grabbed hold of me and tried to push me past my boyfriend and his friends and that's when the trouble started. It seems that these guys had other friends waiting outside in the parking lot and a huge fight broke out.

The police came and from what I could see handcuffed and arrested some of the men who had been fighting with my boyfriend and his friends. I think my boyfriend and his friends had to go to the hospital."

"What happened to you?" I asked.

"I went back inside the bar. The barman locked the door and I waited until the police and everyone else had left then took a cab home" she replied "I've been calling my boyfriend ever since but all I've been getting is his voice mail."

"You know his phone might have been damaged or lost during the melee or he may still be in hospital and unable to use it. You know the people who tried to snatch you only seem to pick on young women who are alone in bars so next time you go out make sure you are with someone.

Hopefully your boyfriend will be alright and hasn't been injured too badly and will be by your side, when you go out from now on, but if he isn't make sure you're not out on your own. I hope you realize how close you came to being viciously raped and murdered last night and becoming another statistic. Please promise me you will be very careful from now on" I said.

"I will and I appreciate you listening to my story" replied Cindy.

"Can you get home alright?" I asked.

"Yes. I feel much better after speaking to you. Thank you" replied Cindy.

I escorted her to the elevators and wished her well.

After completing my editor Simmons edits to my column at close to midnight as I was heading to have a nightcap with Bert the long-time barman at Jules. A sixtyish lookalike for the Dad in Frazier.

It's a bar where I can usually be found in the early hours of the morning several times a week. An attractive woman who'd been standing in the shadows stepped forward and asked me if I was Harry Walsh the Los Angeles Times crime reporter and I reluctantly acknowledged that I was.

She introduced herself as Shelley Green and said she had something compelling to tell me. Although I was not really in the mood for this right now she was insistent. This situation was most unusual. Someone waiting to give me information. I was usually the one foraging for whatever information I could get.

I said "I'm on my way to Jules a bar just up the road if you would like to accompany me we can talk there?"

She said "Okay."

Bert was surprised to see me with a woman but didn't let on.

"Your usual Harry?" he asked as I sat down next to my new found friend at the bar.

"Just a glass of ice water with a lemon. Thank you" requested Shelley when Bert asked her what he could get for her.

I was thinking *what a strange day this has been. I've been sought out by two different women. This was most unusual!*

Shelley began speaking "For a while now I've been mulling over who I could tell about what I know about who is behind the murders of young women here in Los Angeles and figure you're probably the best person to tell. Afterall you've been writing about them for a number of months. I feel I must tell someone before it's too late and I'm murdered too!"

After hearing this I was even more reluctant to hear what she had to say. She looked to be in her mid-thirties, her attractive face was framed with dark brown hair and she was playing down her obvious sexuality with tasteful pastel coloured clothes and makeup.

MON JUL 24

Shelley didn't waste anytime telling me that until recently she had been Head of Prostitution for a Los Angeles based crime boss by the name of Martin Nelson. Who a few weeks ago decided she wasn't up to the job due to dwindling revenues, demoting her to a street prostitute.

Shortly after this she had gone into hiding.

I thought I'd heard the name before but wasn't sure where or when? I didn't know it then but what she had to tell me was going to take days.

"You are saying this guy is responsible for the murders of the young women I've been writing about. I would guess it's his people who have been trying to shut me up from publicizing what they're doing" I commented.

"Yes. Quite likely he's probably put one of his murder teams on to you too" she replied.

"Yes. Perhaps the same murder team I followed out to the Chatsworth Reservoir recently" I said.

"What? Tell me more" queried Shelley.

"I followed a white unmarked cube van out there to the reservoir and directed the police to where they could find the dead body of a murdered young woman. The murderers got my license plate number and have been after me ever since. Anyway please continue" I said.

Shelley started up again telling me that like most corporations, Nelson's criminal organization is multi-level and hierarchical, with he himself at the top of the pyramid, reporting to no one.

She not only told me how his organization ran and operated but also how it began.

She said she'd heard that after leaving New York for Los Angeles soon after graduating from university and briefly toying with a career in advertising. Someone he'd been at college with had contacted him and suggested he come out here and get into the adult film business, where he suggested there were many great start-up opportunities.

Apparently many things about it appealed to Nelson. Particularly the women and the money and although at first it was very exciting, being at movie shoots and dating the adult movie stars. It turned out that it was the darker side of the business that intrigued him more, where even more money could be made.

It seems growing up in Manhattan, overlooking Central Park and never wanting for anything. Had left him bereft of excitement in his adolescent years and he yearned to live on the wild side. Which he began to do, although in a very methodical and careful manner.

The story goes that he turned two of the most attractive adult movie stars into high-end escorts. He provided them with a steady stream of clients splitting the take fifty-fifty which was unheard of and obviously made the women very happy and gave him his first revenue stream.

As you probably know normally at the lower levels of prostitution, the women are usually only provided with food, shelter and drugs of course and very rarely see any of the cash they earn.

After doing really well in this first venture he moved into drug trafficking. Starting up a street drug dealing team which very quickly began making greater profits than his high-end escorts.

With a portion of the profits from these two businesses, he purchased a rundown strip club for a song, quickly turning it into a going concern and making more profits.

From these modest so-called business ventures he rapidly amassed the sufficient funds, to have a multi-million dollar home built in the Pacific Palisades highlands, where he still lives today.

Over the last twenty years he has grown his organization from two to over a thousand employees. He's a billionaire and apart from property sales and investments, his money has all been accumulated from ill-gotten gains.

He is a self-made crime boss with no ties to any crime families which he is very proud of.

Shelley continued.

Telling me that on the next level of Nelson's organization. Are his best friend and right-hand man Brian, his lawyer Ron, Estelle his book-keeper, Sam his purchasing guy and the Heads of each revenue stream. Strip Clubs, Drugs (Clubs and Street), Prostitutes (Clubs and Street), Escorts and Club Sports Illegal Betting.

There are also Heads of Construction and Murder Teams.

It was blowing me away the way everything seemed to be so well organized.

She told me Nelson treats his right hand man Brian James, like a brother and in return he takes care of all of his dirty work.

His lawyer Ron Wells is obviously as crooked as him even though his law firm is well respected.

"I know the name. How interesting" I replied.

Although I probably didn't need to know Shelley told me about Estelle Corby, who she described as a middle aged, sophisticated looking woman. Who she said normally wears horn rimmed glasses, has her long dark hair tied up and a pencil pushed through it. She said she has worked for Nelson for over fifteen years and is the only book-keeper he has ever had.

Apparently although initially wary of taking the job, she has since managed to treat it like any other job in corporate America.

The story goes that back when she joined Nelson's organization, she'd fallen on hard times. Getting fired for cooking the books, for a medium sized company. Which had resulted in her not being able to find another job for over a year.

She hadn't known anything about Nelson's company, Clubs International, before she joined. She had been told by several people in the know, that it was a shell company, for illegal activities.

This concerned her greatly but at the time she'd had no choice. It was start earning money or begin living on the street.

Shelley was relentless.

She told me about Sam Feldman, Nelson's procurement guy. She described him as an energetic and enthusiastic young man who had a receding hairline and could usually be found wearing a tee shirt, shorts and Crocs.

Apparently he is extremely overworked, Nelson's philosophy being it is easier to eliminate one person if things go wrong, rather than several.

Shelley said she thought Sam's is perhaps the most trusted position in Nelson's organization. He is the front man for acquiring everything from condoms to cocaine. Every month he has to get the cash together, to make the payment, to receive the next cocaine shipment. This means going to one or two clubs and filling bags with cash. Then arranging to get them all the way down to Belize.

Talk about trust when your dealing with that much cash. Not just Sam but all the way down the chain. I would think it would be at least $5 million every time and as far as I know, none of it has ever been stolen or lost, which is a tribute to how good he is.

Shelley said "I won't bore you with the names of the revenue generating stream Heads because they sometimes change like in my case. But I will tell you about each stream so if anything happens to me at least someone else knows about Nelson's so called businesses."

This just gets better I was thinking while checking my watch and noticing it was getting on for two o'clock. The bar didn't close until four o'clock, so not wanting to lose this golden opportunity, I asked Shelley to keep going.

"Okay" she said "Let's start with the Head of Strip Clubs, responsible for all fourteen of Nelson's gentlemen's clubs. With approximately two hundred and fifty employees including bar staff, dee-jays, 'dancers', waitresses and cleaners.

The guy who is currently the Head of Strip Clubs, had previously been of all things the general manager of a large grocery store and has twenty-five year's management experience.

He was perhaps a strange choice. But once Nelson heard he had gone to school with Brian he made him an offer he couldn't refuse. Even though he was already in a dream job that paid very well and had excellent benefits.

He was apparently attracted by the challenge of managing something completely different, which paid extremely well and had obvious fringe benefits, if you know what I mean."

She continued "The Head of Drugs is responsible for the dealers at each club and the street drug dealing teams too. He is responsible for over a hundred dealers and is a trusted friend of Nelson's. He has known him since Nelson first got involved in the adult film business."

"Let me see who's next" she sighed.

"The Head of Prostitution, my old job, manages the prostitution in each of the strip clubs as well as street and escort prostitution.

By the way I've also known Nelson since the adult movie days, when there was a lot of prostitution going on even back then. I hear that he has replaced me with a tough career criminal, who has been a pimp for many years in south central Los Angeles, an African-American."

"Moving on" she said "The Head of Club Sports Illegal Betting manages the illegal gambling in each of the strip clubs. He's an ex-Vegas man. Who knows sport betting top to bottom, inside out and runs it like it's his own business."

"Next is the Head of Construction" said Shelley pausing to take a sip of her drink.

"He runs Nelson's construction sites, which account for over six hundred employees and has apparently managed numerous construction projects throughout Los Angeles County. After fifty years in the business I understand he pretty much knows who's who in the zoo.

This is Nelson's only real source of clean money, with profits after costs and expenses of around $240 million.

These clean money profits are being used to buy his toys like yachts, speedboats, limousines, exclusive memberships in country clubs and part ownership of a helicopter and a private jet.

He launders a significant percentage of his dirty money in construction payrolls, stuffing unmarked pay packets with thousands of dollars in cash every week.

There are four levels of pay packets 1, 2, 3 and $4000 which are provided to each worker based on their job level. Millions every year, which if I remember, is about thirty percent of the dirty money he takes in annually.

By the way he literally has racks of bundled of dollar bills, in different denominations, in all of his clubs."

She continued "Although not a revenue stream, we have the Head of Murder Teams. For the ongoing murders he is co-ordinating the selection of victims and handling the communication between the murder teams. These murder teams only work part-time on a when needed basis."

I know all about this because we had meetings every Monday that sometimes took all day. Often going late into the night because Nelson wanted to literally know everything, about everything, so as a result we all got to know everything too.

Perhaps the craziest part of all this was that these meetings were held in a large tent in his back yard.

Which he had swept for listening devices before every meeting."

"This guy is incredibly thorough" I commented.

She replied "You bet. However he did occasionally provide us with an opportunity to enjoy ourselves.

Sometimes after the Monday meeting. He would provide drinks and finger food around the bar out by his pool overlooking the Pacific Ocean.

We all really enjoyed chatting about things that weren't work related, which briefly relieved our stress."

"At the next level …." she went to say.

"Hold on" I interjected "It's getting on for four o'clock and as you can see we're the last ones here, apart from Bert who's closing-up."

"So why don't we go back to where I'm staying? It's within walking distance not far from here and we can continue" Shelley suggested.

She was most alluring especially at four o'clock in the morning after I'd had quite a few and she was obviously quite smart, based on the way she'd been describing Nelson's organization.

"You know it's quite late or early depending on how you look at it" I said.

"Please. I have a lot more to tell you and you are such a good listener. It's important" she pleaded.

Making the assumption that everything was above board I agreed. While we were making our way to where she was staying. She told me her own apartment was in west Hollywood but she was currently staying at a friend's place.

She said her friend travels a lot with her job and is currently over in Europe. Her friend's place was two streets off the main drag in an artsy neighbourhood. When we got there we climbed into an ancient looking freight elevator which took us up to a cozy loft apartment on the top floor. At first glance there were a number of comfy looking couches and a modern kitchen.

We'd hardly got out of the elevator, when Shelley embraced me. She was kissing me hard on the lips while at the same time throwing her coat off onto the floor, starting to get undressed.

Not being one to miss an opportunity I carried her over to the nearest couch.

She finished undressing unveiling a fabulous body which I immediately pounced on kissing her all over as she undressed me.

We were soon fully entangled and pleasuring each other. It lasted until I couldn't hold on any longer and both sweating we lay their side by side.

I asked her if she wanted a cigarette, as I was reaching into my shirt pocket. She said she did so I lit two, passing one to her.

"Let me tell you how I come to be staying here" she said.

"Thursday is usually my grocery shopping day and I always start by getting fruit and vegetables at a farmer's market close to where I live.

Last week as I was returning to drop my bags off. In the distance I could see a white cube van, parked across the street from where I live.

Several guys were standing around smoking, next to it. Alarm bells started to go off and I turned around hoping they hadn't seen me."

"Nelson's guys?" I asked.

"Yes. It looked like they'd found me" she said "So I took a cab downtown here to my friend's place. She more than welcomed me. Telling me I could stay as long as I liked. Especially since I'd brought several bags of fresh fruit and vegetables with me. Which we joked about."

"Do you know why this guy Nelson is murdering young women?" I asked.

"You know I really don't. In the Monday meetings we only focused on the revenue streams. The murders were never discussed" she said asking me if I was ready for round two?

I did my best but it seemed to be too soon after round one. I'd had quite a few drinks and was no spring chicken so it was a bit disappointing, for both of us.

"Now I think its time you told me a bit about yourself" she said.

"Alright let me see. I won't bore you with my life before coming to Los Angeles. Except to say I'd paid my dues before coming to work at the Los Angeles Times, where I've been working for over twenty years now.

I should also mention I was married for five years when I worked in Chicago. However primarily because of the hours I worked and my drinking habits it didn't work out. Fortunately, there were no kids.

Although on my income, I have had all the money I have needed to satisfy my lifestyle. I should probably have done more with it and my time, when I wasn't working or sleeping.

I have a place in a low-rise apartment building not far from here. Where I've lived for the last ten years which has all the amenities and home comforts a single guy could want.

I can buy fresh bread and meat within a block or two. There's a supermarket close by and any number of bars, but Jules where we just were, is by far my favourite.

When I arrived here I started off in a rooming house probably better known to you as a boarding house.

It was small with three bedrooms, a kitchen and a living room with a TV. It was adequate for my needs at the time. I had essentially arrived here with the clothes on my back and a few bucks in my pocket, after the settlement with my ex wife.

I stayed at the rooming house for several years not needing much to get by. Spending most of my time concentrating on improving my reporting skills.

I have never been one for material things as you will see if you ever see my car, preferring social interaction instead, usually in bars.

I really only have acquaintances, people I know from work or bars. I guess you could call me a loner but I prefer it this way. Do you want me to go on?"

"Yes" she replied.

"I moved from the rooming house, a few weeks after someone stole some money from my room. I don't know if it was one of the men I roomed with or one of the friends they often had over. It wasn't much money but it really upset me. I found an apartment in a large house, not far from where I'd been living.

It was at the back of the property and provided me with the run of the back garden. It had a sliding patio door which led out to the backyard. Where there was a glass topped table and two metal chairs, on a square of well weathered patio stones, surrounded by a high fence."

"That's enough. I think I can tell what a boring life you lead outside work" Shelley commented.

Checking my watch I said "Wow! Look at the time. I'd better get going?"

"You don't have to. I told you I still have more to tell you. Please stay" she said, begging me to stay.

"Sorry but I think I need some time to digest what you've told me already. It's been quite a revelation" I replied.

Getting up from the couch we kissed, before I got into the freight elevator and headed for the underground parking where my car was parked.

As I drove down to where I was staying catching up with my smoking I was thinking *how crazy this whole thing has been with Shelley.*

I'd only just met her a few hours earlier and we'd already had sex twice. The first sex I'd had since splitting up with Sally. I was wondering who this woman was and why she had suddenly burst into my life to tell me all this stuff about a guy by the name of Martin Nelson.

On the surface she seemed legit and what she had told me seemed genuine. She was dishing up the person responsible for the young women murders on a plate.

* * * *

Nelson's house phone rang early on Monday morning and to his surprise the voice on the other end was his sister Millie.

She was phoning to tell her brother she was at Los Angeles airport after flying in from New York and was wondering if she should take a cab or would he come and pick her up.

What irony Nelson thought *after he had only just been thinking about the summers he'd spent with her and his parents.* He knew she had been planning to come out to visit him but this was still a surprise.

He told her to go for a coffee or breakfast and in about an hour wait outside Arrivals and look for a red sports car.

After hanging up he phoned Brian and asked him if he could pick his sister Millie, up at the airport. He asked him if he could pick her up in his classic red corvette and give her the grand tour. Nelson hoped this would mean she wouldn't arrive until later that afternoon, by which time he could make sure everyone attending the Monday meeting had left.

Brian enquired what the grand tour was and Nelson suggested the movie star's homes in Beverly Hills, shopping along Rodeo Drive and lunch at the Beverly Hilton. Followed by a slow scenic drive out to Pacific Palisades.

Brian said he would do his best and he'd see him later that afternoon.

Nelson's sister arrived with Brian as planned mid-afternoon and they had lemonade out by the pool.

Nelson thanked Brian for taking care of his sister, who couldn't stop saying what a wonderful time she'd had.

Once Brian had left. Millie asked her brother if he would give her a tour of his home and gardens. Millie was most impressed with everything and the tour ended at the guest house where Nelson suggested she should stay.

A little upset about this suggestion, thinking *he must surely have a number of guest bedrooms in the main house, where she could be staying with him.*

Nelson said he understood this. But still wanted her to stay in the guest house. Telling her. He still had to run his business, even though she had come to visit. He said his home was actually his office.

Still somewhat hurt. Millie remembered how stubborn her brother could be. Usually always getting his own way. So she changed the subject saying "It looks like you're doing really well out here?"

"Not too bad" he replied cutting short any further discussion saying "Let's get you settled in."

"By the way how long are you planning to stay?" he asked.

"I'm not planning to fly back to New York for a couple of weeks. Is that okay?" asked Millie.

"Sure. No problem as long as I have a rough idea" replied Nelson "It looks like your bags have already been brought over, so I'll give you some time to unpack. Come over to the main house whenever you're ready. It's really great to see you Sis."

He gave Millie a hug before heading out of the door.

Nelson had only been back east to New York once since he'd been out on the west coast and then only for a few days. Apart from his sister he didn't really have any close friends or immediate family back there anymore. He'd made the trip to attend his mother's funeral.

Millie still lived in Manhattan where she had a successful career in fashion advertising, freelancing for several Madison Avenue advertising agencies.

Nelson and Millie had both got generous inheritances when their mother had passed away which had been invested for their retirements.

This money didn't mean much to Nelson anymore. But he knew his sister's share would be most important to her. Especially since it looked like she had no plans to get married.

Millie stood admiring the very well furnished guest house thinking *how her brother's home and even his guest house certainly put her tiny upper west side Manhattan apartment to shame.*

As she looked around she was thinking *that maybe her brother was right. It was perhaps better for her to have her own space while she was visiting him.*

Hopefully, she could still spend time with him. She opened the fridge and found a bottle of California white wine chilling. She opened it and poured herself a generous glass to drink while she unpacked.

Millie's impromptu arrival had created a bit of a problem for Nelson because he didn't want her to know what businesses he was involved in.

However he'd already thought of a way to try and hide his shady businesses from her by suggesting she spend time out on his yacht. She could relax, sunbath, swim, snorkel and scuba dive while enjoying some of the finer things in life.

It would mean he would need to hire extra support staff. Normally when he spent time on one of his yachts most of his house support staff accompanied him. He would see if she would like to do it first and then worry about getting the extra staff.

He planned to wine and dine her tonight and suggest it. Mentioning that he would join her from time to time. Thinking *Brian could take care of the daily activities if need be.*

* * * *

When I finally woke up around two o'clock that afternoon. I quickly roughed out a column for tomorrow's edition, while drinking several in room coffee maker made, black coffees.

By seven o'clock I was back in the office discussing what I'd written with Mike Simmons, a chubby, gregarious, larger than life character, who had been working here at the Los Angeles Times ten years longer than me.

I mentioned the two women I'd met yesterday Cindy Samuels and Shelley Green. And told him a little bit about both of them.

I told him Cindy thinks she came close to being abducted Saturday night. By some guys in a white cube van but fortuitously her boyfriend showed up just in time to thwart the attempt.

Shelley I said. On the other hand has provided me with in amazing amount of information about a guy she used to work for. She says he is responsible for the young women murders I've been reporting on.

His name is Martin Nelson.

The name seemed to strike a chord but all Simmons said was thanks for the update.

After my meeting with Simmons. I spent several hours going over the notes I'd made after meeting Shelley last night. I was reviewing them to see if I could use any of what she'd told me in a column later in the week.

*   *   *   *

After having spent most of the day with Millie. Brian had to rush down to the courthouse in the hope he would still have time to bail out the two murder team members, currently in custody.

It would now have to be a quick drink rather than a meal as Nelson had suggested. After bailing them out he took them to O'Malley's an Irish bar just up the road from the courthouse. Brian had arranged for them to meet up with the rest of their murder team there.

After hurried drinks Brian asked the murder team leader to bring his murder team to a local park. He told him they could tell him what had happened Saturday night. To their surprise and concern when they got there they found members of another murder team already there.

When both murder teams had finished greeting each other Brian shouted "Let's get on with it" and immediately, members of the murder team that had been waiting, turned on the newly arrived murder team. They stabbed each one of them, without exception, in the carotid artery on the side of the neck. The five newly arrived murder team members dropped to the ground bleeding to death.

Knives were always the choice of weapon in public places, as gunfire would draw too much unwanted attention.

Within minutes. The murder team members who had just been murdered, were loaded into their own cube van and it left heading for the pig farm.

After the bodies had been dumped the van would be driven to Nelson's property, cleaned and parked in one of the garages.

When a new murder team had been hired they would pick it up there.

*   *   *   *

Nelson's rapid rise in the criminal world had the crime families back east somewhat mystified. The fact he seemed to be outsmarting their chosen family designates was a matter of concern. They were losing revenues to him and he seemed to be becoming more dominant.

Nelson appeared to be much smoother than their own people, who had been hand picked from the ranks of the families back east. They had also heard he had some of the key officials in the city of Los Angeles in his pocket. Something the families had rarely achieved even on the east coast.

The more money Nelson made the more they lost. It was as simple as that and at their occasional get togethers he was always near the top of the agenda. The consensus was that he needed to be taken out but so far it had only been talk.

It was rumoured Nelson's sister was currently visiting him. So this might leave him vulnerable. Providing an opportunity for them to send him a strong message. It was unanimously agreed that they should make the most of the situation.

*   *   *   *

At dinner that evening Millie asked her brother if he was seeing anyone? He responded "Not really" which was essentially true.

He had an impressive array of women at his beck and call but seldom had the time or inclination to date any of them.

Although whenever he did it was usually an all in forty-eight hours that the women would never forget. Being lavished on one of his luxury yachts, having his undivided attention in some of the most exotic places in the world.

He really didn't want to get into it during dinner so changed the subject. He asked Millie if she would like to spend some time out on his yacht. Big Fish. Moored off Marina Del Rey and to his surprise she jumped at the idea.

"I hear you have two yachts. You really are doing well" gushed Millie asking "Can I invite two of my friends. I only ever see them when they come to New York and it would be great to spend some time with them, out here."

Nelson replied "That seems like a great idea. When would you like to go?"

Millie responded that she would arrange it as soon as she could.

"Tomorrow?" Nelson enquired.

Millie outwardly happy responded that she'd call her friends tonight.

This had gone better than Nelson had anticipated and got the impression that she might spend most of her vacation out on the boat which was perfect. He would just have to get Brian to hire the extra support staff.

After dinner he and Millie had a nightcap and he began to relax for the first time since her surprise arrival.

He was no matchmaker so hadn't suggested any male company which would likely only complicate things anyway. Just her and her friends would be perfect. They would just have to find their own men.

His sister's arrival was a little bit problematic but what could he do. Asking her to spend time on his yacht seemed to be the best way to handle the situation. This way he could conduct business as usual. Even though he did feel it was somewhat mean spirited.

At that moment he realized he had become his father. More interested in making money than anything else. Perhaps in fact worse because at least his father had made his money legally.

* * * *

I realized it was almost midnight. So I made my way over to Jules, fitting in a quick smoke on the way. As I entered I could see Shelley sitting at the end of the bar in conversation with Bert.

TUES JUL 25

"Greetings" I said as I sat down on the stool next to Shelley.

Bert asked me if I wanted my usual to which I replied "Yeperr you bet. Thanks."

"So where were we? Was it level three?" I quipped after taking a swig of my beer.

"Hello to you too" she replied "I see you've obviously missed me?"

"Of course I have and I must say you are looking quite lovely this evening, tonight, this morning. Whatever" I responded.

"Yea right. So are you ready to continue?" she asked.

"Sure. I'm all ears" I replied.

She began "Let me see. At level three are the different revenue streams.

I think before I go any further I should tell you about Nelson's employee identification scheme.

When he first started his organization he wanted to stay away from the old Mafia style titles. So he devised a number based coding system, which still serves him well today.

Everyone has a coded identity. Which makes it easy to identify and refer to them. But makes it almost impossible to track what is going on inside his organization, because real names and titles are never used.

An example is CS312 which means Construction Site 3 Worker 12. Another example is CL7D6 which indicates Club 7 Dancer 6.

As you can see. When discussing people, always in code it's impossible to tell what's going on unless you know the coding system. The same system is also used for the payroll.

Ingenious don't you think?"

"I guess in the businesses he's involved in, you can't be too careful" I responded.

She continued "I would think you can already tell he runs a tight ship and on top of this he makes sure everyone who works for him, is a serious professional with significant qualifications including college degrees.

He pays extremely well and fully supports everyone he employs.

Like running any profit-making business he always has challenges in his revenue streams.

Whether it's Strip Clubs, Strip Club Drugs, Street Drugs, Strip Club Prostitutes, Street Prostitutes, Escorts or Club Sports Illegal Betting.

Not to mention Construction or his Murder Teams.

"This guy sounds like a real pro" I commented.

"Oh believe me he is in every sense of the word. Shall I continue to tell you about each of the revenue streams?" she asked.

"Sure this is definitely most enlightening. Just let me get another beer" I said waving to try and get Bert's attention.

"Should I start with Strip Clubs?" she asked.

"Okay" I said.

She started up again "Let me see. Nelson's strip clubs are very clean, compared to most other dirty and dingy rundown premises, often associated with such places.

Whenever he takes a club over he has it completely renovated. To ensure it's exterior and interior is very impressive looking and also easy to maintain.

He ensures his strippers are super attractive and mostly college graduates. Believe me any one of them would be top of the bill at any other gentlemen's club. Because without exception they are all stunning.

Another unique feature of his clubs is regardless of what they are doing, on the hour, every hour, the 'dancers' get up on stage for one dance. This reminds the customers in the club, who is available for lap dances or 'private sessions'.

As far as I know it's been quite awhile since Nelson has been to any of his clubs.

Obviously, the women he's sometimes seen with are of a much higher class than any of the women he employs at his clubs.

The biggest problem he has in his club's is the way the customers behave if they don't get what they want. However, any sign of trouble is usually swiftly dealt with. In extreme cases the customer is taught a lesson in good manners he won't soon forget.

It's quite simple really. The customer causing trouble usually gets pulled out of the club by a murder team, driven and left by the side of a major highway naked.

As for the financials. Nelson reports the take from the credit cards to the Inland Revenue Service. But try's to avoid reporting the majority of the cash transactions."

"You want me to go on?" she asked.

"Yea. Please" I responded.

"Drugs next.

Nelson's cocaine is pure uncut, processed at the source in Columbia, which he purchases for peanuts. I think he was paying nine or ten dollars a gram at the time I left. He has only ever dealt in cocaine which is consistently sought after in Los Angeles and acquiring a regular supply has never been a problem.

Over the last two decades he has been bringing cocaine into the United States and up to Los Angeles using some very ingenious methods.

I'll give you an example of how he has recently been bringing it across the border. Just over a year ago. He bought a construction company based in Mexico. It has a contract to maintain the roads along the Mexico-United States border.

At the same time he purchased an American based construction company. It is contracted to maintain the same roads.

At the Mexican construction company's depot close to the border. Small, 'up from Belize' shipments of cocaine are received everyday. These each consist of seventeen or eighteen kilos, I believe.

Once a week. About a hundred and twenty kilos are loaded into the spare tires of big road rolling machines, owned by the Mexican based construction company and driven to the border on flatbed trucks.

At the open border where the road maintenance work is taking place. The cocaine is transferred from the spare tires into the back of pick-up trucks, owned by the American based construction company.

It is then taken and unloaded at the warehouse of a haulage company, Nelson also owns, on the northern outskirts of San Diego.

In turn it is smuggled onto large haulage trucks and transported to a storage warehouse in Los Angeles, Nelson also owns" Shelley said, with a sigh.

"Gee! This guy is really something" I commented.

She continued "The drug business is by far Nelson's most lucrative revenue stream. Coke heads in Los Angeles have always been willing to pay seventy dollars or more for a gram of high grade uncut Colombian. With a thousand grams in a kilo, five hundred kilos normally yield's revenues of approximately $35 million."

Out of the blue Shelley leaned over and gave me a peck on the cheek. She felt down between my legs, waited a few seconds and whispered "You're ready. Let's go" as she was getting up off her bar stool.

When we got back to the place where she has been staying. She immediately dragged me over to one of the comfy couches, pulled a blanket up over us and moved on top of me skillfully manoeuvring me inside her.

I couldn't control myself as well as I had the last time and within minutes I let out a sigh of ecstasy, much to her disappointment.

Shortly after, she was snoring softly. I fell asleep too.

When I woke and checked my watch it was almost seven o'clock and already light.

Shelley was still sleeping.

I must say I felt pretty good after only getting a few hour's sleep and was finishing a cigarette when Shelley came awake. She immediately began to hug and kiss me.

Pulling free I asked "How about some coffee?"

"Give me a minute and I'll make some" she said getting up and scampering off to the washroom half naked.

I pulled my pants up folded the blanket and lit up another cigarette. Shelley burst out of the bathroom her impressive breasts still exposed. She came over and kissed me. Put the top she'd been wearing back on and headed over to the kitchen.

"Do you want anything to eat?" she asked, looking over to where I was sitting.

"No. Just a black coffee. Thanks" I responded.

Over in the kitchen she started to make a pot of coffee, the aroma wafting throughout the loft. It was such a good smell.

Turning back to me she said "Shall I finish telling you about Nelson's organization?"

"You may as well?" I replied.

"Okay" she said as she was bringing the coffees over. Setting them down on the aped named coffee table, in front of where I was sitting.

"Let me see" she said, sitting down.

"How about I tell you about the club, street and escort prostitutes? The area I used to manage.

Club prostitutes. They usually cater to men who after they've had a few decide they want more than a lap dance or 'private session'. Rooms in the club are available for just this purpose. Club prices depend on what the customer wants.

Street prostitutes. They normally cater to men looking for a quickie. Either in their car, a back alley or park. The prices for these are lower than the clubs.

Escorts. I think you know what they do?"

"What are you implying?" I asked.

"I just meant that I probably don't need me to tell you much about what they do. Just that they normally earn more than regular prostitutes. Even though they are of course prostitutes too" Shelley said.

"Okay. Let's move on please can we?" I said.

"Okay. Next we have Club Sports Illegal Betting" Shelley said "I believe Nelson offers better odds than legal sports betting companies and it's apparently easy money given the infinite combinations of losing bets.

Alcohol and ego always play a huge part in sports betting, especially during the NFL season. When almost everyone at one time or another, after having a few drinks feels obliged to show their expertise, by placing a bet on who they think is going to win the game.

All bets are cash only, so none of them are traceable."

"Amazing" I said "You certainly know Nelson's businesses, inside out."

"As I told you. In the Monday meetings we'd touch on every aspect of them. By the way you should know. Now I've unloaded all of this on you I'm feeling much better" said Shelley.

"Good. I'm glad you're feeling better. I'm not sure I am" I replied.

Changing the subject I asked "How about going for breakfast? I know a great greasy spoon not far from here."

"Sorry but I think you know. I only go out at night. I'm frightened Nelson's men might be out there" she replied.

"Yea. I guess I know what you mean. I haven't been able to go home myself for the same reason. Maybe we can rustle something up between us, if you've got some eggs and stuff" I suggested.

"Sure how do you like your eggs?" she asked getting up and moving over to the kitchen.

"Scrambled would be fine" I replied getting up and moving over to where she was reaching for a frying pan.

We ate scrambled eggs on toast and drank several cups of coffee sitting at the island in the kitchen.

*　　*　　*　　*

Millie was standing outside the guest house waiting for Osvaldo, Nelson's chief bodyguard, to pick her up. She could see her brother walking over from the main house.

"Couldn't let you get off without letting you know that I hope you and your friends have a great time out on the boat" he said as he was approaching her.

"I'm really looking forward to it. Spending time with Donna and Jill, on your luxury yacht" responded Millie.

"I'm sure Osvaldo will take good care of you and your friends but if you need anything don't hesitate to call me" he replied.

A dark shiny Lincoln town car pulled up along side them. Osvaldo got out and came around and grabbed Millie's suitcases and put them in the trunk before opening the rear door for her to get in.

Nelson gave Millie a peck on the cheek saying "Have a wonderful time. I'll see you soon."

Millie gave him a hug and climbed into the backseat and Osvaldo closed the door.

After picking Millie's friends up, when they got to Marina Del Rey they all clambered into a large speedboat and were shuttled out to Millie's brother's luxury yacht.

When they got there Osvaldo was thinking *the ride out to the yacht hadn't taken as long as it taken to transfer Millie and her friends luggage from the town car to the speedboat.*

Once they got out to the yacht. Osvaldo helped them out of the speedboat and told them he would take care of the luggage. He said they should go exploring until he caught up with them.

None of them had been on a luxury yacht before. So they moved from one deck to another, taking in the expensive fittings and furnishings. It seemed no expense had been spared by Millie's brother.

When Osvaldo caught up with them on the lounge deck. He ushered them over to the impressive looking bar and once he got behind it asked them what they would like to drink?

"Do you have champagne?" asked Millie.

"Of course" responded Osvaldo reaching down into the fridge behind him.

"I think we should celebrate being together again especially in such luxurious surroundings" suggested Millie.

Osvaldo put three champagne flutes on the bar and expertly popped the cork on a large bottle of Bollinger. Millie and Donna slowly sipped the champagne. Jill on the other hand gulped it down asking Osvaldo for a refill.

After a while they walked over and sat down on the comfortable blue and white loungers beside the pool.

*　*　*　*

Still sitting at the island in the kitchen. Shelley was sitting next to me, drinking her coffee and smoking a cigarette.

I asked "Do you have anything else to tell me?"

Shelley laughed saying "Yes. Of course I do."

I replied "That's fine by me. I just need to go to the office this evening to put my column together but until then as usual I'm all ears."

Shelly started up again saying "Let me think what's next. Okay. Money laundering and murder are also an integral part of Nelson's organization.

Over the last decade he has built quite a few high end homes in some of the more affluent neighbourhoods of west Los Angeles like Brentwood, Malibu and Pacific Palisades.

This is the way he launders money from his illicit activities. Construction contractors and subcontractors are more than willing to accept cash to pay both their legal and especially their illegal workers. Their suppliers too.

Nelson and Gazzaro have agreements with the contractors, subcontractors and suppliers that they will pay their workers directly in cash.

Like this Nelson can make sure his cash is never visible or tracked. As soon as it comes in. It goes out. I will explain this later but just know everything is being done using cash.

The revenue he gets from the sale of the new properties is clean legitimate money to which the Inland Revenue Service has visibility and collects taxes on. This is Nelson's favourite revenue stream, money that he can make visible and track.

Next we have murder. Inside Nelson's organization it is hardly ever talked about but we both know he has murder teams and these are the ones murdering the young women. Let me give you an example of how he uses these murder teams and how ruthless he is.

A gang of Latino's had been causing trouble from time to time at one of his Desperado clubs. He dispatched his combined murder teams to the club in question to give these troublemakers a message. I heard there were about thirty Latino's, including their wives and girlfriends there at the time.

Apparently Nelson's combined murder teams stormed into the club surprising the Latino's who'd been being rude and hassling the 'dancers', saying their women were better than them and did more than them for free.

The murder teams were all wearing fox head masks which is really scary right off the bat. They apparently rounded up and disarmed the Latino's, amassing an impressive stash of weapons.

Various knives, straight, flick and even big hunting ones, handguns and even a sawn-off shotgun. Knuckle dusters, metal pipes, small baseball bats and the high heeled stilettos, nearly every Latino woman was wearing, were thrown in a pile.

The Head of Murder Teams, Joe Salvatore was there.

While he was instructing the Latino men to line-up everyone in the club could hear a loud crunching sound of metal on metal outside.

It seems Nelson had hired a heavy duty pick-up truck with a V blade snowplough on the front from a Rent-All up in the San Gabriel mountains especially for the job.

Several BMW's and other assorted high-end vehicles had their front and back-ends smashed, leaving them, in most cases undriveable.

Nelson obviously knew how much these fancy vehicles meant to these thugs and it would complete their humiliation. Reinforcing the message he was sending.

Apparently Joe hit the first man in line between the legs with a baseball bat saying "I wonder how your woman will like you now?"

Immediately several women rushed screaming at him but were quickly pushed back.

The next few men in line knowing what was likely coming covered up their privates so Joe cracked them on the head. He hit the rest of them across the knees, most of them crumpling to the floor. Their women were shrieking and trying to intervene.

One of the Latino men lying on the floor shouted "This is not right. We can't fight back."

To this Joe apparently responded saying "Isn't that too bad. I just hope you and your whores stay away from this club from now on. And all the other Desperado Clubs (the name of Nelson's clubs) or we might not be as nice next time."

"Can we go now?" asked another Latino man while being helped up by his woman.

"Yes. But heed my words or you won't be as lucky next time" growled Joe "Your whores can help you get out the door."

I heard that as the Latino women rushed over to help their men up one of them spat at Joe and he hit her in the knees with the baseball bat and she fell to the floor screaming.

Gradually the Latinos limped out of the club their women all with bare feet.

"I'm sure Nelson himself would have been extremely pleased with this show of force. It must have been very scary" I commented.

"I'm sure it was" she replied "Do you want another example of how ruthless he is?"

"Okay" I replied "This guy is really something!"

"Well" Shelley continued "Having dealt with the Latino's he began to focus his attention on a street prostitution problem.

Some of the women working the streets were being roughed up by young punks. One night a street prostitute was badly beaten up which I reported at a Monday meeting.

Nelson wanted to know what was being done about it. When I said nothing so far he laid into me.

Remember when he first started out he had two escorts. Apparently one of them got badly beaten up.

The story goes that he found the guy and kept dipping him headfirst into the sea off the side of a fishing boat owned by a friend of Brian's until he almost drowned. This guy was lucky. He was freed afterwards.

The women were never touched again.

He told me he couldn't have his organization affected like this and asked me to find out who was responsible. He said he wasn't sure what he was going to do but said it would be something for effect.

He said there were things he'd always wanted to try. Like tying someone to railway tracks or pinning them out in the heat of the desert.

Releasing them in a flimsy dingy in shark infested waters. Dragging or keel hauling them behind a boat or penning them in with a rabid dog.

Keel hauling wouldn't leave any visible marks whereas the others would. Shark or dog bites, limbs on the railway tracks and blisters from the desert. He said regardless of what he did. It was time to send out a clear message.

I later heard that he, Ron and Brian had met to discuss what they'd do and had agreed on keel hauling and were interested to know how it would work out. However they had to find those responsible first.

Several weeks later another street prostitute was roughed up. But this time, one of Joe's murder teams were waiting and the two thugs responsible were caught. It seemed it was them who had beaten up the other girl too.

Osvaldo showed up with two bodyguards. The three of them were wearing black balaclavas to hide their identities. They took the captured men to Marina Del Rey.

Their two captives were manhandled out of the back of the car they were in, onto a large powerful looking speed boat and taken out to Nelson's yacht. There they were shackled to the side of the top deck.

The captured men could see the night sky very clearly, the stars never shining so bright before in their lives. They were both very scared wondering what fate awaited them knowing it was going to be bad, whatever it was.

The men who had captured them had obviously been concealing their identities so they hoped this meant they were going to be released and not killed.

They'd both seen enough TV crime shows to know that when captors covered their faces, it usually meant they weren't going to kill their victims. So hopefully this was a good omen.

Neither one of them got any sleep that night.

At first light one of them was unshackled from the railing by the big burly guy who seemed to be the leader. His face was still covered. This first man was taken down to the lowest deck of the yacht and pushed into the same speedboat he was brought out to the yacht in last night.

He was fitted with a life jacket and a small harness which was attached to his wrists. The harness in turn was attached to the end of a long thick rope.

While this was going on he was asking what was going to happen to him? But the men still wearing balaclavas, doing the harnessing didn't say a word. He figured he was going to be dragged behind the speedboat but couldn't do anything about it.

The speedboat started up and headed out to sea. After several minutes it slowed down and came to a stop. The sun was just emerging from behind the snow covered mountains off to the east. The sea was calm, small waves lapping against the side of the boat. It was a scene of serenity.

The rope and the captive were thrown over the side and the speedboat's powerful twin outboard motors started up again and began to churn up the warm water of the Pacific Ocean.

The speedboat sped up bouncing into and over the waves. It was most unpleasant for the victim, the sea water hitting his face hard, hurting him. The water was flowing up his nose and into his mouth at an alarming rate.

He was drowning and couldn't do anything about it.

Osvaldo was watching him closely from the back of the speedboat and could see the victim was struggling, his head bobbing up and down and from side to side.

Osvaldo shouted to the driver to stop the speedboat.

Osvaldo could see the life jacket was keeping the victim up in the water, otherwise he would have sunk below the waves.

He was just floating and looked lifeless.

Osvaldo took his balaclava off and jumped over the side and swam to where the man was floating. When he got to him he grabbed his hair and lifted his head up. His face was beet red and it was obvious he was dead. Osvaldo checked for a pulse anyway but there was none.

Osvaldo hadn't planned to kill him but it looked like he had. He would have to be more careful with the second man.

I assume the dead man was taken to the pig farm.

The second man was happy to have survived to tell the tale to anyone who would listen, except the police, after being threatened with a quick death if he did."

"Wow" I gasped "This guy really is ruthless almost like the mob?"

"In a way" Shelley replied "But his organization is tiny compared to the mob's west coast operations. Although Nelson's year over year profits are slowly rising every year. Allowing him to continue to take great satisfaction from knowing he is a self-made man, who answers to no one."

Nelson knows he is only as good as the weakest link in his organization which is why he personally watches over every single one of them. A thousand and four at the time I left. He continually wants to know how every person in his organization is doing, right down to the cleaners.

There is not a job that is more valuable than any other to him. If you work for him you are as important a link in the chain as anyone else regardless of what you do.

Before you get a job working for him he personally interviews you. Interviews take up most of his day on Tuesdays. He knows how important it is to have the right people, which I think you would agree is the key to every successful enterprise, anywhere in the world.

Around a thousand people is the most he has ever had working for him at any one time. It is the number he has settled on and maintains and includes his own staff, bodyguards and crews whenever needed on both yachts.

He keeps an up to date coded list of everyone who works for him and if they are ever suspected of anything untoward they are confronted.

Good communication skills are of great importance to him because to him it shows character and a good level of intelligence.

"I just remembered. One thing I didn't tell you about is the cash and is there ever a lot of it!" said Shelley "This may be a bit of a patchwork summary but I'll tell you about it as it comes to me."

"Okay. As Nelson became more and more successful, great amounts of cash began to amass. This is a problem he has always had, although you might think it is a good problem to have.

Protecting it from theft, organizing it, keeping track of it, counting it and storing it has always been a challenge and it is only very recently that he has really started to get to grips with it.

When Nelson started his first business he was the one organizing and controlling the cash. I understand he rented an apartment in Palisades village just for this.

As the number of escorts increased and he got seriously involved in the drug business. While at the same time acquiring and opening more and more strip clubs. The cash suddenly started coming in, at an exponential rate.

He was no longer able to control and manage it himself. Also the apartment was too far from downtown.

So at that point management of his cash became the responsibility of the managers at each of his clubs. Overnight they became drop off centers for the street drug dealers, street prostitutes and escorts.

The clubs were also storing the cash their own workers were bringing in.

Think of the cash coming in. Six or seven drug dealers bringing in around ten thousand dollars a day. Street prostitutes bringing in between five or six thousand dollars every few days. Not to mention the cash being taken in at the clubs themselves.

Hundreds of thousands of dollars were accumulating each week. It was crazy money. Nobody unless they were directly involved would believe how much cash there was.

Within a short while. Large piles of bags of cash were forming in many of the rooms in the clubs and the tracking of the cash coming in was primitive.

And boy was the money ever dirty. Anyone handling it had to wear gloves as mountains of cash began to accumulate. Anyway this is the cash coming in.

Now we have the cash going out. Listen to this. From what I understood at the time. Most club workers were being paid in cash purely at the club manager's discretion, based on how good a job they had done that week.

Obviously, as you can imagine, there were some very happy workers and perhaps a few unhappy ones. But regardless, I think they were all well paid.

Prostitutes kept an agreed percentage of the cash they earned. It was twenty two percent while I was there. Drug dealers also skimmed an agreed percentage off the top of their take. I don't know exactly what it was.

It was paying the construction workers that was the challenge, because of the number of them. The piles of bags of cash had to be sorted and stuffed into wage packets, in the four different amounts, based on the employee's identity code.

I believe the club managers or their designates did this themselves as the construction workers arrived to get paid, every Friday evening. Not an easy job. I heard it often took until late into the night before everyone had been paid.

Fortuitously, while the workers waited they could enjoy the entertainment in the club, running up tabs until they got their wage packets.

Nelson apparently tried to discourage this, because the parking lots at the clubs would get jammed up and he was concerned it would draw attention.

It was never clear if the regulars realized what was happening every Friday night at the clubs, but they certainly knew it was going to be busy.

Scribbled notes were kept on sheets of paper every week. The persons identification code and amount paid out noted. Crazy though it sounds this is how it worked for many years. Nelson only ever had a rough idea of how much money was coming in and going out.

Asking employees to pick up their wages up at the clubs every week had an unthought of positive side to it. Because many of the construction workers spent a portion of their pay there. It boosted each clubs take. Even though, like I said, Nelson wanted them to be in and out as quickly as possible.

Things gradually got better, becoming more organized. The cash began to be stashed in cardboard boxes, in the different denominations. Although for awhile only one hundred or fifty-dollar bills were being used. The cardboard boxes full of the lesser denominations were being put aside and no one could be bothered to open them and use twenty, ten, five or one dollar bills.

Soon the multitude of boxes of the smaller denominations, started to become a big problem. As they began to take up more and more space in the clubs. I believe burning them to free up space, was seriously considered at one point.

How about that. Having so much money that you were thinking of burning it. Crazy, Crazy.

Money counters and money racks were introduced a few years back and since then the management and control of the cash has been much improved. The cardboard boxes were all emptied and the smaller bills sorted and separated and are now being paid out along with the larger bills."

"Phew" I said "I think you've literally just described his cash flow."

"Something else. Everyone in Nelson's organization is asked not to deposit over two thousand dollars in cash into the bank. The same with big cash purchases, nothing over two thousand dollars. Nelson also asks everyone to use their cash sparingly and to never flaunt it.

Everyone on his payroll finds it easy to follow these rules. They buy groceries with cash and on a monthly basis deposit enough in the bank to cover their rents, mortgages, car payments, phone, cable and utility bills.

Other purchases like furniture and appliances can also be purchased within his guidelines. So being paid in cash is very workable.

Nelson had often toyed with the idea of setting up centralized storage for all the cash. But up until I left he was continuing to have it controlled in the clubs.

I estimate each club is regularly holding around $100 million in cash. Well over a billion in total.

A few months back Nelson asked us to bring cash to his Monday meetings. So it could be distributed amongst us, Ron, Brian and Nelson himself.

We could take as much cash as we liked. I was just taking a small amount every week. I don't know about anyone else. Before we started doing this I used to go to one of the clubs to get cash every month. In fact I was still going to a club every week to get cash to bring to the Monday meetings.

I'm not sure why Nelson started doing this. Maybe it's the beginnings of his central storage plan."

"Perhaps some paranoia creeping in on his part" I said.

"Would you like more coffee?" Shelley asked.

"No, I'm good. What I could use is a few hours' sleep. My brain is starting to hurt. Would that be alright?" I asked.

"Yes. Be my guest. I'll be joining you once I've cleaned up here a bit" she replied.

I had a good long sleep and didn't wake up until just before eight o'clock in the evening and after we'd had a quickie. I told Shelley I needed to go to my office. I quickly got myself together before hopping into the ancient freight elevator.

*   *   *   *

"Is everything ready for tonight?" asked Nelson quite sternly as he sat next to Ron beside his pool looking out at the Pacific Ocean and the large bright orange sun that was setting.

"Yes as far as I know" responded Ron.

Nelson hadn't been able to get the blonde that got away out of his mind. Knowing he'd had to sacrifice a whole murder team and a Head because of her. He hated leaving loose ends and had asked Brian to finish the job tonight.

At the time Brian had questioned whether it was wise to attempt a murder outside the usual Saturday night window. But Nelson said he wasn't concerned. Because he knew Brian could pull it off without a hitch. Anyone else he said he might worry.

A murder team was waiting for Cindy when she arrived home from work that night. They knew where she lived. Because after the botched abduction, the murder team members that hadn't been arrested, had followed the cab she took home early on that Sunday morning.

She lived above a convenience store not far from the large mall where she worked. To the murder team's surprise two men were accompanying her, one of them her boyfriend they assumed.

The murder team discussed what they should do and knowing Brian was pushing to get the job done tonight they called their new Head, Jimmy the Fixer. He told them to still go ahead, even though they may need to take on the two men who'd arrived with the blonde.

They really didn't want to murder any additional people and thought it might be an issue, if they murdered anyone other than the blonde.

Originally they had planned to intercept her as she went in through the door to her upstairs apartment, but now they would need to get in some other way. This was something else they hadn't planned for but knew they couldn't fail as Brian would be most upset.

They waited as long as they could before buzzing up to the apartment. When someone came on the intercom one of them said "Pizza delivery". They hoped this would confuse those upstairs enough that one of them would come down to investigate.

A back and forth ensued with those upstairs saying that no one had ordered a pizza until eventually the blonde's boyfriend came down to discuss the matter. Opening the door he found a tough looking guy standing outside with no pizza.

More men suddenly appeared and wrestled him down to the floor just inside the door.

While this was going on Cindy was feverishly shouting "What's going on down there?" from the doorway at the top of the stairs.

By now her boyfriend had been overwhelmed and was being restrained. Cindy continued to peer down the stairs asking what was going on and getting no response yelled "Ben are you alright?"

She thought she heard Ben's muffled voice say "Lock the door."

Cindy could see her boyfriend was being held down by several men against his will. So she decided to shut and lock the upstairs apartment door. She told Ben's friend that there were men downstairs holding him down and asked him what he thought they should do?

"Shouldn't we call the police?" responded Ben's friend.

"Yes. Can you do that please?" asked Cindy.

Josh, Ben's friend went into the kitchen to phone the police but found the phone line was dead.

"The line is dead!" shouted Josh.

"Use your mobile" shouted Cindy.

Cindy could see the apartment door handle being turned one way then the other which was very scary and she could hear someone shouting "Open the door or your boyfriend's arms will be twisted out of their sockets."

She could hear muffled screaming.

The apartment door was being banged into and suddenly there was a loud bang and the it came crashing into the apartment. The two men who had landed on it, quickly got up and rushed at Josh wrestling him to the floor.

Cindy seeing this ran down the hall and locked herself in the bathroom. Ben was dragged through the doorway over the broken door and pushed down onto the floor next to Josh. They were both handcuffed to a radiator.

Cindy locked in the bathroom was trembling with fear. Remembering what the reporter had told her about these men. She began to see moving shadows under the bathroom door. Could see the door handle being turned backwards and forwards.

She already knew the bathroom window was too small to crawl through and even if she could there was a sheer drop from the second floor to the ground.

She had seen movies where women had locked themselves in bathrooms then overflowed the bathtub to try and attract the attention of those below. So she quickly turned both taps full on and placed a towel along the bottom of the bathroom door.

Hearing the loud sound of the water running spurred the killers into action. They were taking turns running and banging into the bathroom door. But the frame, door and lock were holding firm.

The bathtub was rapidly filling up. Cindy stuffed a face cloth into the overflow outlet and not long after water began to flow over the side of the bathtub.

Cindy could see a sharp knife protruding through the door next to the locking mechanism making a narrow slit beside it.

Water continued to overflow onto the bathroom floor. Cindy hoped the tiling hadn't been installed too perfectly. But it began to look like it had. Warm water began to get higher and higher reaching up to Cindy's ankles.

The knife blade was now below the lock and hadn't got too far to go before it looked like the locking mechanism was going to fall out.

Cindy started to panic even more and looked for something to damage the tiles with. The warm water was almost up to her knees now. But there didn't seem to be anything heavy enough to crack the tiles.

Shampoo bottles, razors and packages of soap wouldn't be any good so she focussed on the toilet. The seat and cover were made of wood so these wouldn't be much good.

Frantic now she wondered if she could remove the toilet bowl. She reached down into the warm water and took off a plastic screw cover. She found that the screw underneath was rusted and wouldn't budge.

Looking back at the bathroom door. She could see a square had been cut all around the locking mechanism, which was now being pulled out. The bathroom door flew open and the warm water rushed out.

"Well. Hello Cutie" commented an ugly tough looking man standing in the doorway.

"What do you want with me?" Cindy yelled.

Another man rushed past her and pulled the plug out of the bathtub and turned the taps off.

Cindy was dragged out of the bathroom into the bedroom opposite, thrown on the bed and stripped naked. Her panties were shoved in her mouth and tied in place with a nylon stocking that had been lying on the floor.

She was begging her captors to let her go in a muffled voice. She already knew this wasn't going to happen. She was pinned, face up, on the bed feeling extremely vulnerable.

"Okay. Let's see who goes first?" shouted one of the men excitedly.

"There's some change here on the dresser" said the leader.

The leader lost the first toss so would go last which he commented was perfect as he could finish the job.

The man who had won quickly dropped his pants and climbed up onto the bed kneeling between Cindy's legs while the other men held her down.

He felt for her breasts which were firm, well formed and felt really good. Then he applied some spit to his member and pushed it into her.

One at a time each man came down from the bed and another one got up until it was the leaders turn. He took a hand towel and wiped away what the previous men had left behind.

Cindy was squirming and crying out and the leader could see she was raw and bleeding. He felt sorry for her and asked if she would prefer to use her mouth. She shook her head violently.

"I know what we'll do then. Help me turn her over" shouted the leader.

Once turned face down the leader penetrated her from behind making her shake the whole time until he had finished.

Once he was done she lay face down, motionless. Cindy's boyfriend Ben and his friend Josh were still handcuffed to a radiator. They had been listening to what had been going on and heard one of the men say "How about seconds?"

"No. We're already an hour behind schedule" growled the leader as he turned Cindy over and untied the nylon stocking around her mouth.

"Alright pretty little Miss Muffet what are we going to do with you?" asked the leader knowing full well what he was going to do with her.

After what Cindy had been through she wished she were dead and feared it wouldn't be too long until she was. Although in a lot of pain she had come up with the idea that she could be their permanent sex slave. Doing whatever they wanted, whenever they wanted.

She figured they could keep her somewhere and whenever they wanted sex she would be there for them.

She was obviously trying to appeal to their primitive instincts. But the leader wouldn't have any of it and quickly quashed the idea saying "There are plenty like you whenever we feel like it."

"Yes. But you'll murder them after. If you keep me alive. I'll always be there for you" pleaded Cindy.

"If we got caught we would be killed by our boss for disobeying orders" replied the leader "Anyway the fun and games are over. Boys hold her down."

Cindy's arms and legs were pinned and the leader asked one of the men to hand him a pillow lying on the floor. He began to smother her with it pressing down with all his strength.

Cindy struggled to move but couldn't and was finding it hard to breathe. Soon she was losing consciousness. The leader kept this up for several minutes until her body became limp and lifeless.

The men having had their fun with her, more than with any of the other young women they had raped and murdered, were sad to see she was dead. But were happy in the knowledge, that they had done what Brian and Nelson had wanted.

Although it had taken a while. Water had now seeped through the ceiling of the store below. The young Korean in the store had been closing up for the night. But he was now stealthily making his way up the stairs, to Cindy's apartment, to see what was going on.

He saw the broken apartment door lying in the doorway. As he stepped over it he saw two young men, one of them beaten and bloodied, handcuffed to a radiator and could hear talking down the hall.

What he saw and heard scared him. He wasn't sure what to do. Until a man came striding out of one of the bedrooms and shouted "Hey guys we've got company."

The young Korean turned and quickly made his way back downstairs.

When he got back into his store, he tried to phone the police. But found the store's phone line was dead. While he was starting to dial on his mobile. Two men came through the door to the store, rushed at him and wrestled him to the floor.

After getting the better of him and tying him up one of the men flipped the OPEN store sign to CLOSED before making his way back upstairs. The other man remained standing over him.

When he got back upstairs and told the leader about the guy downstairs he calmly said "We need to get rid of the three of them. They have seen our faces."

With that said. Two of the men in the murder team stabbed the young men handcuffed to the radiator. A steady stream of blood started to flow from under their bodies.

"Okay" said the leader "Now go and take care of the guy downstairs."

The murder team members although giving the appearance of being quite jovial. Inwardly they were worried about what Nelson's reaction might be. Given they had murdered three more people than planned.

They knew he had killed other murder teams for less. So figured it would all depend on how he thought it would affect his organization. If he thought they had done the right thing they should be alright. But if on the other hand he thought they hadn't they might be in big trouble.

Several hours later the murder team leader met the new Head, Jimmy the Fixer. They met in a park that was often used for discussions like this. The leader provided Jimmy with the details of what had happened.

Explaining they couldn't avoid murdering the two guys who arrived with the blonde and the guy downstairs in the convenience store.

Jimmy said he knew the guys who came home with Cindy might have to be killed but hadn't anticipated the guy in the store below would have to be murdered too.

As it turned out when Nelson heard what had happened he thought the murder team had done the right thing. Then and there he decided on a new rule.

From now on anyone who could identify murder team members should also be killed. He said these ancillary murders wouldn't become cold cases as quickly as the murdered young women. So it would add to the caseload of the Los Angeles Police Department keeping them even busier.

WED JUL 26

I couldn't believe it when I read that Cindy Samuels and three others had been murdered. I felt sick to my stomach and felt compelled to do something to try and entrap this guy Nelson. Even though he was at the top of his own food chain and pretty much untouchable.

I needed to expose what he was currently doing and the things he was controlling. I knew it was going to be difficult because he wasn't actually directly involved in any of the illegal activities.

That afternoon when I got into the office. After repeatedly getting his voice mail for almost an hour. I eventually managed to get through to Nelson's lawyer Ron Wells. I told him about a proposal I had.

I was willing to pay $10 million to spend one night with Nelson's latest lady friend, even though I didn't know who she was. I obviously didn't tell Nelson's lawyer this.

He laughed and said he would let Mr. Nelson know. If he was interested he'd call me back. He asked me for my name and a number where I could be reached.

This threw me for a bit of a loop. Remembering the cigarette brand I smoked were called Winston's and were originally manufactured by the R.J. Reynolds Tobacco Company of Winston-Salem, North Carolina. I told him my name was Reynolds and said I'd prefer to call him back later to get the answer.

When I called back that afternoon. I got through straight away. Wells informed me that Mr. Nelson is most interested in my proposal and would need the $10 million in cash up front. He asked me to be outside Grauman's Chinese Theatre in Hollywood at 10.30 pm sharp tomorrow night.

I was amazed how easy it had been to set this up. I realized I needed to clean myself up and probably buy a new suit in order to look the part. So I went shopping.

Nelson wouldn't normally touch anything like this that had come completely out of the blue. But it was $10 million for one night with a silly immature young woman who he'd already gone off. So figured it was easy money.

Even though he had gone off her. His current lady friend was an absolutely stunning blonde, tall and shapely, with a body to kill for.

She came from a well-heeled family in the Hollywood Hills.

Nelson had hooked up with her at Santa Anita Park racetrack on a big race day. She had stood out from all the other gussied up young women in eye catching hats.

He had invited her to join him in his club house box seats for the remainder of the race card. He had immediately impressed her with his charm and good manners.

He had offered her champagne and Carol Bromley had fallen head over heels for him within the first hour of meeting him.

He exuded class and wealth. He had shown a keen interest in everything she'd talked about. This was very unusual, based on her previous dates, with other successful self-centered men.

He hadn't even had to woo her to start the relationship which disappointed him a little. On several other occasions he'd had to pull out all the stops to get the women he wanted. Flying them over to Europe first class. Spending the weekend with them on his other luxury yacht in St Tropez on the French Riviera.

Lavishing them with every luxury possible including spa treatments. The best food and drink money could buy along with very extravagant gifts.

If this didn't work. He'd fulfilled whatever fantasy they had. Including weekends at the most expensive hotels in London and Paris.

He'd even taken one to Rio.

Within only a few weeks of knowing him they had probably ticked off several items on their bucket lists. Plus some other things they hadn't dreamt of. By then they were hooked and always available.

The lyrics from the song "The Sweetest Taboo" by Sade. "Every day is Christmas and every night is New Years Eve" might best sum up how they had been pampered.

Nelson himself was indifferent to women. On occasion thinking he might even be gay, but knew he wasn't. It was important for him to always have an attractive, shapely woman on his arm at least for appearances sake. Even though he normally wasn't interested in having sex with them.

On occasion when he decided he wanted to have sex. He arranged a session with a high-class escort. Always a different one to ensure there was no chance of an attachment of any kind. It happened very infrequently these days as he seldom had the time or inclination. Instead making money excited him a lot more than having a sexual encounter.

Nelson wasn't planning to mention the proposal to Carol. Instead he planned to spring it on her, knowing she would be able to deal with it. Because he knew what she was like, when she got drunk and coked up. Although on the surface she was a high society type. Under this façade. She was a common slut, addicted to cocaine, alcohol and sex.

* * * *

Out on Nelson's luxury yacht. Osvaldo and the extra support staff, including two bodyguards and a catering team were taking care of Nelson's sister Millie and her friends. So far they'd been having a great time with one small exception.

Jill had got sunstroke from a combination of too much sun and champagne yesterday. But she seemed to be over it this morning having just eaten a hearty breakfast with Millie and Donna.

Today Millie and her friends were planning to lie by the pool. Soak up the California sun and catch up with what had been happening in each other's lives since the last time they'd met up.

Since arriving on the yacht yesterday they'd been having a fabulous time. Osvaldo had been constantly checking on them and providing them with snacks and drinks.

Last night. Their first night on the yacht. They'd had an amazing steak dinner, accompanied by a selection of some of the best California red and white wines.

THURS JUL 27

Early on Thursday morning a suspicious looking speedboat started circling Nelson's yacht. Leaning down over the side Osvaldo could see three dark-haired men with sinister looking ashen faces. They looked to be Italian and didn't appear to be looking for fun.

Osvaldo quickly moved along the railing to where Millie and her friends were. They were also looking down to see what was going on. Watching the men in the speedboat. Osvaldo suggested they go below while he figured out who these unfriendly snoopers were.

Millie and her friends were a little upset about this. But complied making their way down to Millie's cabin.

Not long after. They heard a loud volley of automatic gunfire which was most unnerving.

Millie said she'd go and ask Osvaldo what was going on. But found the hatch leading up to the deck above had been locked.

The gunfire stopped as quickly as it had begun. Leaving Millie and her friends wondering what was going on. It wasn't long until they heard the hatch being unlocked.

Osvaldo appeared saying "I don't know who these people are that have been circling the boat but they are not friends of Millie's brother. However they have been dealt with for now. I would ask that you stay down here until I get further directions. By the way Brian, who Millie knows, is on his way to join us."

"Why is that?" asked Donna.

"He's just coming in case we have to further deal with these people who we assume are jealous of Millie's brother. Nothing more than that" responded Osvaldo dismissively.

"Are we in danger?" asked Millie.

"No. Not at all. Please just stay down here for the time being. Thank you" replied Osvaldo. Making his way back upstairs and locking the hatch behind him.

"I guess I'll go and get a coffee" said Jill heading for the galley.

Nelson had already gotten word about what had just happened out on the yacht. He had asked Brian to go and investigate the incident. Telling him he would join him later.

What Nelson didn't realize was the thwarted attack on his sister and her friends was part of a bigger plan. To try and leave him vulnerable and less well protected. Depending upon how he reacted to the situation.

This was a false premise. Because he had hired extra staff and bodyguards out on the boat. He still had his usual compliment of staff, with the exception of Osvaldo and now Brian. Lenny was filling in for Osvaldo.

Since early this morning. Nelson had been contemplating postponing or even cancelling the harebrained idea of offering a Mr. Reynolds a night with Carol for $10 million. But he was now going out to the yacht anyway.

When he had agreed to the proposal. It had slipped his mind that his sister Millie and her friends were staying out on the yacht. But didn't really see that as being a problem.

Brian arrived out on the yacht in an attempt to calm the situation. He briefly met with Osvaldo. Then went below to meet with Millie, Donna and Jill to tell them everything was alright now.

"Surely it's more than jealousy" suggested Millie to Brian.

"What? Oh yes that's all it really is" responded Brian remembering Osvaldo had just told him this was the excuse he'd used. "Just know you are safe and please continue to enjoy your vacation. You can go back up now."

"Why are you guys being so serious? Come on. Brian says everything's alright now so let's go party. We're missing the best part of the day" shouted Jill, as she put her coffee down and started up the stairs.

When they got up on deck they saw a United States Coast Guard vessel heading away from the yacht.

Millie asked Brian what was going on?

Brian said the United States Coast Guard is on routine patrol. Millie thought it was suspicious and there had to be more to it. But knew there was nothing she could really do.

She went over and joined Jill and Donna lying by the pool. Settled back with a freshly poured drink and began to read her novel.

There was no sign of the speedboat, with the unfriendly looking men, they had seen earlier.

Nelson was surprised about what had happened out on his yacht. Something like this had never happened while he had been on-board. He wondered why his sister and her friends were being targeted?

An incident like this was something he had not expected and wondered *how he could explain it away when he saw his sister later tonight.*

He wondered *if the people who were targeting the yacht thought he was on-board. This might explain it better. He knew he had enemies because of the success of his illegal ventures. He would have to think up an excuse to explain it away. He hoped Millie and her friends would not link it to his illicit activities.*

Apart from the incident today Millie and her friends were continuing to have a great time.

Donna and Jill were constantly congratulating Millie, on how well her brother had done since coming out to the west coast. Even though she could only tell them he was in the construction business.

Thursday night arrived and circumstances had somewhat overtaken Nelson. He knew he would be setting the guy with the $10 million up with Carol and also needed to deal with what had happened out on the yacht earlier in the day.

He was thinking *if Reynolds turned out to be a social guy he might provide a nice diversion for his sister and her friends.*

Brian had called Nelson to tell him he had calmed the situation and was planning to stay out on the yacht until he got there.

That evening Nelson had arranged for Carol to be picked up and brought to his private club in Malibu. Towards the end of their dinner Nelson made an off-the-cuff remark about spending some time with her out on his yacht tonight.

He said he had arranged a meeting with an oil man from Houston and would be mixing a little business with pleasure. He mentioned that Brian, his sister Millie and two of her friends were also out on the yacht.

This was quite a surprise for Carol. She said she didn't have a problem with it because she enjoyed meeting new people. Inwardly she hoped it might be a chance to sleep with Nelson. Which hadn't happened since they'd been dating.

*　*　*　*

I'd completed the edits Simmons had requested to my column before being picked up outside Grauman's Chinese Theatre on Sunset Strip in Hollywood. After a comfortable ride to Marina Del Rey. I was shuttled out to Nelson's yacht in a big speedboat.

Nelson's yacht was lit up like a Christmas tree, red, white and blue against the night sky. Each deck was lit up giving the effect of a floating hotel. It was most impressive, almost mind blowing.

As I climbed out of the speedboat I was greeted by a big burly guy who welcomed me on-board. He introduced himself as Osvaldo. We made our way to where a group of people were sitting talking. I was greeted by someone who introduced himself as Brian. I'd heard of him from what Shelley had told me.

Osvaldo introduced me as Mr. Reynolds, to Nelson's sister Millie and her friends, Jill and Donna. I was as surprised to see them as they were to see me. I told them I was here for a business meeting with Martin which they quickly accepted. As I sat down the big guy asked me if I would like a drink?

I asked for a gin and tonic and seeing an ashtray full of butts asked if it was alright if I smoked and Jill said no problem, her and Donna smoked.

Brian got up almost immediately and excused himself. After he'd left I seemed to become an instant hit. Likely because apart from some heavyset bodyguards who were obviously working. I was perhaps the only eligible man on-board. Millie's friends were all over me excitedly asking what my meeting was about and when would Millie's brother be arriving?

I wasn't sure if they knew he was bringing his date with him. I was unsure now if anything was going to happen in regard to my proposal. But thought *perhaps this is the way Nelson had planned it.*

I'd never been on a luxury yacht before and it was unbelievably impressive. The deck we were on overlooked the stern where there was a pool, hot tub and beyond that a helipad.

I later found out that in addition to Nelson's palatial suite with an adjoining office. There were five guest cabins all with their own ensuite bathroom facilities. So there was ample room for him and his guests.

In addition there was apparently a captain's cabin, two bodyguard cabins, four crew cabins and two staff cabins. They all had bunk beds in them except the captain's cabin. There is also a galley, dining room, several bars and a Cinema/TV area.

While I was chatting with Millie and her friends we heard a helicopter approaching. It's lights coming into view as it hovered and landed.

Nelson and his date jumped down out of the helicopter. Protecting their ears from the noise, of the rotor blades, they ran over to where we were sitting.

Like on que Brian appeared and he and Nelson briefly spoke before he disappeared again.

Nelson's date blew me away. She was young in her late twenties. I guessed. Was a natural blonde with a body like a playboy centerfold and was extremely attractive.

Nelson shook hands with me while introducing me and everyone else to Carol Bromley. She was busy trying to get her hair back into place. Almost immediately she excused herself saying she had to go to the little girl's room.

Nelson said "Good evening ladies. I hope you've been enjoying your time out here on Big Fish. If you would excuse me for a moment I need to speak with Mr. Reynolds."

As I was getting up. Nelson came around to where I'd been sitting and gently took my arm, leading me over to the bar. On the way he whispered "For your information everything is still a go with Carol tonight!"

I immediately broached the subject of a contract for what had been agreed over the phone with his lawyer. He dismissed it saying there was no need because he trusted me and it was a cash deal anyway. Which didn't require any agreement or contract.

He asked Osvaldo standing behind the bar to setup two tumblers and get the bottle of single malt Scotch whisky he had recently acquired.

Nelson said the Scotch whisky is a single malt called Oban and aged for thirty two years and he wanted me to try it to see what I thought.

Only rarely having sampled some of the finer things in life, including single malt Scotch whisky. I took a sip and it pretty much tasted like any of the other Scotch whisky I'd ever had. But I lied and told Nelson it was amazingly smooth and he looked very appreciative as he clinked my glass with his saying "Cheers!"

"So about tonight" Nelson commented "This is what's going to happen. It's been arranged that I will be called away along with Brian, who I assume you've met, to deal with an urgent matter. We'll be taking the helicopter.

Carol will not have a say in the matter and will be left with you, Millie and her friends. Don't worry about having your way with her this won't be a problem. Once she gets into the coke and booze she turns into a nympho. I bet right now she's downstairs getting her fill of both.

I have asked Osvaldo to make sure she has sufficient quantities of both to ensure she won't remember a thing when she wakes up sometime tomorrow."

I was lost for words.

"I hope you agree that this is the best way to achieve what you want and ensure you get your money's worth?" Nelson enquired.

I was thinking to myself *"What I want is for you to sign a piece of incriminating paper. I still wasn't sure what I was going to do with Carol."*

Nelson continued "I normally try to keep away from her whenever she gets too stoned or drunk because she's so demanding. But for you tonight it will be perfect for what you want. Just humour her. Tell her some of your best stories and she'll be happy and all yours."

"Does this work for you?" Nelson asked.

"Yes. But can we sign a contract of some kind?" I responded waving the piece of paper I wanted him to sign.

"What?" he asked somewhat taken aback.

"I was wondering if we need to sign some kind of agreement. After all it's $10 million we're talking about" I replied.

"Don't worry about that. It's not necessary just have the cash ready when I get back" he replied walking away carrying his drink.

I was about to disagree when Carol reappeared at the top of the stairs and shouted "Dry vodka martini, please Osvaldo. Thanks". She sat down to chat with Nelson's sister, Donna and Jill.

She looked incredibly sexy and enticing.

Nelson and I joined them, me sitting between Jill and Millie across from Donna, Carol and Nelson. I'd never been this close to such a stunning woman in the flesh and I was thinking *my god this should be good.*

Millie and her friends only wearing bikinis were complimenting Carol on the outfit she was wearing. A low-cut white blouse, short black skirt with a large white belt separating the two garments and black and white stilettos. I was wondering how she could even walk in them, especially on a swaying boat.

"So have you ladies caught up?" asked Nelson.

"You certainly look very relaxed" commented Carol, as she took a sip of her just delivered dry martini.

"We've been having a wonderful time" responded Millie.

"Nice to meet you Mr. Reynolds" said Carol "You know I really know very little about Marty's business affairs but he certainly knows how to treat a lady. Will you be staying on-board tonight?"

"Please call me John, which I thought *seemed more appropriate than R.J. which I had looked up and stood for Richard Joshua Reynolds.* Yes. I've been invited to stay overnight" I replied.

"So please tell us about yourself John?" suggested Carol.

This was the part I'd been dreading in case I fluffed the lines I didn't have.

I began by telling them that I'd made my money in the oil refining business in Houston. Hoping none of them knew anyone there or anything about the oil business. This seemed to be the case and Carol seemingly not being much of a listener immediately tried to switch the discussion to what I'd been doing in Los Angeles.

I responded by saying I'm here in Los Angeles to drum up venture capital for a new refinery in Latin America.

Carol asked Nelson if he was planning on getting into the oil refining business but before he could answer. Osvaldo approached him and whispered something in his ear.

Nelson got up immediately and said "Excuse me."

Brian was waiting for Nelson in his office and told him from what he had found out he thinks the guys in the boat were San Diego mobsters. Working for a guy called Moretti who has been trying to establish himself in Los Angeles.

He is likely aware of our operations down on the border and in San Diego. Maybe he is targeting you as a test. Perhaps given to him by the other mob families here or perhaps even back east.

"But why now?" Nelson asked.

"He's obviously trying to get at you while your sister is here. I'm not sure if it's part of a bigger plan. I'll try and find out?" responded Brian.

Back on the lounge deck Millie realizing it was getting late and finding Carol somewhat overpowering said she was going to call it a night. She said goodnight, got up and left. Soon Donna and Jill got up saying it had been a long day and said their own goodnights.

This left me talking to Carol until Nelson and Brian suddenly appeared. Nelson shouted over to Osvaldo at the bar to refresh our drinks. He told us something had come up and he and Brian had to leave immediately but he hoped to be back soon.

He gave Carol a peck on the cheek and as she was starting to ask him something cut her short.

He said "Sorry. We have to go" and he and Brian ran towards the helicopter. It's propeller was already beginning to whirl.

It quickly took off heading for the well-lit California shoreline.

"Oh well, no reason for us not to have some fun. Right Mr. Reynolds, sorry John" said Carol as she stood up.

"I'll be right back" she said walking over to the bar and talking with Osvaldo before disappearing.

She was a knockout alright.

Following his brief exchange with Carol, Osvaldo turned on some smooth jazz music. I sat and listened to it while looking around thinking *this is certainly the life*.

I was racking my brain to try and think of some stories I could charm Carol with when she returned. It wasn't long until she came back.

"Alright John. Tell me more about what you've been doing since you've been here?" she asked.

I rambled on about the people I'd supposedly met during my stay. Including Hollywood film and TV stars, leading politicians, including the Governor of California and many other affluent people she had heard of.

This was easy for me. I'd lived here for almost twenty years now and was up to date on the comings and goings of Californian celebrities. I also knew who was currently hot.

The gossip seemed to very much intrigue and interest Carol. Right up until she checked her impressive looking diamond studded watch and acting surprised said "Oh look at the time. It's almost one o'clock. I think I should be turning in for the night."

She stood up and was a little unsteady on her super high heeled stilettos. So I jumped up and assisted her across the deck and down to what I assumed was Nelson's suite.

She invited me in and once inside immediately began to undress. Throwing her stiletto's, belt, blouse, bra and skirt on the floor. While all the time leaning on me to support herself.

I was trying to stay calm with this dream girl now only wearing panties hanging on me. I was taking deep breaths while trying to ignore her advances. I could see the remains of several lines of cocaine on a mirror on the dressing table and a half empty bottle of vodka.

"See you tomorrow" I said as I began to untangle myself from her. But she hung on to me. Putting her arms around my neck, pleading with me to stay, constantly kissing me.

I managed to break away from her again. As I was heading for the door she ran and jumped on my back, piggy-back style, begging me to stay.

I was thinking. *Why am I resisting this gorgeous, voluptuous woman who is so irresistibly sexy and smells so good, when I'm supposed to be paying $10 million to go to bed with her?*

I locked the suite door and carried her still on my back over to the bed. I dropped her on the bed and as I bent down to kiss her mountainous breasts she grabbed my head burying it between them.

I quickly got undressed and in those early hours of the morning we did everything you would expect to see in a great adult movie. Without a doubt it was sexually the most memorable night of my life.

When sleep eventually overtook Carol. As I lay next to her I was thinking *about what would happen in the morning knowing I didn't have the $10 million.*

Perhaps I could delay things by telling Nelson I would have the money wired to one of his bank accounts. What I really needed was his signature on my damning one page contract.

Thinking *I shouldn't be found sleeping with Carol, in Nelson's suite. I found an empty cabin and got a few hours' sleep.*

FRI JUL 28

The following morning I was sitting up on the lounge deck talking with Millie when Nelson's helicopter circled and landed on the yacht.

Carol, Donna and Jill had not surfaced yet.

As Nelson ran from the helicopter, Osvaldo went to speak to him. Probably to tell him what had happened last night. Nelson waved him away showing no interest in what he was trying to tell him.

As he approached Millie and I, where we were sitting. He waved me over to the bar. When we met there he asked me how it had gone last night. I told him I had thoroughly enjoyed myself and was ready to complete the transaction. My stomach was churning knowing at any moment I could be found out for perpetrating a fraud.

Nelson commented that he hoped I'd got my money's worth in the time he'd given me and said "So now I believe we need to discuss the ten million smackeroo's?"

I told him I was currently working with two electronic money transfer companies Western Union and Wells Fargo. To see who will give me the best rate on the money transfer. By suggesting I was supposedly working with these two companies I was trying to create the illusion that I had the money. I hoped it would give him the impression that it was only a matter of time until he got it.

Meanwhile I was thinking *I still needed to get his signature on an incriminating piece of paper. Afterall, it was really the only reason I was here.*

"I thought you agreed with Ron that it would be cash?" Nelson queried.

"I don't know about your business. But in mine, when I'm paying out millions of dollars, I always do it using electronic money transfer. I know cash was mentioned with your lawyer but I thought the cash would be in the form of a money transfer. I never carry that much cash around with me and I'm sure you don't either?" I replied.

"I was hoping you would have a suitcase or a bag with you. But I guess this is not the case and you don't have the cash with you?" laughed Nelson, before asking Osvaldo to make three Mimosa's.

When the drinks were ready he took one over to Millie saying "Cheers Sis!" before coming back over to the bar.

I continued "When we discussed it last night you didn't seem to be that concerned about the timing. I still need the paperwork to go with the transaction for my records."

"Is this a trick you're trying to pull?" shouted Nelson angrily "Are you trying to trap me?"

At that moment he was interrupted by one of Osvaldo's men who whispered something in his ear. Nelson said "Excuse me" and quickly walked away.

I carried my drink over to where Millie was sitting my stomach churning. I was also starting to sweat.

"You look somewhat hot and bothered and a little pale. Is everything alright with you and my brother?" asked Millie.

"Everything is fine. Thanks. I think the bright morning sun and not the best night's sleep are making me feel a little woozy" I replied.

Last night Nelson had asked Brian to check me out becoming very suspicious after hearing I hadn't brought any suitcases or bags on-board with me.

Nelson picked up the phone in his office and Brian told him he had not been able to find any information about a Mr. John Reynolds in the oil business in Houston.

Brian also said "Ron has been doing some digging as well and traced the source of Reynolds phone calls. He thinks the guy is Harry Walsh. The crime reporter for the Los Angeles Times."

Nelson told Brian he had begun to suspect he was being fooled by an imposter and would take care of it.

While waiting for Nelson to return I began to observe the shoreline and wondered *how far it was from where the yacht was anchored and if I could swim that far.*

Although I knew I wasn't a great swimmer. I figured this might be my only chance of staying alive now that Nelson had become suspicious about the money. There didn't seem to be any other options.

I could see quite a lot of small boats between Nelson's yacht and the shore which I thought might be of help to me. I was concerned about what Nelson might be doing and wondered if he might be getting information about who I really was.

I was still sitting with Millie when suddenly we heard Carol's voice loudly calling out.

Millie got up and started to make her way over to the stairs. One of Nelson's overweight bodyguards also began to waddle over to see what was going on. Osvaldo ran out from behind the bar. Suddenly we all heard a loud sequence of obscenities. The only discernible word being Vodka.

With everyone on the deck distracted. I got up from the table and stealthily made my way to the shoreline side of the yacht. I dived over the railing fully clothed. I tried to minimize the sound of my splash as I hit the water and immediately began to swim underwater.

Osvaldo, Millie and the bodyguard who had been looking down at Carol ran over to the side of the yacht where they'd heard a splash. Looking down they could only see bubbles and ripples.

Not seeing me on the deck anymore, they figured it must have been me who'd gone over the side.

Nelson appeared at the top of the stairs asking "What's going on?"

Osvaldo who'd been looking over the rail turned and shouted that I'd gone over the side.

Nelson asked him to launch the speedboat and go after me. Osvaldo and a bodyguard went down to the lower deck. Climbed into the speedboat and started up the two high-powered outboard motors. Launching it.

Fortunately for me they were on the other side of the yacht.

By now reluctantly. I'd ripped most of my newly purchased suit off and was treading water next to the bow of the yacht. I was trying not to bang into it as the waves pushed me around.

I started to hear the loud noise of a speedboat. I assumed it was the same one, I'd been brought out to the yacht on, the night before. I took several deep breathes and dived down next to the yacht's hull as it sped by. When I came up for air it was nowhere in sight. Although I could still hear it so figured it couldn't be too far away.

Osvaldo and the temporary bodyguard hadn't spent much time on the water and their search so far, had consisted of circling the yacht.

Nelson was shouting down at them to slow down and move further out. But they couldn't hear him over the noise of the two high-powered outboard motors and continued to speed around the yacht.

After swimming underwater for as long as I could. I reached the boat closest to Nelson's yacht. It seemed to be unoccupied so I hid behind it.

The shoreline looked to be no closer.

I hid here treading water the speedboat occasionally speeding by. Each time it came by I dived down under the surface until I could no longer hear it. Coming up gasping for air.

There were smaller boats off in the distance closer to the shore but I knew it would take a Herculean effort on my part to swim to even the closest one.

However, I knew I had no time to waste so setoff swimming underwater as best I could in the direction of the small boats. From time to time I heard the speedboat as it sped by.

After what seemed like an eternity I reached a large buoy. It was bobbing up and down in the channel between the boats. I clung on to it, on the shoreline side.

I could see Nelson's yacht quite a distance away now and could see the speedboat heading in my direction. I submerged. The sound from the speedboat was momentarily very loud before it gradually began to fade away. When I came up for air. I could see it off in the distance. Heading back towards Nelson's yacht.

I noticed the sun was quite low in the sky and should be setting soon. So I decided to keep hanging onto the buoy until it got dark thinking *surely they couldn't search for me at night.*

I saw the lights all along the shoreline gradually coming on. On some of the boats too.

Nelson's yacht was lit up like a Christmas tree again and I could see a powerful searchlight criss-crossing the surface of the water all around it. The sun had almost set and I began to feel cold so swam towards the boats closest to the buoy.

Nelson was fuming as he sat in his office.

When Osvaldo had returned. Nelson had blasted him for the unprofessional way he'd conducted the search. He didn't know where the person who had called himself Reynolds was but knew he had been tricked.

He felt completely helpless. He phoned Brian and told him to hire men and position them along the shoreline. He told him to ask them to look out for anyone who resembled a fifty-year old man, in tattered pants, stumbling out of the sea.

SAT JUL 29

I awoke at dawn on the deck of a small sailboat. I'd obviously ended up here last night after what must have been the longest swim of my life.

I collected myself and wondered what I should do next.

I decided to stay where I was for now. But be careful not to let anyone see me. In case those with boats nearby could see I wasn't the owner.

The boat I was on had a small outboard motor and there seemed to be all kinds of folded sails lying on the deck. I setup a wind breaker of sorts. Moving into the diminishing shade as the sun rose and slowly moved across the cloudless blue sky.

Lying inside the wind breaker no one could see me unless were in the air. I figured any flight plans that had been filed with the local aviation authorities had to be from A to B not circling surveillance type flights.

I was thinking *how easy it had been to trick Nelson. So perhaps he wasn't that smart after all, just greedy.*

Although I'd had the best lay of my life. I hadn't come close to accomplishing what I had set out to do. Which was to get something in writing that could incriminate Nelson.

I had decided once it got dark I would continue to head for the shore. But right now I really needed something to drink. I'd already searched the boat I was on. But hadn't found any water. In fact I hadn't found any provisions whatsoever. So I assumed the boat was only used occasionally and whatever was needed was brought on-board at the time.

I was tasting salt whenever I swallowed and it was getting dark on that Saturday night. My goal was obviously to try and get to the shore. I tried to start the boat's small outboard motor, but it wouldn't catch.

Great I thought. *The boat is too big to use paddles and I don't know how to sail it. I don't know anything about outboard motors so was at a loss as to what to do. Except maybe swim to another boat to see if there was any drinking water on-board.*

There were lights on several of the boats close by. So I figured there must be people on them. I swam past them underwater to avoid making splashes that someone might hear.

It was very dark now. I found a boat that seemed to be unoccupied and climbed aboard. I went below and gradually began to make out shapes. Feeling around I found an unopened case of bottled water. I drank five or six of them in quick succession.

After quenching my thirst. I realized I was exhausted after all the swimming I'd just done. So I cleared the junk off a bunk bed and as soon as I lied down. Fell asleep.

* * * *

On that very same Saturday night. One of Nelson's murder teams, without a doubt, murdered the wrong young woman. Dahlia Rossini, the wife of west coast mafia boss Johnny Rossini's youngest son, Joey.

The story goes. After having a fight with her husband, Joey, she took off and drove downtown fuming. She came across one of Nelson's Desperado clubs and out of spiteful curiosity decided to go in.

The place was hopping that night. Although reluctant at first. Dahlia allowed herself to be plied with free booze by several different guys. Each one doing his best to pick her up. Having sent each one of them packing. She ended up sitting at the bar on her own.

She hadn't gone unnoticed and Jimmy the Fixer was called. He was told there was a potential candidate for one of his murder teams at this club. No other victim had been selected so far that night so he contacted one of his murder teams and told them to check out the situation.

When two murder team members arrived. They couldn't believe their luck.

Dahlia Rossini was very attractive. Wearing expensive clothes and jewelry which worried them a bit. She was certainly the classiest potential victim their murder team had preyed upon and they couldn't wait to get her into their van.

After getting the go ahead from Jimmy. They followed their usual protocol. At the end of the night, although Dahlia insisted she had her own car. They convinced her she'd had too much to drink to drive and got her to accept a ride with them.

It seems at some point she had let Joey know where she was. Just as he showed up he saw her being bundled into a white cube van. To late to stop what was going on he followed the van as it made it's way out into the country.

After about an hour. The van slowed down on a deserted road and Joey saw something being thrown out from the side of it.

Joey stopped where he thought the van had slowed down. After getting out of his car he looked down into a drainage ditch and saw Dahlia's naked lifeless body.

Joey immediately called his father who told him to stay where he was and call 911. Once the police arrived Joey gave them what information he had. Identifying his wife's body and telling them about following a white cube van out here. He also told them about seeing Dahlia being pushed into the same van outside a downtown Desperado club.

He told them he had stayed quite a distance behind. So much so that he didn't get the license plate number. He said he realized now it would have been of great help to the them.

The police at the crime scene asked Joey who was very distraught if at his earliest convenience he could go downtown to the Los Angeles Police Department headquarters building and ask for Detective Sergeant Stone. They said he who would assist him to complete a Witness Statement.

Detective Sergeant Stone was a thoughtful, career cop who had a very positive attitude. He was someone who always had time for others.

SUN JUL 30

I awoke to daylight streaming in through a porthole. I drank several more bottles of water before going up on deck. After several minutes I managed to start the outboard motor. Regardless of who saw me I headed straight for the marina.

One of the hitmen Brian had hired positioned at Marina Del Rey noticed a man in a small boat was having difficulty lining it up with a berth. He looked to be half naked and seemed to match the description he'd been given. A man about fifty years old with torn and tattered pants.

After docking the boat. Leaving the marina I wasn't sure where to go. So I staggered north until I came to the Marina Hotel. Where even though I looked like a castaway. I managed to get a room after pulling a credit card out of my soaking wet wallet.

I stupidly checked in under my fake name. I purchased some smokes with a soggy five dollar bill. Lighting one up as soon as they were handed to me.

There were several stacks of newspapers on the counter. I noticed there was a photo of an attractive young woman under the headline Dahlia Rossini Murdered. I thought to myself *Nelson has really gone and done it this time.*

I'd only just got into my room on the second floor of the hotel when the door came crashing in. A heavy-set man, in a crumpled suit stood on top of it, pointing a gun at me.

He told me to lie face down on the bed while he got the door back into place. After wedging the door back in it's frame the big man came over to where I was lying and said "Turn over and let me get a good look at you."

He picked up the phone on the bedside table and started telling whoever was on the other end that I looked like George Clooney. I was wearing torn and tattered pants and he'd seen me as I'd sailed into the marina. He finished by saying it's the Marina Hotel, room 217. Before hanging up.

After he got off the phone he told me to keep lying face down on the bed. He went and sat on the end of the bed, watched TV and waited.

After receiving a call from one of the men he had hired to watch out for Reynolds. Brian phoned Jimmy the Fixer and told him to send one of his murder teams to pick up the guy Nelson has been looking for. He said he's at the Marina Hotel, room 217 and said it's just up the road from Marina Del Rey.

About half an hour later there was a soft knock on the damaged motel room door. The big gunman still with a gun in his hand got up and walked over and pulled the door aside. Out of the corner of my eye I saw two men enter the room. *More of Nelson's men I assumed.*

"You think this is the guy?" one of them asked.

"He matches the description and sailed into the marina about an hour ago looking like he'd never sailed a boat before" replied the big gunman.

"Good. We're supposed to be getting a phone call from our Head so we need to sit tight until then. We'll let him know you did a good job" said the other man.

The three of them sat on the end of the bed and watched TV while I continued to lie face down wondering what was going to happen to me. The phone rang and one of the newly arrived men picked it up and after several okays hung up.

The guy who had been on the phone tapped me on the shoulder and said "Okay Sailor. Up you get we're going for a ride."

He put a pillowcase over my head and pulled me up off the bed. I guess that was so I didn't know where I was being taken. He led me out of the hotel room, assisted me down some stairs and pushed me into the back of a van. I heard the big gunmen who had spotted me being thanked as the doors were slammed shut.

I'm not sure how long the journey took. But when we arrived I was manhandled out of the van. Assisted up some steps, the pillowcase removed and there I stood face to face with Martin Nelson.

I figured *I was in Pacific Palisades. The pillowcase hadn't been necessary because Shelley had told me where he lived but I didn't say anything.*

"Well I must say it's nice to see you again Mr. Reynolds or should I say Harry?" laughed Nelson.

"I'm sure it is" I quipped.

"I thought I was a good swimmer but you must be an even better one?" chuckled Nelson.

"Desperation makes us do things we never thought we could do" I said.

"Is that a famous quote?" asked Nelson.

"I don't think so. I just came up with it" I said.

"You sure pulled a fast one on me. I understand what you were trying to do by getting me to sign your piece of paper. You almost had me fooled which is quite unusual for me. So I must say I'm most impressed. Given that you are such an inventive person. I think we should have some more fun. What do you think?" Nelson asked.

"I must admit you have me on pins and needles" I replied.

"Come on now there is no need for such sarcasm Mr. Walsh" responded Nelson.

He asked one of his men to frisk me. He found my still soggy wallet, a pack of cigarettes and a book of matches which he put in a plastic bag handing it to someone else. He in turn handed me a bundle of dry clothes before escorting me to what turned out to be a nicely decorated day room at the end of a long hall at the front of the property.

As we'd walked down the hallway. I'd caught glimpses of the ocean off in the distance. I imagined this was probably wasted on Nelson. Who probably like most of the men in this high end neighbourhood likely rarely took the time to smell the roses. The smell of money being much sweeter to them.

Nelson and men like him were usually only interested in power and money. Regularly working eighteen hours a day and likely looking at an early death which seemed to be fine for them. Even though to most of us it seemed like they'd never really lived.

I was thinking *it is funny how the best places around the world are owned by super rich self-centered ego maniacs who rarely have the time to appreciate them.*

Sitting in the day room I was surprised that I hadn't been tied up or handcuffed. Nelson was definitely showing me a great deal of respect. Considering a few days ago I had tried to do my upmost to trap him into signing a document that I hoped could be used in a court of law to convict him of at least pimping.

Now alone I couldn't stop thinking *about how it used to be a constant struggle between the haves and have nots. But now seeing and being inside Nelson's mansion it was pretty obvious the haves have won.*

We used to talk about the landed gentry through the centuries but it has gotten even worse these days with most of those at the top having no breeding or gentlemanly manners whatsoever. They have been acquiring their wealth and fortunes in new ways. Accumulating more and more assets at an alarming rate.

World revolution is all the billions of impoverished people living on planet earth have left. But the question is how can it be accomplished. The super rich these days are so well insulated in military states that it will almost take an act of god to dislodge them.

Cindy's death still haunted me. I still wanted to do something to avenge it. Even though my first attempt had failed miserably, almost resulting in my own death.

I was kicking myself that I hadn't told anyone what I was planning to do last Thursday night but even now I didn't know who I could have told.

I didn't really have any close friends. In fact if I thought about it *Bert the bartender at Jules was probably my closest. Certainly, a sad state of affairs. Maybe I should have told Shelley but I'd really only just met her.*

I knew Mike Simmons my editor would be pissed off with me because I hadn't submitted a column on either

Friday or Saturday. What I didn't know was that after not receiving my draft columns or hearing from me he'd become very concerned. I'd never missed a printing cut-off deadline in all the time I'd worked for him.

I found out later he'd e-mailed me and phoned both my home and mobile numbers but had only got voice mails. *He obviously didn't know my mobile was at the bottom of the Pacific Ocean.* Not being able to reach me he'd even sent someone from the office to look for me at my apartment.

They'd got no response when they buzzed me. So waited and followed someone in but got no answer when they knocked on my apartment door.

They reported back to Simmons who immediately phoned the Mayor a long time friend of his to let him know one of his reporters had gone missing. He asked the Mayor if he could ask the Police Chief to get his officers to look out for me.

The Mayor asked Simmons to fill out a missing person report at police headquarters, just up the road. He said he would speak to the Police Chief. He asked Simmons if he had any idea where the police should start looking?

He replied "Unfortunately I don't. He's been moving around a lot lately."

"Leave it with me but please fill out that missing person report as soon as you can" said the Mayor before hanging up.

I had already settled into my new surroundings. I was sitting in a comfortable armchair flipping through a coffee table book. It was a book about of all things the French Revolution, which I was finding to be most interesting reading.

An hour or so later I was taken to Nelson's opulent looking office where we briefly exchanged pleasantries. Him telling me he still couldn't believe what I'd tried to pull off and me asking him when he was going to let me go.

He gestured towards a laptop on his desk, telling me he would like me to write a column for tomorrow's newspaper. He said it should say that it still remains a mystery as to who has been committing the murders of young women, since the beginning of the year.

"You know I saw the headline in the newspapers this morning. I assume you did too?" I asked.

"You're talking about Dahlia Rossini? What does that have to do with me?" he replied.

"Just another one of your murders?" I responded.

"Let's get back to tomorrow's column about not knowing who is doing the murders" he mumbled.

"We both know you are responsible for the murders" I responded.

"I'm holding all the cards right now so you'll be writing this for your own well being" he said.

"You know I can't do that" I replied.

"Okay. Just give me the e-mail address where I can send it. We'll leave it at that" responded Nelson handing me a pen and a paper.

I scribbled Mike Simmons e-mail address down and handed it back to him saying "There you go."

"After this I think we'll be even. You pretending to be someone else and me pretending to be you. What do you think?" he laughed.

"Good luck" I said.

Nelson made a phone call and within a matter of seconds someone had arrived to escort me back to the day room.

A short while later I was taken back to Nelson's office and he asked me to read what he'd written which he was planning to send to my editor.

The gist of what he had written was that despite my thorough investigating I still did not know who was murdering young women in downtown Los Angeles which was about as far from the truth as you could get.

He said he was happy with the column and asked me what I thought of the style and whether my editor would think I'd written it?

"You know I really can't comment because this whole thing is so bizarre" I replied.

"I think we need to wait to see if it's printed in tomorrow's paper before we move on to the next step with you" he commented.

"Which is what?" I asked.

"To be honest I'm not sure yet. All I know is people in high places are concerned with your disappearance which would appear to be a problem for me" he replied.

"This is news to me. But good news all the same" I replied.

"Let's wait to see if the column is in tomorrow's paper. So for now I'll have to ask you to go back to the day room" replied Nelson, calling someone to come and get me.

One of Nelson's bodyguards showed up and escorted me back to the room. Not long after I had a nice dinner and slept intermittently on a lumpy futon that Sunday night.

Simmons was most surprised when he received my draft column in an e-mail. It had come from a nondescript google e-mail address, late on Sunday evening. He was even more surprised when he read what I'd written and immediately knew something wasn't right.

My e-mail started by saying the reason for missing the previous printing cut-off deadlines was a close friend had recently become seriously ill. This didn't make any sense to Simmons because he didn't think I had any close friends.

He made the decision that until he could speak to me face to face he wouldn't be printing anything sent from me. It seemed so out of character that I still hadn't contacted him other than via this phony e-mail.

Simmons called the Mayor to see if he had any news.

The Mayor asked Simmons if he'd filled out the missing person report and he said he had. The Mayor said so far he hadn't heard anything, but he would let him know if he did.

Simmons wasn't satisfied with the Mayor's response knowing he could tap into the most influential people in the city. Some who had voted for him and some who hadn't. I asked the Mayor what the Police Chief was doing to find his missing reporter. The Mayor informed him that All Points Bulletins were being sent out regularly, with the reporter's description. So the whole police department was on alert.

Simmons was pleased to hear this and thanked the Mayor before ending the call.

*   *   *   *

Since being informed about Dahlia's murder early on Sunday morning, Johnny Rossini had begun to make plans on how to take Nelson out. He knew his daughter-in-law had been murdered by one of Nelson's murder teams. It was common knowledge in the criminal underworld that he was the one murdering young women, even though no one knew why.

Rossini already knew a lot about Nelson. Including that he rarely left his home and whenever he did he was closely guarded. Always travelling in his bullet proof Mercedes.

It was known that Nelson liked to discuss most matters in his gardens. Where there was no chance of a conversation being overheard or recorded. So Rossini figured the best place to take him out would be in his own backyard.

Rossini was so angered by what Nelson had done he planned to carry out the hit himself, which was most unusual. He figured he couldn't trust it to anyone else and his Capo's knew better than to try and dissuade him.

He had learned that the accessible perimeter of Nelson's property was protected by deep ditches and high fences. The only way in was through one of the two gated entrances.

Rossini had discovered that there was a regular delivery of beer and liquor tomorrow. Also that Nelson liked to get the perspective on how things were going from Brian before chairing his Monday update meetings, usually outside in his gardens.

By late Sunday night Rossini was satisfied he had covered all the bases and was ready.

MON JUL 31

Monday morning Nelson was out by his pool flipping through the early edition of the Los Angeles Times. He didn't see my column anywhere. So he had me brought out to join him.

"Take a seat. How do you take your coffee?" Nelson asked

"Just black. Thanks" I replied.

"That's easy" he said. He got up and moved to where a coffee making machine was located. It was on the counter behind his impressive looking bar off to the side of the pool. He operating the machine and brought the coffee over to where I was sitting.

"Would it be possible for me to have a cigarette now I'm outside?" I asked.

"I don't smoke but I'll see if I can find someone who does. Hold on" Nelson replied leaving me alone drinking my coffee.

Looking at the pool and it's surroundings, the Pacific Ocean off in the distance. I thought to myself. *Perhaps I was wrong about Nelson and he does appreciate and enjoy where he is living.*

Nelson soon returned with, I assumed, one of his bodyguards. He handed me a cigarette and lit it for me before trundling off.

Nelson sat down at the table opposite me and stated quite angrily that my column was not in today's early edition.

"As you know you sent it to my editor from a google e-mail address and he likely figured it hadn't come from me. He is probably still wondering where I am" I responded.

"Yes. I am beginning to realize abducting you is not without its challenges. You seem to be being missed by quite a few prominent people in the city. By the way you haven't given me all the details of how your night with Carol went? We only briefly discussed it out on the yacht" Nelson enquired.

"It was by far the best lay of my life. Let's leave it at that" I responded.

"Not bad for a freebie then? I'm still trying to figure out how you can pay me back" replied Nelson.

"You know it was inevitable that you and I would meet again in circumstances that were unfavourable to me" I said.

"I know you are responsible for the murders of over twenty young women and you are obviously not happy that I know this.

I'm sure that's why your people have been trying to take me out for the past few weeks. However, I think you realize murdering a crime reporter from the Los Angeles Times is a lot different from murdering careless hapless young women.

Even those running the city might not be able to turn a blind eye. My editor knows all about you and is friends with a lot of influential people in the city. He can also easily get access to my files if he wants to.

So you could soon be approaching your Al Capone Inland Revenue Service moment" I said.

Nelson said laughing "Is that right? Well I should tell you I've thought of something you can do before I let you go. I will tell you what it is later."

After I finished my cigarette and coffee I was escorted back to the room I was being kept in. Once back there I went back to reading the coffee table book on the French Revolution.

Having a cigarette had temporarily suspended my need to quit smoking cold turkey. I'd often heard it was the best way to quit but at the moment I didn't feel too bad.

*   *   *   *

Johnny Rossini and his most trusted captain Cosimo Giordano were faking that their car had broken down. It was on the road not far from the south entrance to Nelson's property.

They were both wearing skin coloured balaclavas and hiding under the hood of the dark Lincoln town car. A brown National Liquor delivery truck slowed down to see what was going on.

As the driver was rolling the window down Rossini rushed at him pointing a gun at his head. He shouted at him to turn the engine off.

In short order. Both delivery men were dragged from their truck and told to take their caps and coveralls off. Leaving them only in their underpants. They were then pushed into the back of the supposedly broken down car.

While this was going on. Rossini's driver also wearing a skin coloured balaclava. Had moved the liquor delivery truck off to the side of the road.

Rossini and Giordano quickly put the coveralls on over the clothes they were wearing. Both of them being a lot thinner than the two husky looking delivery men.

Rossini threatened the two delivery men. Telling them that they and their families would be killed if they ever mentioned what had happened here. Rossini told the driver to drop the men off somewhere in the country.

After the town car had left. Rossini and Giordano clambered up into the delivery truck. They took their balaclavas off. Put the National Liquor caps on and setoff for Nelson's mansion. Rossini grinding through the gears.

As they approached the entrance to Nelson's estate. The gates automatically opened. This amazed them both as they drove onto his property, without being questioned by the men on the gate. It seemed that because they were in the brown National Liquor truck and it was a regular delivery day. Everything was good and normal but they were still surprised as to how lax Nelson's security was.

As they got close to Nelson's house. Rossini steered the delivery truck off the driveway and drove across a manicured lawn. They were leaving deep ruts as they made their way to the gazebo where they expected to find Nelson.

They took their National liquor caps off and put their balaclavas back on. As they continued to drive across the lawn they startled two gardeners who started sprinting away from the truck.

Rossini anticipated there would likely be bodyguards close to Nelson. He didn't know how many. He figured regardless. He and Giordano would have the advantage of surprise.

Sure enough. Nelson and Brian were where they were expected to be. In the gazebo on the south side of the property.

There was a long rectangular pond, full of lilies in front of the gazebo and walking paths and shrubbery all around it.

Nelson and Brian were startled when they saw the National Liquor truck heading towards them. As were the two bodyguards standing either side of the gazebo. And they were all even more surprised when two men jumped out and started firing automatic weapons at them.

Both bodyguards were quickly hit. Falling to the ground in pain holding their legs. Nelson and Brian unhurt. Ran out of the gazebo as fast as they could. Splashing into the pond in front of them. Brian was talking on his mobile as he started to wade through the lily pads. Nelson was right behind him. The gunfire stopped once they both ducked down and hid under the lily pads.

When Rossini and Giordano reached the pond they started spraying bullets across the lily pads. A stray bullet hit Nelson in the shoulder where he was submerged and he almost cried out in pain.

The gunfire stopped and Nelson and Brian could hear splashing nearby and knew it was only a matter of seconds until the killers would be on top of them.

All of a sudden they heard a lot more gunfire starting up. Looking out from under the lily pads Nelson could see Ron and several Heads firing at the killers who were wading out of the pond as fast as they could to get back to their truck.

Nelson sat up just as the killers were climbing into the delivery truck the gunfire aimed at them continuing.

Nelson holding his shoulder made his way out of the pond. Brian was assisting him. The two of them looked like drowned rats. Some of the Heads were helping the bleeding bodyguards who both had leg wounds.

"Who the hell was that?" remarked Brian to Ron who had come over to help Nelson.

"Thank God you got here in time" groaned Nelson.

"You can thank Brian. He phoned me and we came running" replied Ron.

"Let's get you patched up" said Brian as he and Ron supported Nelson as he staggered towards the back of the main house.

Rossini and Giordano had both been hit making their way out of the pond.

Rossini in the left leg and Giordano on his right side and although they were both bleeding Rossini drove on.

Rossini was speeding through shrubs and flower beds to get to the gate on the north side of Nelson's property. No one was pursuing them. They could see the Pacific Ocean on their left side and could see a parked car blocking the gate as they were hurtling towards it.

The men hiding behind the car started firing at the truck. Giordano was returning fire. Rossini didn't slow down. The truck smashed into the rear of the parked car at full speed. It spun the car around scattering the men hiding behind it. The truck continued on. Splintering the gate as it rammed through it out in to the road.

They could see a town car waiting for them. Rossini pulled the truck off to the side of the road. They both jumped out. Ran and got into the car and it took off.

Rossini had thought of everything including locating get away cars outside both gates.

During the fire fight on Nelson's property. A stray bullet had hit a passing car. A call had been made to the local police. Patrol cars began arriving. Their flashing lights on and their sirens blaring. Questions were being asked about what had been going on.

Apparently several neighbours had also called the police saying they had heard a lot shots being fired.

One of Nelson's men lied saying they had been carrying out target practice and was sorry if a stray bullet had hit a passing car.

One of the police officers commented "I can see it is quite a large property but you are very close to the road here. Do you have a target practice permit for this property?"

"Yes I believe we do" replied another one of the guys standing near the gate.

"Well. We'll need to report this incident. Another police officer will be coming back to check your permit and discuss the matter further" responded another police officer.

The guys at the gate knew this would never happen as the police rarely visited Nelson's property. If they did it was usually the Police Chief himself who seemed to be quite friendly towards their boss.

*   *   *   *

Nelson was outraged that someone had almost killed him in his own backyard. He already knew he had to

127

have some kind of revenge but needed to find out who it was before he could go after them.

Nelson was sitting in the big kitchen at the back of the house talking to Brian and Ron. He was waiting for his physician Dr. Charles Ross to arrive.

Some of the kitchen staff and gardeners were fussing around him. He was telling them not to worry that he was going to be alright.

He had seen Dr. Ross only a few weeks earlier for his annual check-up when he had got his usual clean bill of health.

Nelson was obsessed with his good health. He felt feeling good physically and mentally was a necessity for a leader. You always had to be there for those you were leading was his thinking.

Nelson thanked Brian for making the call to Ron as the Heads were assembling for the Monday meeting. He said the call had without a doubt saved their lives.

He asked what had happened to the delivery truck and was told it had smashed it's way out through the north gate and been found abandoned not far up the road.

He asked Ron to cancel today's meeting adding "Who the hell were these people who almost killed Brian and me?"

Nelson was grimacing in pain holding his shoulder which was hurting even though he'd already taken some pain killers.

"Whoever it was had obviously commandeered the National Liquor delivery truck and taken the place of the regular delivery guys" replied Brian.

"We need to find out who it was and return the favour as soon as we can" replied Nelson defiantly.

That afternoon Dr. Ross examined Nelson and said he had a superficial flesh wound.

After he'd been patched up Nelson asked Brian to free me in the way they had discussed earlier in the day.

I'd heard a lot of gunfire and it was a relief when a calm looking Brian came through the door into the room I was in.

Looking up from my book I asked "Is everything alright?"

"Yes. We're going for a ride" he said as he handed me the plastic bag containing my wallet, cigarettes and matches.

He asked me if I wanted what was left of the clothes I was wearing when I arrived.

"You mean what's left of my new suit?" I responded laughing.

"I believe it's what's left of your pants and boxers" laughed Brian.

"No. I don't want them" I said.

"Stand up so I can put this pillowcase over your head" said Brian. It was the same one from the motel.

With Brian's assistance I moved through Nelson's house before being bundled into the back of a car and off we went.

The drive took quite a while and when we got there as I got out of the car I could smell manure. After my hood was removed I could see I was on a farm which turned out to actually be a pig farm.

"We're going to put you to work before you go back to your old life" said Brian laughing as we walked around to the back of the farmhouse. A big tough looking guy approached us and asked if I was the cleaner?

Brian told him I was and asked him if everything was ready?

"I just need to clear the pen and he can go to work" replied the big man "That's after we've given him the demonstration if I understood you on the phone?"

"Yes. We want him to see the show before he gets to work" responded Brian.

The stink was getting stronger the closer we got to the pig pen. The pen was full of large grunting pink and white spotted pigs.

"Okay" said Brian "Let's show him the pigs feeding."

The big man who I'd figured out by now was the pig farmer disappeared into a nearby barn. He came out carrying what looked like a beef round. He threw it into the pen.

There was a great deal of grunting and commotion as the filthy squealing pigs fought each other to get to the meat. Within a matter of minutes it was gone. Bone and all.

"You can let the pigs out now. I'm sure Harry gets the message" commented Brian.

I guessed *I would be replacing the beef round if there was a next time and shuddered at the thought.*

The pig farmer opened the gate and wielding a big stick got the pigs out of the pen into an adjoining fenced off area.

"Okay" said Brian "There's bins over there, a shovel and a hose. Let's get this pen cleaned out right down to the concrete."

I was only wearing the tee shirt and shorts I'd been given when I'd arrived at Nelson's place and had bare feet.

I was thinking *Nelson sure is something if this is what he thought up for me to do ahead of my release. Nice guy!*

Shelley had mentioned this place and now I was seeing it for myself in full smelling colour. I guess Nelson was sending me a message to play nice.

After what I guessed was about an hour of shoveling and hosing the pen down it was clean right down to the concrete. The pig farmer seeing this tossed several bales of fresh straw into the pen and asked me to spread it around.

After I spread the straw. I stripped naked and cleaned my self off using the same hose I'd been cleaning the pen out with. The farmer threw me a towel, a faded John Deere tee shirt and an old pair of shorts. After drying myself off. Shivering. I changed into the dry clothes. Transferring my wallet, cigarettes and matches from my wet shorts.

I asked Brian if I could have a smoke and he said I could. After I finished my smoke, still shivering, after a short walk I was asked to climb into the trunk of the car. I assume they didn't want the car to smell inside.

After what seemed like an eternity. The car came to a stop. The trunk was opened and after climbing out my legs felt really stiff and I was barely able to stand.

Brian closed the trunk. Wished me good luck. Got back in to the car and it took off leaving a cloud of dust.

As I began to walk I lit up a cigarette. I was walking along the sandy unpaved road in my bare feet. The sun was low in the sky and it looked like it would be setting soon.

The landscape was desert like and it wasn't long before an old beat-up Chevy truck drove by stopping up the road ahead of me. When I reached it the driver asked me where I was going?

I told him it was a long story. But I could really use a ride to the nearest pay phone. This turned out to be outside a Denny's in the town of Lancaster. I later found out it is about eighty miles north of Los Angeles.

I called Mike Simmons collect and told him where I was and that I was alive and kicking. I told him I could use a ride and I'd like some clean clothes including runners size ten. He said he would send someone to pick me up.

I told him I had been kidnapped which is why I'd been unable to contact him and asked him not to print anything he had received because it had not been written by me.

He told me to sit tight before hanging up.

Fortunately, I still had my wallet so was able to get a coffee. Although I got strange looks from people noticing I had bare feet and if they got close enough could smell pig manure. I thought it best to stand out in the parking lot while I waited.

* * * *

That same night Nelson summoned Lenny to his office and told him he needed him to drive him somewhere. This came as a surprise to Lenny who suggested it might not be the best time to leave the property.

The very same day he had nearly been killed. But Nelson insisted saying his car was bulletproof and whoever it was who had tried to kill him was long gone.

He confided in Lenny that not only had he been physically wounded. But felt as if he had been emotionally wounded too. He said he had never felt so vulnerable and needed him to do this. Lenny could see he was upset and agreed.

* * * *

During the drive back to the city I told Bill Mason. The guy the editor had sent to pick me up. That I wanted to get dropped off at a certain address which was where Shelley was staying.

Bill however said he had strict instructions to take me straight to see Mike. So now here I was sitting opposite Simmons in his cluttered office.

"What the hell happened to you? You look like shit" said Simmons.

"I smell like it too" I responded.

"So what's the story?" he asked.

Putting it as succinctly as I could. I told Simmons I had gone after Martin Nelson and he had won. With it finishing up with me cleaning out a pig pen.

"So I guess we can call the dogs off?" Simmons asked.

"What dogs?" I laughingly enquired.

"How about the Mayor, the Police Chief and their Deputies" replied Simmons.

"This guy Nelson mentioned people of significance were helping to look for me. I didn't realize it was those at the very top" I said.

I was thinking *until the murders began at the beginning of the year my reporting job had been pretty mundane and nobody was trying to kill me.*

I had reported on all kinds of murders during my time working at the Los Angeles Times. Mafia hits, serial killers, machete murderers but not until now had I ever felt in danger for my own life. I'd obviously touched a nerve.

Becoming so involved was something new for me. Like following a murder team out to the outskirts of the city where they dumped a dead body or trying to trap a crime boss.

I could tell Simmons was concerned that I may have become too involved and potentially a liability in all senses of the word.

He had recently been on my case to cover anything except the young women murders. Surely he too wasn't being paid off.

It appears those running the city are extremely sensitive to anything that might tarnish it's reputation.

For almost a century it has been known as the home of the movie stars. Much has gone on under the surface but the face of Los Angeles and particularly Hollywood has pretty much stayed the same. Unlike New York and Chicago where the underworld has been much more visible.

I began to realize it might not only be Nelson but the whole of the city's upper echelon that might want me gone. It was becoming very clear that politics is more than politics here in Los Angeles.

Above all the city's reputation must be preserved regardless of what was happening. Even the movies stars of yesteryear understood that they were privileged to live here and if they stepped out of line their careers could be ruined. It is all about promoting the right image.

Examples of recent falls from grace are once big stars Mel Gibson and Charlie Sheen.

Beginning to understand where I stood in the pecking order made me even more worried. I was an example of someone who'd tried to do the right thing but it wasn't appreciated and likely considered reckless.

I wondered why Simmons hadn't intervened but I guess he didn't know I was going to take on Nelson until my attempt had failed. I hadn't told him about the other attempts on my life so he didn't know the whole story with regard to what I'd been going through.

Only when I went missing and he started informing those in the know did I become a potential problem. I had obviously been sticking my nose in where it wasn't wanted.

"So what are your plans?" asked Simmons "I think your next column can wait."

"My immediate plans are to go back to the motel where I'm currently staying and crash" I replied.

Simmons suggested I go to the police first to let them know I was no longer a missing person. He told me he'd filled out a missing person report yesterday.

I agreed. Even though I knew the very first place I was going was to where Shelley was staying.

As I came out of the ancient freight elevator Shelley jumped up from one of the comfy couch's and shouted "Oh Hi" and came over and hugged me.

She started to kiss me before quickly pulling away, holding her nose, asking me where the hell I'd been?

"Could I please use your shower to get cleaned up?" I asked "It's a long story."

After having a soapy shower. As I emerged from the bathroom I could see Shelley lying on the bed naked. A sheet was partially covering her body.

"Over here big boy. Come and show me how much you've missed me" said Shelley.

I dived onto the bed and we kissed and hugged each other. It was so good to be in Shelley's arms again after what I'd just been through. The sex was wonderful making me feel happy all over.

Afterwards we moved to one of the comfy couch's. We lit up cigarettes and I told her where I'd been for the last four days. Shelley couldn't believe it.

The fact that I'd been face-to-face with Nelson blew Shelley away. I told her I needed to go to the police to tell them that I was no longer a missing person and report what had happened to me. I said she should come along to tell them what she knows about Nelson's illegal activities.

She responded by saying I should know Nelson is in cahoots with the prominent people in the city. Like the Mayor and Police Chief.

I didn't tell her that I'd already figured that out.

She said "For years Nelson has been donating to their re-elections and attending fund-raising dinners. He knows it's hypocritical. But uses these opportunities to keep up the façade that he is a fine upstanding citizen.

Several times a year he attends these dinners even though he doesn't give a hoot about the arts or the city. He uses these occasions to be seen hob-knobbing with the most powerful people in the city, corporate sponsors and lobbyists.

Giving the impression he is a caring person even though he is the epitome of a wolf in sheep's clothing.

He and his date usually sit at the same table as the Mayor, Deputy Mayor and Police Chief and their wives. Most people in the room will at least know him by sight.

None of them except the men sitting at his table will have any idea he is the owner of the Desperado Gentlemen's Clubs and is the mastermind behind a slew of illegal activities taking place in the city."

I continued to insist that we should go to the police but Shelley seemed to be reluctant and not very keen on the idea.

In telling the police what she knew about Nelson's illegal businesses she might have to explain how she knows about them.

Shelley was thinking *this could perhaps leave her open to backdated charges relating to her own involvement in prostitution.*

Despite Shelley's reluctance, late on Monday night we found ourselves sitting opposite Detective Sergeant Stone of the Los Angeles Police Department. I already knew him from previous cases we had worked on together over the years.

Stone said "Pleased to see you're not missing anymore Harry. We can close out your missing person paperwork."

I told him about being held unlawfully by someone called Martin Nelson. Stone said he knew who he was.

I suggested he was responsible for the murders of a number of young women including Cindy Samuels and three others.

Stone said he had suspected this based on his own investigation.

I told him that my friend Shelley here knows a lot more about Nelson and his illegal businesses.

Stone looked up at the clock on the wall. He suggested it was getting late and assumed what Shelley had to tell him would take awhile. So he said we should meet again when we had more time.

Shelley was inwardly relieved.

He said he was working the late shift all week so we should come by one afternoon.

We said we would and left heading for Jules.

As soon as we sat down Bert came over and said "Howdy stranger! Haven't seen you for awhile. What have you been up to?"

"It's a long story which I might tell you sometime but not tonight. Shelley and I just want to catch up" I replied.

Once we got our drinks Shelley asked "Why didn't you tell me you were planning to try and trap Nelson? How did you expect it to end?"

"I guess I arranged it on impulse after hearing about Cindy's murder thinking someone needed to do something. I wasn't really thinking about how it would end. I just wanted to get his signature on a piece of paper that could be used as evidence against him" I replied.

"Now the big question" Shelley asked "Did you sleep with her?"

"Yes. I won't lie. I did" I said sheepishly.

"Okay. I understand" Shelley responded pecking me on the cheek "I'm not going to get all high and mighty about it. Knowing I've been in the pay for sex business for years."

"Anyway I think you agree we need to nail him one way or another even though it's not going to be easy" I remarked.

Shelley lifted her glass of water saying "I'll drink to that."

"So when are we going back to speak to the police?" I asked.

"Later today I guess?" she said somewhat unenthusiastically.

This confused me a little until I checked my watch and noticed it was almost one o'clock in the morning.

Shelley said she was here last night.

She said "Bert said he hadn't seen you for a few days so I had one drink and left."

Our drinks were almost done so I asked her if she wanted another and she responded that she would rather go back to the place she was staying.

I jumped off my stool and threw enough cash on the bar to cover our drinks and said "Let's go!"

We said goodbye to Bert who looked surprised that we were leaving so soon.

When we got back to where she was staying, we climbed into the bed and made mad passionate love. It was amazing how good it was.

During the time we were making love. I blocked out everything that was going on in my life. It was if I was someone else without a worry in the world.

Afterwards both sweating we lit up cigarettes and gradually began to return to reality. Both soon falling asleep.

TUES AUG 1

The Police Chief in uniform. A tall, rigid looking figure of a man was knocking on Nelson's front door early Tuesday morning. He was bringing with him the knowledge that a mystery guest had arrived at the very same front door last Sunday lunchtime. He was not aware that Walsh had been released yesterday.

The Police Chief was welcomed and asked in like always and shown great respect even though today was Nelson's busy 'Interviewing Day'.

Sitting in Nelson's office the Police Chief told him he had come to see him in person because the Mayor was putting pressure on him to find a missing reporter from the Los Angeles Times.

Nelson told him he hadn't heard anything about this. He said if he did he would let him know.

Nelson reached down into a bottom desk draw and retrieved four bulky envelopes which he put on his desk.

"Can you take care of these?" he asked the Police Chief.

The Police Chief was reluctant to bring up the matter of the half-naked man who had been seen arriving at his front door last Sunday lunchtime. Because it might tip Nelson off to the ongoing surveillance of his house.

Because it was rumoured in the press and Detective Sergeant Stone himself suspected Nelson was behind the murders of young women. He had put surveillance in place several weeks ago.

The Police Chief asked Nelson if he had any guests staying with him at the present time. He knew he often did and normally wasn't shy to mention them or show them off.

Nelson responded that he didn't.

He did however mention his sister Millie was visiting him from New York. He said she was staying out on his boat, as he often called his yacht, with some friends.

Because there were no obvious signs of anyone staying at Nelson's place. The Police Chief began to make a move.

He asked Nelson if he had a bag he could put the envelopes in. Nelson searched around and found one. He put the envelopes in it and handed it to the Police Chief. He said his goodbyes and left.

It was only when the Police Chief got back to his office that he found out the reporter from the Los Angeles Times was no longer missing as of early this morning.

*   *   *   *

After hearing Walsh's story regarding his attempt to collect incriminating evidence against Martin Nelson it gave impetus to Detective Sergeant Stone's investigation and he met his most senior homicide Detectives to bring them up to speed.

Detective Biff Howell a tall goofy looking guy with thick black glasses and Detective Mac McShane a somewhat overweight young guy with a happy disposition.

"Okay" commented Howell "This maybe the breakthrough we've been looking for."

"Hopefully, Shelley will soon come back and tell us what she knows about Nelson's illegal activities" offered McShane.

"Let's start with Harry Walsh's story about what happened out on the yacht" suggested Stone.

"Can you go and interview Carol Bromley to see if she can corroborate Walsh's story. About what supposedly happened out on Nelson's yacht. I think this is the first step in following up on what he told me last night" suggested Stone.

A woman in a black and white maid's uniform opened the front door of the mansion where Carol Bromley lived in the affluent Hollywood Hills. Detective Howell told her. He and his partner were there to speak to Miss Carol Bromley.

Over the maid's shoulder. He and Detective McShane could see two women hurriedly striding towards the door. The younger one was an absolute knockout and the other an extremely attractive older version.

The maid stepped aside as the two women took her place in the doorway. Detective Howell flashed his badge saying "I'm Detective Biff Howell of the Los Angeles

Police Department and this is my partner Detective Mac McShane. We're here to speak with Miss Carol Bromley."

"What is this about?" asked the older of the two extremely attractive women.

"We'd like to ask Miss Bromley a few questions about her whereabouts at the end of last week" replied Detective McShane.

"Why did something happen?" asked who they assumed was her mother.

"It's just routine" replied Detective Howell.

"Is she going to be arrested and charged with anything?" asked the mother.

"No. We'd just like to ask her a few questions" responded Detective McShane.

"You know this is most unusual. The police coming to our door" replied the mother as she began to walk away with a look of disdain on her face saying "Go ahead."

"Hi. I'm Carol would you like to come in?" asked the younger woman who been standing patiently waiting.

"Yes. Thank you" responded Detective McShane.

The room they were ushered into was almost as impressive as Carol Bromley herself.

There was a lavishly upholstered dark brown leather couch, matching love seat and armchair. These were surrounded by brightly polished dark mahogany bookshelves and accent tables adorned with fresh flowers. The room exuded affluence.

"Please take a seat. Now how can I help you gentlemen?" asked Carol Bromley "I was just on my way out but I can spare you a few minutes."

She was a natural blonde, wearing a tight almost see through white top with a black bra underneath. A black leather skirt, black stockings and high heeled red stilettos. The way she was dressed was accentuating her womanly attributes.

Her makeup had been perfectly applied including bright red lipstick. She was the sexiest thing either of them had ever seen in the flesh.

Both Detectives wondered where she was going dolled up like this.

"Miss Bromley" opened Detective McShane.

But before he could continue Carol Bromley asked him to call her Carol.

"Okay. Carol were you on a Mr. Martin Nelson's yacht last Thursday night? asked Detective McShane.

"Yes. I was" replied Carol Bromley.

"Did you meet a Mr. John Reynolds?" asked Detective McShane.

"Yes I did. I must say he was a most charming gentleman" responded Carol Bromley.

"Do you remember when this was?" asked Detective Howell, just as the woman they assumed was Carol's mother entered the room.

She was carrying a tray of mugs and pastries which she put down on the coffee table in front of them. Her strong smelling perfume almost overpowering them.

These women really like an audience thought McShane.

Carol's mother had changed and was wearing a very provocative low-cut red dress showing off all of her womanly assets.

"Sorry to interrupt but I thought you gentlemen might like some refreshments" commented the older Bromley asking what they took in their coffees?

"By the way" said Carol Bromley "This is my mother Caroline."

Detective McShane responded first saying "That is very kind of you. Just cream for me."

"Me too" chipped in Detective Howell.

Caroline Bromley added the cream to the Detective's coffees and passed them over to them. She asked Carol if she would like a coffee and she replied "No thank you".

Caroline commented "There are pastries here too."

"I guess I'll leave you now" suggested the older Bromley dying to be asked to stay as she slowly left the room.

"Where were we?" asked Carol Bromley.

"Okay. I remember. Yes. It was on Thursday night. Marty told me he had a business meeting with Mr. Reynolds" she said.

"Did you see Mr. Reynolds other than on Thursday night?" asked Detective McShane.

"No. That was the only time I saw him. He was gone the next day" responded Carol Bromley.

"Do you know how he left?" asked Detective McShane.

"Yes. I heard he jumped overboard. This was most unsettling and distressing to all of us. Especially Marty's sister Millie and her friends who were also staying on the yacht at the time" replied Carol.

"Do you know why Mr. Reynolds jumped off Mr. Nelson's yacht?" asked Detective Howell.

"No. Nobody explained why he'd done it" replied Carol innocently.

McShane asked Howell if he had any other questions to which he said he didn't.

"Thank you Carol. I think that's all the questions we have for you right now. We might need to speak with you again. If that's okay?" asked Detective McShane.

Carol feeling relieved replied "Oh okay. Yes. That would be alright. Please don't rush off. Enjoy your coffees. Excuse me for a moment" she said as she left the room.

She returned within a few minutes and sitting down asked "Has something happened I should know about?"

"No. Mr. Reynolds is fine. We'll be going now. Thank you for your time and the coffees" replied Detective Howell standing up.

Detective McShane and Carol Bromley also stood up and Carol led them out of the room to the front door her perfume wafting in the air.

Both of them were both thinking *what a lucky bastard this Nelson is.*

They didn't know that he had never slept with her but Walsh had.

Once outside they both thanked Carol Bromley again. Both of them taking one last look at a living doll.

McShane was the first to speak as they headed for their car "These broads really know how to lay it on thick. I guess it's always worked for them no matter what."

"They certainly live in a different world and I noticed there was no sign of any men around. Not sure why?" responded Howell.

*   *   *   *

Out on Nelson's yacht that Tuesday morning Millie and her friends were being given scuba diving lessons in the pool. Nelson had asked Brian to hire an instructor to ensure everyone was safe while they were trying out different water sports. Nelson assumed for the first time.

They had already tried snorkelling. They thought it was fun and quite easy once they got the hang of it. The scuba diving on the other hand was a lot more difficult. With the heavy tank and the need for rhythmic breathing while you were trying to slowly maneuver around the pool underwater.

After they'd each had a turn they told the instructor they would likely be sticking to snorkelling. None of them said they wanted to go scuba diving because it seemed too much like hard work rather than fun.

Later that day they were fitted with rope attached lifejackets and went swimming beside the yacht. They had a great time treading water, swimming and just talking. Just knowing they were in the Pacific Ocean was enough for them even though it was still quite challenging with the waves constantly buffeting them.

When they'd finished swimming and dried off. Back on the lounge deck having cocktails at the bar. They felt as if they'd accomplished something by swimming in the ocean.

All in all it had been a good day out on the yacht with everyone safe after their little adventures.

* * * *

Brian had managed to track down the two hijacked delivery guys at one of National Liquor's warehouses. Although reluctant to say very much because of what they had been threatened with. They did say they were driven and dropped off somewhere in the foothills of the San Gabriel mountains.

All they knew was they were driven in a fairly new looking Lincoln town car. After hearing this Brian headed for Nelson's place where he found him sitting out by the pool in conversation with Ron.

He told them that the car was the likely connection because it was the daughter-in-law of Johnny Rossini that had been found murdered so it was likely to have been two of his men.

Nelson said they should confirm it somehow. As Brian was leaving he said once he got home he would check with Jimmy the Fixer on a secure phone line. Jimmy seems to know a lot of mob people said Brian. Maybe he can put his ear to the ground and find out something.

Jimmy called Brian back a few hours later and told him he'd found out it was Rossini himself and his right-hand man who had carried out the hit. Apparently he is extremely upset about the death of his son Joey's wife and word on the street is he is not done yet.

Brian drove back to Nelson's. He told him what he'd found out and suggested the murders of the young women should stop. He said with the murder of the daughter-in-law of one of the west coast's most powerful mob bosses it was obvious they were no longer murdering homeless hapless young women.

Nelson didn't agree saying this was a separate discussion. He was still incensed that he'd almost been killed. He wanted to send Rossini a strong message.

To let Rossini know, he knew it was him, who had tried to kill him.

"I'm not sure that's possible." responded Brian "You have twenty killers on your payroll. He has over a hundred. I don't think we want to take on that much firepower, even though it sounds like he is still gunning for us."

"Well. We need to do something" Nelson barked angrily.

You're right we at least need to let him know that we know it was him who tried to kill us and we can return the favour anytime we want" suggested Brian.

"That works for me" Nelson replied excitedly "What do you have in mind?"

"Let me find out if he has any pets or real passions and go from there" suggested Brian saying "Leave it with me" as he was getting up to leave.

"Good" said Nelson "Thanks."

That evening Brian showed up at Nelson's yet again and while they were walking around the well lit gardens. He told Nelson he'd found out that Rossini has a passion for fine Italian wine. And that apparently he has an extremely well stocked wine cellar that includes a collection of rare and expensive wines.

I would think he would be gutted if his wine collection were destroyed. It would surely send him the kind of message you have in mind. It would mean someone had got into his home with devastating consequences. All we need to do is figure out how to do it.

"I like it" responded Nelson "Can you make it happen?"

"Leave it with me" replied Brian "I'll take care of it. He got onto your property so we'll get onto his."

*   *   *   *

To my surprise I was arrested at work late on Tuesday over Simmons protestations.

When I asked why I was being arrested? I was told it was for Impersonation. I was frisked and what few personal belongings I had were put in a plastic bag. I signed a sheet that listed them.

As I was being read my rights and being handcuffed Simmons was talking to me as if he was my lawyer. Telling me to keep silent and that the charge was bogus.

The most embarrassing part of the whole thing was being taken out of the office and building in handcuffs.

Also later at the police station being finger printed. Having my photo taken and providing a DNA saliva swab. This is apparently standard procedure if you are arrested. Regardless of where the case goes from here.

I was sitting in a holding cell after being charged with impersonating another person which was something I hadn't realized was a possibility at the time I was trying to trap Nelson.

I was thinking *how everything had gone so wrong. There was always a possibility of this.*

It seemed the Los Angeles Police Department and even the California State Police were turning a blind eye to Nelson's illegal activities.

Perhaps the Feds could be brought in somehow even though they were usually reluctant to get involved in local or State affairs.

I was waiting for a bail hearing and was trying to sleep to overcome the utter boredom of being in a jail cell.

*   *   *   *

After being briefed by Detectives Howell and McShane about Carol Bromley's interview. Detectives Howell and McShane having confirmed Walsh was on Nelson's yacht last Thursday night.

Detective Sergeant Stone asked them to go and check out what had happened at the Marina Hotel close to Marina Del Rey last Sunday.

WED AUG 2

Early on Wednesday morning after showing his identification Detective Howell asked someone wearing a badge that said 'Jake' if he had checked in a half naked man last Sunday morning?

Jake Wilken's said "Yes I did. The guy showed up dripping wet with bare feet wearing only tattered pants."

This corroborated Walsh's story.

Jake said an hour or so later a cleaner noticed the door to one of the rooms up on the second floor had been damaged.

This was suspicious. I called the police and when they arrived found the door had been broken and no one was in the room. It was that guy's room, number 217.

"Thanks for this information Jake" responded Detective McShane.

"Yes. Thanks" said Detective Howell.

As they were leaving Wilkins said "Although it might not look like it right now. This place is usually very busy. Especially early in the morning when people are checking in and out. Usually there's only me, a cleaner and one of the cooks here, first thing in the morning."

McShane called Stone to tell him what they had found out during their visit to the Marina Hotel. He commented that at least another part of Walsh's story checks out.

Stone suggested "Perhaps it's time you went and visited Martin Nelson. You may as well get to know him and see what he looks like up close and personal. You can get his take on what happened out on his yacht. See what he has to say about meeting Harry Walsh masquerading as Mr. John Reynolds last week. I am not sure if he will help us in anyway but we don't have much else."

McShane commented "We have our surveillance people who saw a half-naked guy arriving at Nelson's last Sunday lunchtime and leaving the next day. We are fairly sure it was Walsh.

We also know that his editor sent someone to pick Walsh up in Lancaster on Monday night."

"I guess you're right we do have a few things" replied Stone "but I doubt Nelson will tell us anything that will help us.

If Nelson wants his lawyer to be present before he will talk. Tell him to come downtown with his lawyer to speak to us here.

If he is willing to speak to you without his lawyer see what he has to say."

*　*　*　*

Detectives McShane and Howell arrived at Nelson's impressive property late on Wednesday morning. After flashing their badges a number of times they finally met up with Nelson out by his pool.

They were immediately in awe of the spectacular view. The Pacific Ocean off in the distance.

"What can I do for you gentlemen?" asked Nelson in a friendly manner. He stood up and asked if he could get them a drink?

Detective McShane responded saying "No thanks. We're working."

Detective Howell said "We'd like to ask you some questions about a Mr. John Reynolds. We understand you had a business meeting with him out on your yacht off Marina Del Rey last Thursday night?"

"I'm not sure I can answer any of your questions without guidance from my lawyer who as you can see is not here at the moment" Nelson replied.

"Well. We would really appreciate it. If you could help us with our enquiries regarding a Mr. John Reynolds. If you are unable to answer any of our questions today. We would ask that you bring your lawyer down to Los Angeles Police Department headquarters downtown at your earliest convenience" responded Detective Howell.

Nelson agreed and Detectives McShane and Howell were escorted to their car in the parking lot.

Nelson was surprised that the detectives who had just visited him were keeping up the pretense that John Reynolds was real. Even though they must know by now it was Harry Walsh the Los Angeles Times crime reporter.

Being asked questions about John Reynolds seemed disingenuous. It didn't make sense to be asked questions about someone they knew only existed in name.

That afternoon Brian arrived at Nelson's and found him in conversation with Ron out by his pool.

He informed them that the Rossini job had been done.

He said Jimmy the Fixer had found a hardened criminal who was willing to do the job and he apparently destroyed nearly every bottle of wine in Rossini's cellar before being killed. All he wanted for doing the job was for his wife and boys to be taken care of. Something he hadn't been able to do while he was alive.

Brian said "Jimmy told me this is how it went down. Rossini's wine cellar is on the second basement level of his property. It is right below where his bodyguards stay. Where apparently there is an ample selection of weapons readily available to any of them.

Our man got in as a new bodyguard and was supposed to have a chaperon at all times but managed to slip him. He was able to grab an automatic weapon and once he got into the wine cellar pretty much smash every bottle of wine down there. Apparently by the time he was mowed down in a hail of bullets he was ankle deep in expensive wine.

"Good job! Make sure the dead guy's family are looked after" said Nelson seemingly content.

"We'll assume Rossini is devastated and knows things are even between you and him now" chipped in Ron.

"We can only hope" replied Nelson "Now Ron. You and I need to go downtown to visit the Los Angeles Police Department."

After waiting for awhile, which Nelson was unaccustomed to, he and Ron were ushered into an interview room where Detective Sergeant Stone and Detectives McShane and Howell were waiting.

"Please take a seat gentleman. I'm Detective Sergeant Stone and I think at least you Mr. Nelson have already met Detectives McShane and Howell" said Stone.

"This is Ronald Wells my lawyer" responded Nelson.

"Pleased to meet you Mr. Wells" offered Detective Sergeant Stone "I don't know all the details of this case so will ask Detectives McShane and Howell to ask you the questions they are looking to get answered if that's okay?"

Ron Wells spoke saying "Just to be clear my client is not going to be arrested or charged with anything. Is that correct?"

Detective Sergeant Stone responded saying "Yes. We'd just like to ask him a few questions. Mac please go ahead."

"Mr. Nelson have you met a Mr. Harry Walsh who was posing as Mr. John Reynolds?" asked Detective McShane.

Nelson thought to himself. *So they have changed their tact and are being up front about Walsh being an imposter and are no longer asking questions about the non-existent John Reynolds.*

Wells leaned over and whispered something to Nelson.

"I have 'No Comment' to this question" Nelson responded.

Detective McShane asked "Mr. Nelson will this be your answer to all the questions we have pertaining to Mr. Walsh when he was posing as Mr. Reynolds?"

Wells whispered to Nelson.

"Yes" said Nelson.

Detective Sergeant Stone chirped in "For your information we have arrested Harry Walsh for Impersonation and he is currently in custody."

"No comment" said Nelson.

"It looks like there is no point in continuing the interview then. Thank you for coming in" responded Detective Sergeant Stone.

With that everyone stood up and Nelson and Wells left.

Stone commented to McShane and Howell that things had gone about as well as he had expected they would. In that Nelson was not going to provide them anything that was going to help them in anyway.

"We may as well release Walsh" said Stone "Nelson didn't respond to him having been arrested.

Regardless. I only had Walsh arrested to teach him a lesson and use him as bait to try and get Nelson to open up. In California, the law is 'It is only illegal to impersonate a real person not a fictious one'.

I've also decided to close the case against Nelson due to the lack of conclusive evidence."

*　　*　　*　　*

Bored stiff lying in my cell I was surprised when I heard my cell door being unlocked. When it was opened a uniformed police officer. Detective Howell standing behind him. Told me I was being released and was free to go and should collect my personal belongings.

Still surprised I asked Detective Howell if something had happened?

Detective Howell said chuckling "Nothing has happened. That's the problem. Martin Nelson was just here with his lawyer and said 'No Comment' was going to be his response to any questions he was asked. That's all. You might also like to know that Detective Sergeant Stone has closed the case against Nelson citing a lack of credible evidence."

I said "I need to find Shelley because she has all kinds of information that might be considered to be evidence."

"Yes. If you can. I believe she was here with you the other night. I understand she didn't have time to make a statement. If you can bring her back it might really help" replied Detective Howell.

"Okay. I'll see if I can track her down" I replied.

"Thanks" said Detective Howell as he was walking away.

I was escorted to get my belongings and not long after released into the cool air that Wednesday night. Because I was downtown and close to where Shelley was staying I made my way there.

I took the ancient freight elevator up to her friend's loft. On my last visit Shelley had given me the code. I entered the loft. Looked around but she was nowhere to be found.

I called out her name thinking *perhaps there was a chance she might be in the bathroom* but got no response.

Her friend's loft looked like it always did everything in it's place.

Everything looked normal except Shelley wasn't here. I wasn't sure what to do? So I decided to wait for a while and sat down on one of the comfy couches and flipped through some old magazines.

I was racking my brain as to where she might be and realized she had never mentioned any family or friends so I didn't even have anyone to check with. If I thought about it I really knew very little about her.

I didn't know if she was married, had kids or even a boyfriend. All these things were probably doubtful given the business she'd been in for the last twenty years. I didn't even have a phone number for her because she'd always met me at Jules.

I waited for a while feeling completely inadequate. I'd been aloof to this woman who had slept with me and confided in me everything she knew about crime boss Martin Nelson's organization.

Feeling there was nothing else I could do. I went to tell Simmons I'd been released. Then I drove out to where I was staying.

That night as I tried to sleep. I had a bad feeling about what might have happened to Shelley, knowing Nelson ruthlessly took care of both the big and small stuff. I was really scared for the first time since I'd escaped from Sally's place.

THURS AUG 3

It turned out that Rossini had not got Nelson's message.

Thursday morning Nelson played eighteen holes of golf, at his exclusive club in Malibu, where he was a long-time member.

That day he had played with Brian, Ron and Lenny. The addition of Lenny to the golf foursome achieved two things. He was a scratch golfer so added to the competition and he was also Nelson's protection.

Numerous lessons over the years had almost brought Nelson up to Brian and Ron's level who had both grown up playing golf from a young age.

Brian had won today's round as he often did and was having a beer with Ron in the club house lounge rehashing each hole.

Nelson as was his custom was taking a shower in the locker room when suddenly he saw a fully dressed tall man approaching him from behind. Although initially apprehensive he quickly gained his composure and confronted him asking him what he was doing there?

He had never seen the man before but because he had a tanned bronze Italian complexion and tattoos on his neck figured he'd likely been sent by Rossini.

While wondering how he had managed to get into the club Nelson began calling Lenny's name but he didn't respond or appear either. He normally sat and waited for Nelson on the bench in front of his locker so Nelson wondered *why when he'd called him, he hadn't come.*

Nelson wasn't aware that the tall man had crept up on Lenny and held him in a head lock until he'd become unconscious. He was currently lying on the floor in between the lockers.

Nelson turned to the tall man and asked him "What are you doing in here?"

"I'm here to see you" replied the tall man.

"What do you want?" Nelson asked standing naked in the shower.

"Mr. Rossini asked me to tell you that you will never be safe even with all your bodyguards and murder teams" replied the tall man.

"Fine. I understand the message. Is there anything else?" asked Nelson.

"Yes. He asked me to give you this" the tall man said as he punched Nelson in the stomach.

It caused Nelson to slip down on to the tiles on the floor in the shower.

The tall man said "Mr. Rossini also told me to tell you he still plans to kill you. For killing his beautiful daughter-in-law and destroying his valuable wine collection."

The sucker punch had winded Nelson and he was in a lot of pain as he lay on the wet tiles.

The tall man was leaving the shower when a voice shouted "Marty are you in here?"

Brian had just found Lenny in the locker room and was standing at the entrance to the shower stalls and could see Nelson lying on the tiles moaning.

The tall man was nowhere to be seen but Brian and Nelson suddenly heard a loud crash.

Brian helped Nelson up and as they rounded the corner of the lockers saw the tall man lying in a pool of blood. Lenny was standing over him. The tall man looked like he had been stabbed multiple times and appeared to be dead.

Brian asked Nelson "What's been going on in here?"

Now able to speak Nelson said "This guy was sent by Rossini. He threatened and assaulted me to make a point."

Nelson wasn't happy that Lenny had murdered the guy sent by Rossini.

But at the same time understood that Lenny didn't know what had happened to him in the shower. That Lenny may even have thought he had been murdered.

"Okay. So how do we explain this?" asked Brian.

"It shouldn't be a problem. Just let Laurie know" replied Nelson.

Brian found Laurie Walters the owner of the club. He explained the situation to him and he said he would take care of it. He told Brian that he and Nelson should leave the club immediately. Which they did with Ron and Lenny in tow.

*   *   *   *

Early that afternoon I was back in the office sitting opposite Simmons.

"So, what happens now?" he asked.

"I guess I start writing again" I replied.

"Is that wise after what's recently happened to you? Why don't you take some time off? Take a vacation" Simmons suggested.

"Okay. I think I'll do that. Thank you" I replied thinking *this would give me more time to look for Shelley.*

The first thing I did was head over to Jules. Bert was just starting his shift. When he saw me he asked sarcastically if I'd lost track of time? Telling me there was still daylight out there.

I responded saying "I'm just starting a well-earned vacation. I thought I'd start it off with a cold one. If that's alright with you Mr. Smartass?"

"Vacation! Wouldn't that be nice. I haven't been anywhere for years. Although why go anywhere else if you live in California?

People come here from all over the world on vacation" responded Bert walking behind the bar and reaching into a beer fridge.

"I know what you mean but I'm a bit too old to sit on a noisy crowded beach or even swim in the ocean. It also costs an arm and a leg to stay in a hotel anywhere near the beach here. Instead you can always get a cheap Las Vegas deal for a few days where there's lots to do no matter what age you are" I replied.

"By the way I haven't seen your lady friend for a few days" commented Bert before I had the chance to ask him if he'd seen her.

"I know. I'm not sure where she is?" I remarked.

"So when are you heading to Las Vegas?" asked Bert.

"Right now I'd like to see Shelley again but if I can't it will likely be next week. I still need to book a hotel and get a flight" I said.

Walking down to the end of the bar Bert grabbed a flyer off a pile of them. He came back and handed it to me saying "This looks like a good deal. Three days and nights at the Bellagio. Airfare included for $299."

After reading the flyer I commented to Bert that this would work for me. So much so that I phoned the 800-number getting through almost immediately to Southwest Airlines who were offering the deal.

I booked to leave next Monday evening, returning Thursday lunchtime. Thinking *Shelley would surely have shown up by then.*

"Well Bert I must say you've found the perfect get away for me. Why don't you come too?" I suggested.

"Wish I could but the wife would want to come too and I'm not sure if that would be part of your plan?" replied Bert laughing.

"You're right it's a men only trip unless Shelley shows up by then. If she does. I'll change the rules" I said "I wish I knew where she is. I've been to the place she's been staying but there is no sign of her."

"Have you phoned her?" Bert asked.

"No. I don't have her number" I sighed.

"I guess you really don't know much about her" replied Bert.

"I guess not" I responded.

"Well. Check in with me when you get back from Las Vegas and I'll let you know if she's been in" said Bert going off to serve a newly arrived customer.

Waving to Bert I said "I'm going to get going. I'll see you later and thanks for finding me that deal."

I paid my bill and headed out thinking *about where Shelley might be* as I drove back to the motel where I was staying.

FRI AUG 4

While they continued to relax around the pool. Millie, Donna and Jill were still talking about the mysterious boat that had circled the yacht. The gunfire they'd heard and the nice man Mr. Reynolds who had jumped overboard.

Millie occasionally caught a glimpse of the United States Coast Guard ship and wondered why it hadn't got involved in the search for Mr. Reynolds.

She was thinking *that the incidents were very strange. But hadn't been given explanations for any of them.*

Jill was planning to leave this afternoon to help organize a Segal Foundation fund raising event this coming weekend. So the girls were having a farewell party of sorts indulging in strawberries and cream and glasses of bubbly.

By now they'd caught up, all had fabulous tans, had read numerous novels and been wined and dined on some of the finest cuisine Millie's brother's money could buy.

* * * *

Detectives Howell and McShane were disappointed that Detective Sergeant Stone had put Nelson's case on ice. It was almost to the point where they were beginning to suspect fowl play of some kind.

Afterall they'd collected what they considered to be corroborating evidence about Walsh being on Nelson's yacht. Also him checking in to the Marina Hotel looking like Robinson Crusoe.

They'd also heard that the surveillance team had video of Walsh. In the same half naked state. Arriving at Nelson's place on the Sunday lunchtime and leaving Monday afternoon. If he was being held against his will that could be considered kidnapping. They thought Detective Sergeant Stone must be aware of this but had never mentioned it?

Detectives Howell and McShane had decided whenever they had any spare time. They were going to start reviewing the online young women murder case files to see what they could find in the way of evidence.

They weren't even sure anymore if Shelley's statement would be enough to reopen the case.

Detective Sergeant Stone's own reasoning for closing the case was. If it was kept open it would require a far reaching coordinated effort. Bringing together each of the young women murder case files. Sifting through what little evidence there was. Requiring resources he currently didn't have.

Those doing the killing had been very careful. Leaving minimal evidence which would make it even more difficult.

Even if he got a statement from Shelley it would be basically informational in nature. She obviously had knowledge of Nelson's illegal activities but directly connecting him to any of them was going to be very difficult.

She had not personally witnessed any of the murders and had no direct knowledge of any of them. So she had no evidence that linked Nelson to any of them.

This was similar to Al Capone. Who the criminal justice system could only get for tax evasion. Even though they knew he had orchestrated a number of murders. Massacres even.

Solid proof is what Stone needed.

Detectives Howell and McShane knew the abductions usually took place on a Saturday night. So were planning to spend the next few weekends seeing what they could uncover.

They planned to canvas as many dive bars as they could to try and dig up any information about those carrying out the young women murders.

This was all unbeknownst to Detective Sergeant Stone of course.

They had checked the online criminal database with regard to the two men who had been arrested on the Saturday night Cindy Samuels was almost abducted.

They had found out that after being bailed out they hadn't shown up in court when required and even though a bench warrant had been issued they had never been located.

Both men had nothing more than petty crimes on their Record of Arrests and Prosecutions or RAP sheets.

As for the night Cindy, her boyfriend, another friend and a store keeper were murdered. It seems anyone who might have known anything had been killed.

*　*　*　*

Nelson had chosen today to visit his office in Palisades Village. Lenny was accompanying him.

There was a small Clubs International sign on the door that led to a flight of stairs leading up to an office above a strip mall.

Nelson had an apartment converted into an office a number of years back and visited it periodically to look over the books.

Before it was converted to an office Nelson was using the apartment to handle and manage the cash from his escort business.

Estelle his book-keeper and Sam who managed purchasing worked out of here, as did Brian occasionally.

After Nelson and Estelle had exchanged pleasantries they got down to business.

He told Estelle he wanted to know where the profits stood. Knowing they were almost two-thirds of the way through the year.

He said he wanted her to extrapolate out what they should look like by the end of the year. He knew how much he'd made last year and wanted to make sure everything was on track.

"Start with drugs please Estelle" he said.

Estelle started to hammer away on the keyboard of her laptop while he sat waiting patiently flipping through an old Forbes business magazine.

"Let me see" said Estelle "Club drugs profits look like they'll be about $45 million the same as last year. Street drugs profits should be about $239 million up $7 million over last year."

"Okay. I'm good with this. Now can you please give me the combined club, street and escort prostitution numbers?" Nelson asked.

More hammering away on her keyboard.

"Let me see" said Estelle "Combined prostitution profits should be $35 million. $13 million off the estimates."

"Yes. I figured that. That's why I've had to make some changes. Hopefully, the new guy Hustle will get us back on track" responded Nelson "How about the grand total for the year?"

"Let me see" replied Estelle banging away on her keyboard again.

While Estelle was getting a number he got up and went to visit Sam.

He went over to the other side of the office and asked him how things were going? Sam's desk was piled so high with stacks of paper and stuff Nelson could only just see the top of his head.

Sam stood up and reached out and shook Nelson's hand saying "Everything's going good thanks boss. Although I know you wouldn't think so looking at my desk. But believe me everything's under control."

"Glad to hear it. I just came over to say Hi" said Nelson before heading back to see if Estelle had a number for him yet.

"Right" said Estelle as Nelson rejoined her "Home sales profits should be about the same as last year $240 million, clubs should be $23 million again, club drug profits should be the same $45 million, street drugs profits should be about $239 million as already mentioned this is up about $7 million, sports betting profits should be about the same about $7 million. As discussed combined prostitution profits look like they'll be down about $13 million to $35 million as you know. The overall total profit should be around $589 million. Down $6 million from last year."

"I was hoping profits would be up but then I always do. We really need to focus in on club, street and escort prostitution where our numbers are off. I'm glad to see we have increased our profit number in street drugs.

Thank you Estelle" responded Nelson getting up and heading down the stairs. Lenny followed after him.

*　*　*　*

I wasn't feeling too good this afternoon after just getting up. I had almost emptied a suitcase of cans of Bud and smoked nearly a pack and a half of Winston's last night.

There were a number of crushed beer cans on the floor. I could remember at sometime sitting out on the porch and welcoming my neighbours home from wherever they'd been. I guess I was due for a binge session given it was the start of my vacation.

Although likely still under the influence I decided I wanted a decent cup of coffee rather than one made with the in room coffee maker.

There was a Starbucks just up the road not far from where I was staying. I'd seen it when I was travelling backwards and forwards from work.

It was the middle of the afternoon and the place was empty. I ordered a black coffee much to the disappointment of the pretty Asian girl serving behind the counter.

I'd never been into ordering those fancy Espresso or Mocha Frappuccino types of coffees. A plain old black coffee has always been good enough for me even at Starbucks.

Seeing several sections were completely empty I decided to stay for awhile and try and let the pain killers

I'd taken before leaving the motel take hold. It was at times like this that I wished I had a couple of good buddies I could hang out with especially when I wasn't working.

I was thinking *friend wise Shelley might be my best hope with regard to someone to spend time with. But didn't feel well enough at the moment to go and see if she was back at the place where she'd been staying.*

After returning to the motel. I took some more painkillers before going back bed in an effort to clear my head.

I awoke just after nine o'clock. Cleaned up my room a bit. Had a smoke. Fortuitously found an unopened can of beer and had a 'hair of the dog'. I hoped this would help to further clear my head. Soon after I went back to bed.

SAT AUG 5

On Saturday night Detectives Howell and McShane were downtown to see if they could dig up any evidence of their own. They hoped they might be able to use it to get the case against Nelson reopened.

It was still early comparatively speaking. It was just after ten o'clock when they entered a Desperado Club. There first impressions were good. It was clean, had modern décor and the 'dancers' were definitely worth buying a cold beer to sit and watch for awhile.

The detectives were looking to speak to anyone who might have been there last Saturday night when Dahlia Rossini was abducted. But as they had anticipated. No one working there had seen anything or knew anything.

After finishing their beer's they left and started checking out other bars in the area. They were looking to find anyone who had seen anything no matter how insignificant.

It was now after midnight. They had struck out so far but hit pay dirt in a quiet bar on a side street off the Sunset Strip, called Smokey's.

After they'd introduced themselves to the barman. He said he recollected a blonde drowning her sorrows a few weeks back. He thought it was on a Saturday. He said two of his regulars were buying her drinks and chatting her up.

He said he was fairly certain it was the Petrescu brothers, Dimitri and Victor who seemed to be toying with her and the three of them left together at the end of the night.

"What can you tell us about these two brothers?" asked Detective McShane.

"Let me see" said the barman. "I think they are muscle for a guy called Joe Salvatore who is on Marty Nelson's payroll, two men you certainly don't want to cross."

McShane and Howell just looked at each other.

The barman continued "They grew up in rental accommodation not far from here. If you can believe it. They are a couple of hunks with tattooed lily white arms."

An interesting description thought both Howell and McShane.

"How do you spell their name?" asked Detective Howell.

"I think its P E T R E S C U. Their parents came over from Romania during the revolution when that dictator was overthrown" replied the barman.

"Thanks. Much appreciated" responded Detective McShane and he and Detective Howell left.

Although it was early in the morning they went straight to their office to check the online criminal database. They found out that both Petrescu brothers had convictions for assault and were currently out on probation.

"They're for real! This could be our break. Let's go back there tomorrow afternoon when the barmen said they're usually in" suggested McShane "I'll meet you there at two o'clock."

"Alright" replied Howell "I need to go and get some sleep."

"Me too" responded McShane.

They went out of the door together.

*　*　*　*

The murders were continuing and that same night one of Nelson's murder teams murdered the wrong woman again.

As if Rossini's daughter-in-law's murder wasn't bad enough. The murder of Police Chief Hillman's niece, Sandy Palmer was going to be a big problem for Nelson.

SUN AUG 6

While Nelson sat in his family kitchen early Sunday morning he was thinking. *His sister had been in Los Angeles for almost two weeks now and she was flying back home to New York this coming Wednesday.*

So as soon as he'd finished his coffee he found Lenny and asked him to get ready to take him out to the boat.

Nelson and Lenny arrived by speedboat and found Millie and Donna wearing their scant bikini's.

Lenny immediately sauntered off to speak with Osvaldo.

"Well ladies. I hope you are continuing to have a great time out here on Big Fish?" asked Nelson.

"You bet" replied Donna "It's been fabulous spending time with Millie and Jill on your floating palace."

"I've never heard that one before. I'll have to remember it" Nelson responded "So what are you ladies up to?"

"We're having breakfast. Why don't you come and join us?" asked Donna walking back over to where her and Millie had been sitting.

As Nelson sat down Osvaldo came over and asked him if he would like a coffee?

"Oh Hi Osvaldo. I think I've already had my fill of coffee today so I'll have a Perrier on ice please. By the way how are you doing? Nelson asked.

"Fine thanks Mr. Nelson. Would you like me to ask the chef to make you some breakfast?" asked Osvaldo.

"No I'm good Just the Perrier for now" Nelson replied.

While she was finishing her breakfast Donna said "You seem to be doing really well. What business are you in?"

"Didn't Millie tell you? Construction. We've built a number of gated communities over the last twenty years and the business has proven to be most lucrative" Nelson responded.

Donna continued "Millie told us you have two yachts, this one and another one on the French Riviera?"

"That's right in St Tropez actually, but enough about me. What about you?" Nelson asked as Osvaldo brought him his drink.

"I'm the Vice President of Human Resources for Global Health Care where I've worked for almost twelve years now. I really enjoy it" offered Donna.

Millie chipped in "You missed Jill she is the Executive Assistant and Board Liaison for the Chairman of the Segal Foundation. She had to leave to help organize a fund-raising event this weekend."

"Donna you and Jill certainly have impressive jobs" Nelson commented continuing to make polite conversation.

"Did you find out who those men in the speedboat were?" asked Donna.

"No not really" replied Nelson adding "Brian thinks they were just checking the yacht out. Maybe they're planning to make me an offer."

Millie asked her brother if there was any news about Mr. Reynolds and did he know why he had dived off the yacht yet?

"You know it sounds crazy but I haven't heard anything. I know the United States Coastguard were informed about the incident but I haven't heard anything from them either" he replied "Anyway, let me hear how you've been enjoying yourselves out here under the summer sun?"

"We've been sunbathing getting great tans, snorkelling, talking, reading and being looked after by Osvaldo who has been a wonderful host" replied Donna as Nelson was amazingly quick on the draw. Whipping a Zippo lighter out of his sports jacket pocket and reaching over and lighting her cigarette.

"I see you are still the consummate gentlemen, brother" commented Millie.

"Of course" he said "It's good to hear Osvaldo has been looking after you. So what are you planning to do this afternoon?"

"We're happy to just hang out together on our loungers with our books and drinks" responded Millie.

"Sounds like a plan" he replied "I just have to check on a few things then I'll be back to join you."

With that he got up, waved over to Osvaldo and disappeared below.

Osvaldo followed him down to his office and Nelson asked him if there had been any other incidents. He said there hadn't.

"Good" said Nelson "I'll be back on deck soon. Make sure you refresh the lady's drinks. Thanks."

Osvaldo went back to the lounge deck and asked Millie and Donna if they needed anything and they asked for some bottles of cold water.

* * * *

Sunday afternoon Detectives McShane and Howell were back at Smokey's just off the Sunset Strip.

There were several muscular, heavily tattooed men sitting at the bar and after finding out who the Petrescu brothers were. The detectives introduced themselves and began asking them questions.

"We understand you were here a few weeks back late at night and met a young woman. Do you remember this?" asked Detective Howell.

"We're often here chatting to young women, what was so special about her?" asked Victor in a deep eastern European accent.

"We are looking for her to help with our enquiries and think you may have been the last people to see her" interjected Detective McShane.

The brothers looked at each other and Victor asked Dimitri if he remembered this. Dimitri said he didn't.

McShane looked at Howell then back at the Petrescu's.

"We might need you to come down to the Los Angeles Police Department headquarters building as our investigation proceeds. Would that be alright?" asked Detective Howell thinking *this may put pressure on them to open up a bit.*

"Where is that?" asked Victor.

"Downtown on West First Street" replied Detective McShane.

"The big police building. Yes I know where it is" said Victor before speaking to his brother Dimitri in what they assumed was Romanian.

"Why do we need to come down there? We've told you everything we know" said Victor.

Essentially ignoring Victor Petrescu's question McShane said "Thank you for your help."

He and Detective Howell made their way out of the dimly lit bar into the briefly blinding bright afternoon sunshine.

Once outside Howell commented to McShane that getting anyone to admit to anything regarding the abductions, rapes and murders was going to be almost impossible.

It seemed like anyone who might know anything were expert at keeping their mouths shut and deny was the watch word.

This included the Petrescu brothers.

Howell said "Don't forget we are investigating this unofficially so anything we get is a bonus."

"You know maybe Detective Sergeant Stone was right to put the case on ice" replied McShane based on what little we've found so far.

*　*　*　*

Sunday evening I was chilling in my motel room. I was still wondering where Shelley could be. I'd packed a few clothes into a small newly purchased suitcase ready for my Las Vegas trip. I was really looking forward to getting away for a few days.

I was thinking *that while I'd been working in Los Angeles I'd never been on a real vacation.*

A few years back I'd taken a bus trip to see the Grand Canyon and Hoover Dam. Both were mind boggling. Apart from this some might say I'd wasted my vacations in beachfront bars.

MON AUG 7

At his Monday meeting Nelson said he had just reviewed the anticipated year end profit numbers with Estelle so was right up to date on how things were going.

He said he wanted to focus on club, street and escort prostitution an area that was currently problematic. He wanted to know how Hustle, the new Head of Prostitution, was planning to improve things.

Nelson said he and Brian had formulated the estimates for prostitution several years back and thought this would be a good time to go over them again.

"A bit of a refresher for everyone I guess" he said "Brian you have the floor."

Brian began projecting information onto a large white screen which was a challenge to read due to the amount the sunlight that was coming into the tent.

He began "Several years ago after getting the fourteenth Desperado Club up and running. Marty and I spent several days coming up with these estimates.

Okay. Let's start with prostitution in the clubs.

We estimated that prices for club prostitutes could vary between $50 to $200 depending on what the customer wants.

Our estimates were based on having six prostitutes in each club, two working the afternoon and four the night shift.

We estimated the average price of a trick in a club at $125. With an average of 60 tricks a day. This should bring in $7,500 per day.

Over a year at each club this would equal 365 times $7,500 or $2,737,500 a year.

Multiplying this by our fourteen clubs we estimated club prostitution should bring in a total revenue of $38,325,000 a year.

By the way as most of you know. We have always used the twenty five percent rule for costs and expenses for all our estimates across the board.

So with costs and expenses estimated at around $9,581,250 we estimated club prostitution should be bringing in a profit of $28,743,750 a year, all in cash.

So just to be clear this is profit from prostitution that only takes place in our fourteen clubs.

Next we have street prostitution.

We estimated that prices for a street prostitute would vary between $30 to $120 depending on what they were asked to do.

We based our estimates on having forty women out on the streets night and day. Doing an average of sixteen tricks each.

It was assumed none of these women would be associated with a club in anyway.

Averaging it out at $75 a trick. With forty women times sixteen tricks came to a total of $48,000 a day.

Multiplied out over a year or 365 days. Street prostitution revenues should be $17,520,000 a year.

With costs and expenses of around $4,380,000. Street prostitution should bring in a profit of $13,140,000 a year, all in cash.

Next we have escorts.

Based on our own experience. Marty and I knew that escort service prices can vary from $120 to $300 a visit.

We figured with twenty escorts doing six tricks a day. Averaging out at $200 a trick this should bring in $24,000 a day.

Over 365 days this should bring in revenues of $8,760,000 a year.

With costs and expenses of around $2,190,000 a year. Escort services should bring in profits of $6,570,000 a year, all in cash.

So based on our original estimates. Combined prostitution. Club, street and escorts. Should be bringing in a total profit of $48,453,750 per year.

"Excuse me Brian. Estelle. Are we anywhere close to this number?" Nelson asked.

"No. We discussed this when you visited last week. Our projected combined prostitution profit number looks more like $35 million this year. Down $13 million from Brian and your original estimates for a year. By the way last year we were only off by $8 million from your original estimates" replied Estelle.

Brian looked over at Nelson and asked him if he wanted him to go through the rest of the estimates for the other businesses?

"Eventually I do but not yet" Nelson replied.

"So Hustle just to keep it simple. Tell me why you are not going to meet your escort profit numbers for the year?" asked Nelson.

Hustle stood up and said "Right now we only have seventeen escorts and on average they are only doing four tricks a day. Some of them make more than $200 a trick which complicates things a little bit.

Anyway if we stick to $200 a trick. On average then the numbers are seventeen women times four tricks a day. Bringing in revenues of $13,600 a day.

If we compare this to Brian and your estimates. Twenty escorts doing six tricks a day at $200 a trick. That's $24,000 a day.

As you can see from the numbers there is a shortfall in revenue of $10,300 a day.

It's really that simple.

When you multiply your estimates out the profit for the year is $6,570,000.

My profit is projected to be $3,723,000 for the year.

A significant shortfall of $2,847,000 a year.

A similar shortfall can be observed in the projected club and street prostitution profit numbers. They are also going to be below your estimates for the year. The main problem here is similar to Escorts, a shortage of women.

I'm sure you know it has always been difficult to attract and keep high quality escorts who normally only do it for a few months on average anyway. At the moment we're also having difficulty attracting women to work as club and street prostitutes.

The business is unpredictable, conventions and big sporting events lift the average numbers significantly but on normal days we are often below your estimates.

Perhaps the estimates need to be revised?"

"It would seem that way. What do you think Brian?" asked Nelson.

"No. Certainly not. They are targets. Whether we meet them or not. This is what we need to aim for." responded Brian.

"So Hustle tell us what your plan is to get us back on track?" asked Nelson.

"Okay. Across all three prostitution areas we need to boost the number of employees. This is where it begins. So please be prepared to do lots of interviewing as we ramp up and send more and more potential candidates your way. Once we get a full complement of workers we can go about increasing their productivity. That's my current plan and thinking" said Hustle.

"Sounds good. Send has many as you want my way. Let's get moving on this. Thanks Hustle. Let's take a break everybody" replied Nelson.

When they resumed after the break Nelson said "Brian you have the floor again if you'd like to go over the rest of the estimates."

"Alright let me see" said Brian.

"Our fourteen clubs" he said.

"We figured each club should bring in around two hundred people a day. Each spending on average $30.

For just one club in a year this should mean a take of $6,000 a day. Multiplied by 365 days this equals $2,190,000 a year.

This is mainly money that's been spent on alcohol and the 'dancers'.

Multiplying this by the fourteen clubs. Total revenues should be $30,660,000 a year essentially just from walk-ins.

With anticipated costs and expenses of around $7,665,000. We estimated the fourteen clubs should bring in total profits of $22,992,000 a year.

We estimated this would likely be seventy percent cash and thirty percent credit card transactions. The latter being reported to the Inland Revenue Service.

Okay. Now Club Sports Betting.

Back when we started we decided to keep things simple and only take bets on the four major North American sports. Football, baseball, basketball and hockey. To use Las Vegas odds and take a ten percent commission on all winning bets. We would obviously pocket the money from losing bets.

We figured that in sports betting there are usually many more losers than winners, even though the odds are meant to balance both sides of the bet. With the ten percent commission on every winning bet it ensures a significant profit, no matter what the outcome.

The winner of the bet is quite often too drunk or high by the time he claims his winnings to care about what we have skimmed off the top.

We figured we would take in about a hundred bets on a good day with a minimum of $20 cash being bet each time.

This would give us a hundred times $20 a day at each club for revenue of $2,000 a day.

Multiplying this by the fourteen clubs it gives us $28,000 a day.

Sports betting was only really setup in the clubs so customers could show off and hopefully forget about putting a bet on any other way.

Estimated over a year or 365 days with daily revenues of $28,000 across all clubs total revenues should be $10,220,000 a year.

Minus payouts, costs and expenses of $2,555,000. We estimated sports betting should bring in an annual profit of $7,665,000, all in cash.

Next we have drugs sold in clubs.

As you probably all know poor quality cocaine has always sold for around $40 a gram with high grade pure uncut Columbian selling for around $70 a gram.

Columbian high grade is the only snow, blow, whatever you want to call it that we have ever sold.

We estimated each club should be able to move 125 grams a day at $70 per gram.

This should bring in $8,750 a day at each club.

Multiplied by the fourteen clubs this should bring in a total of $122,500 a day.

When multiplied by a year or 365 days it becomes $44,712,500 in revenue a year.

With very minimal additional costs and expenses because it is being sold out of clubs.

The profit figure should almost be the same as the revenue figure $44,712,500, all in cash of course.

Next we have Street drugs.

We planned there would be about a hundred street dealers each able to push 125 grams a day at the same $70 a gram price which totals $875,000 a day.

When multiplied out by a year or 365 days this totals $319,375,000 in revenue a year.

Subtracting costs and expenses of $79,843,750.

We get a profit of $239,531,250 for street drugs, all in cash.

Next we come to construction, essentially where our only clean legitimate money is being realized.

As most of you know over the last twenty years our construction business has grown steadily. We have specialized in building spacious homes in gated communities.

These usually consist of a community of thirty two mansions with a selection of eight different models. Each has several acres of land.

Each home is priced at $10 million regardless of which model is selected.

This brings in revenues of $320 million a year.

After subtracting costs, expenses and taxes of $80 million. Profits here should be around $240 million, all in clean money.

That's it. That's all I have."

Thanks Brian. That's a lot to digest so I think we should call it a day. Thanks everyone. We'll meet over at the garages in a few minutes" said Nelson.

After the meeting Nelson suggested to Brian that it might be time to wind down most of the businesses. Apart from street drugs and construction. Perhaps keeping one murder team.

"So you will be just left with street drugs and home sales?" queried Brian.

"Yes" replied Nelson "When you look at the bottom line it doesn't make sense to keep the other businesses going. We have gone with the flow for too long and it looks like it's not worth it anymore. I really think the time has come to cut back.

Think about it!

We have projected profits for the following businesses. Combined prostitution $35 million. The fourteen clubs $23 million. Club drugs $45 million. Sports betting $7 million, for a total of $110 million this year.

This compared to street drugs and home sales. Which are projected to bring in revenues approaching

$700 million a year and profits of almost half a billion dollars.

I think these are the two businesses we should start giving all our focus to from now on. We should seriously consider starting to close the others down."

*   *   *   *

On Monday I made my way to the airport to get my flight to Las Vegas. When I landed, I took a cab to the Bellagio, a so called Luxury Resort and Casino. All I planned to do was sit by the pool, enjoy some good food and get a good night's sleep, in air conditioned luxury. I thought *maybe that's where the Luxury comes from in the name?*

I rarely gambled and if I did it was usually on the nickel or dime one armed bandits. The other types of gambling seemed too much like hard work. Remembering or even counting cards or trying to figure out the roulette table. I thought *maybe on the last night I might give it a try if I have any spare cash left.*

I planned to eat well and go through the cocktail menu, so having any spare cash left seemed somewhat unlikely.

I would pay good money to see a good show but Celine Dion, Cher or Elton John were not really my thing. Even though I've heard their shows are really good. If I could find an Elvis tribute show. I'd definitely go to that.

When I got into my room on the sixteenth floor I unpacked and connected my laptop up to the free hotel Wi-fi.

As it was quite late I ordered room service. A club sandwich and a six pack.

I didn't plan to remove the seal from the mini bar during my stay. Knowing that if I took almost anything out it would likely cost an arm and a leg. I'd got a smoking room with a balcony and was planning to smoke out there.

I couldn't do justice to the club sandwich and was only able to polish off two of the triangular shaped slices. I took care of the beer while watching a couple of TV dramas before climbing into bed.

TUES AUG 8

I was up early on Tuesday morning. I put my swim trunks on under my shorts and headed down to the hotel's buffet restaurant to have bacon and eggs.

After I ate I went to find the Mediterranean themed pool to see if I could get a good spot next to the cocktail bar.

With my lily white skin I was reluctant to strip down to my trunks but knew I had no choice if I wanted to get any kind of a tan over the next few days.

Within short order the blue and white loungers were quickly snapped up either with towels thrown on them to try and reserve them or by bronze bodies of all shapes and sizes.

There seemed to be an equal number of men and women around the pool. The only loungers still available being on either side of me.

I guess no one wanted to lounge next to a middle aged, overly white guy. I guess they didn't know I was feeling quite perky after getting eight hours sleep for the first time in a long time.

Although it was only nine-thirty it was already quite hot. The sun's rays shining down over the pool. I could already tell that finding shade during the day was going to be a challenge. So I tried to cover every inch of my body with suntan lotion. I stretched out and started reading the novel I'd purchased at the Los Angeles airport last night, which I was halfway through.

I planned to finish it today as long as I didn't start drinking too early, fall asleep or get into conversation with the people lounging around me.

I was wearing my sunglasses lying on my stomach with the book held high out in front of me. I was doing exactly what I had planned to do back when I'd discussed the vacation with Bert.

If I began to get distracted I planned to insert my earbuds and listen to my selection of songs which covered a wide spectrum of golden oldies.

The real keeners were already doing laps. As soon as the cocktail bar opened the noise level began to rise. So I figured it was time to insert my earbuds.

*   *   *   *

Millie and Donna were packing their suitcases and bags on that Tuesday morning.

Their time on the yacht had come to an end.

Millie was flying home to New York tomorrow morning. She was disappointed that over the two weeks she'd been in Los Angeles she'd probably only spent a few hours, if even that, in the company of her brother. She'd certainly caught up with Donna and Jill though, was well tanned and felt very relaxed.

On one occasion Jill had suggested she could phone some guys she knew if they liked? Millie and Donna had said they were fine with the way things were and didn't need any male company.

Millie had said they shouldn't be inviting anyone onto her brother's boat. Not without checking with him first and Jill dropped the idea.

Millie had always heard that California's climate was perfect but now had experienced it for herself. In fact she wasn't sure if it had even rained while she'd been out on the yacht. If it had it must have been during the night while she was sleeping.

Millie figured she must have read at least a dozen novels in the two weeks she'd been out on the yacht. She always knew she was a fast reader but now she had proof.

After dropping Donna off. Osvaldo and Millie arrived back at Nelson's house just after twelve noon. Millie had lunch with her brother out on the patio next to his pool. The Pacific Ocean was shimmering and looked amazing off in the distance.

"So how did you enjoy your time out on the boat with your friends?" Nelson asked.

"It was wonderful. I just wish you'd had more time to spend with me" replied Millie.

"Yes. I'm sorry but I tend to be terribly busy these days and I wanted to give you your own space" Nelson responded "I just have a few more meetings this afternoon after which we can have a relaxing dinner and fully catch up."

"That sounds great. I still have to sort out a few things and finish my packing" replied Millie before getting up and starting to walk over to the guest house.

Nelson conducted several interviews that afternoon. He was looking to hire two new club managers. The previous ones having quit saying the job had become too much for them.

Anyone without a criminal bent always had trouble managing the numerous activities that took place on a daily basis in his clubs, especially managing the cash.

Nelson was being very careful these days when screening potential candidates, exactly because of this. When he had concluded his final interview he sent word to Millie to join him for cocktails before dinner.

He was standing behind his poolside bar when Millie arrived wearing a sparkly pink "I Luv LA" tee-shirt, white shorts and purple flip-flops. Nelson couldn't help noticing her great tan and commented that he liked her tee-shirt.

"So what can I get you to drink Sis?" he asked.

"I'm not sure. Why don't you surprise me" responded Millie.

"Something alcoholic?" asked Nelson.

"Are you kidding? All I've been doing for the last two weeks is drinking alcoholic cocktails. By the way please thank Osvaldo he was wonderful to us" she said.

"One of my specialities coming right up. I give this to all my lady friends" Nelson said laughing.

"Close your eyes" said Nelson as he placed the drink on the bar and put Millie's hand around it. "Take a sip and tell me what you think?"

Still with her eyes closed Millie took a swig and said "Oh! It's really nice" opening her eyes she looked at the tropical cocktail and asked "What is it?"

"It's a Mai Tai. It's a very fashionable drink out here on the west coast these days" he replied.

"I don't think Osvaldo offered us one of these out on the yacht" replied Millie.

Maybe it's not one of the cocktails he knows how to make. I'll have to show him" replied Nelson as he was putting some ice in a glass and pouring a bottle of Perrier over it.

Millie knew he seldom drank alcohol.

"Looking around Millie said "You have a beautiful property here. Can you tell me more about your business?"

"There's not much more to tell really. You know I'm in construction, building gated communities and it began with the building of this house. My home" he said.

Nelson hated lying, especially to his sister but said "I have meetings every Monday to allow me to get updates on how the construction is going. On Tuesdays I interview potential new employees. That's about it" he said.

"Well you've certainly done well. You have an amazing home and gardens and a fantastic yacht" commented Millie.

"Thank you. Should we discuss the arrangements for your trip home tomorrow?" Nelson asked.

"I'm on a Delta Air Lines flight first thing tomorrow morning which gets into New York late in the afternoon" replied Millie.

"Osvaldo will take you to the airport. Can you be ready for 6 am?" asked Nelson.

"Yes. Providing I don't have too many of these Mai Tai's before dinner" laughed Millie "By the way what are we having?"

"I'm glad you asked" gushed Nelson.

"Because it's your last night and we haven't spent much time together. I thought we could take our time over dinner.

Ideally I would have liked to have taken you to the finest Japanese restaurant in Los Angeles, in Beverley Hills actually.

But unfortunately it only has ten seats and you have to make a reservation months in advance. So I have got the next best thing. Getting them to cater in.

Everything has it's price.

So soon you can expect to be choosing from a selection of soups, rice, sushi, noodles and bread. Along with deep fried, grilled, pan fried, stir fry and stewed dishes, sweets and deserts.

All Japanese style of course, compliments of world famous Chef Urasawa who owns the restaurant."

They didn't have to wait long for the food to arrive. It was laid out by two members of Nelson's staff, in his impressive dining room.

Millie wasn't disappointed and couldn't believe the amazing selection of great looking dishes in front of her on the massive dining table.

Nelson opened a special 2002 bottle of Cabernet Sauvignon. He said it was from a boutique, family owned winery in the Napa Valley. He and Millie thoroughly enjoyed it while picking at the vast selection of Japanese food.

Millie told her brother she was still very happy living in New York and had lots of friends. She said some were friends from as far back as when he and her had spent their summers in the Hamptons and she still got invited out there occasionally during the summer months.

She said she was really enjoying her job and always had lots of interesting and original advertising challenges.

The evening turned into night. It was almost midnight when her brother suggested perhaps they should turn in for the night, because she had a 5 am wake-up call.

Millie reluctantly agreed and her brother walked her over to the guest house where she gave him a big hug and said "You know I miss you. It's only me in New York now."

"Yes. I know. I promise I'll come and visit more often Sis" he said.

"I'll see you in the morning" he said as he left the guest house.

WED AUG 9

Early Wednesday morning Nelson was standing next to his sister as Osvaldo was loading her suitcases into the trunk of a shiny new Lincoln town car. Nelson and Millie silently hugged each other before she got into the back and Osvaldo closed the door.

Millie rolled the window down saying "Thank you again for a fabulous vacation. I have never felt so relaxed. Too bad we didn't get to spend more time together but I realize your business requires a lot of your time" said Millie.

"Give me more notice next time and I'll shuffle things around so we can spend more time together" Nelson responded.

"Will do" replied Millie as the car began to move off down the driveway.

It was still dark. Nelson turned the lights on around his pool, got changed into his swim suit, dived into the pool and began to do laps.

He was thinking *today might be a good day to meet with Sam to find out what had happened down on the Mexican border.*

There had recently been an incident so it seemed things weren't going quite so smoothly anymore.

Several days ago a drug smuggling pickup truck had been stopped and searched by United States Border Protection officers.

One hundred and twenty bricks of cocaine were found under a tarpaulin in the back.

The guy driving the pickup truck had been arrested, the drugs seized and the truck impounded.

Fortunately, it was far enough away from the border and the road construction work that the officers who stopped the truck didn't put two and two together. But it was still a serious situation.

The young guy who'd been arrested obviously had a very distant connection to Nelson.

He worked for a subcontractor who had been engaged by Sam. It still posed a potential problem to the supply chain. Border Protection officers would now be watching the comings and goings in this area more closely.

* * * *

Sam arrived mid-morning. He met with Nelson out by his pool. Nelson was wearing a bathrobe and his hair was wet. It looked like he'd just got out of the pool.

As he usually did. Sam looked like a tourist in a plain blue tee shirt, black shorts and orange Crocs.

Nelson asked Sam if he would like a coffee but he declined saying it was too late in the day.

"You know I love it here" said Sam "It's so peaceful and the views are fantastic!"

Nelson ignored the compliment quickly getting down to business.

"Brian told me what happened. You realize we're talking about a loss of around $6 million in profit here. Not exactly chump change. But I guess there's no point in crying over spilt milk. Does it compromise the organization in anyway?" Nelson asked.

Sam responded saying "The only way it could is if the guy talks. I've been speaking with Jamie who runs things down there. He told me the guy is fairly new and knows very little about our operation. Certainly not the big picture.

He's just a pick up guy who makes one trip a week. Jamie says he is not any kind of a risk to us. He says the guy already knows what will happen to him if he talks."

Nelson said "Given this is the first time anything like this has happened. Can we trust this guy Jamie? You know we could send Jimmy the Fixer and one of his murder teams down there."

"If you do then there will be a stronger link to us. The fewer people involved the better" commented Sam.

"Good point. Let's leave it to this guy Jamie. Afterall it's his neck that's on the line. Let him take care of it" Nelson responded adding "So Sam do we have anything else to discuss while you're here?"

"No. I don't think so. This is really the only thing" responded Sam.

"Okay. Thanks for coming" said Nelson getting up and disappearing into the pool house.

Sam got up and sauntered off to the parking lot.

*   *   *   *

Early Wednesday morning I was back beside the pool with the obligatory sunburns on my shoulders, back, chest and legs.

Today I would be working on turning them brown. I didn't think bronze would be achievable in the two days that were left. But I was going to try.

It was nice to be in a completely different environment. Away from everything I'd been dealing with lately. I had finished the book I'd been reading yesterday. I'd purchased another action adventure novel from one of the gift shops and was already a third of the way through it.

Even though I was trying to embrace my new temporary environment. I was still was worrying about what could have happened to Shelley. I couldn't get her out of my mind.

She had come into my life like a whirlwind and disappeared just as quickly. It was all so strange.

I put my earbuds in and began to concentrate on my reading. I'd taken it easy with the booze so far, drinking more water than beer and planned to do the same again today.

I was thinking *about what my next move should be.*

I was seriously contemplating leaving Los Angeles. I'd certainly had a good stint at the newspaper. But it looked like I'd worn out my welcome sticking my nose in where it wasn't wanted.

I wasn't sure if it was only Nelson that was gunning for me or those who ran the city as well. Who Shelley had said were all in bed with Nelson.

All of them probably wanted me gone now that I had potentially upset their cushy arrangement.

THURS AUG 10

The murder of Police Chief Hillman's niece, Sandy Palmer. Was splashed all over the front pages of the daily newspapers that Thursday morning. The Police Chief was in shock after reading about it. He immediately went down the hall to Jim Stone's office with the newspaper in his hand, looking incredibly angry.

The Police Chief entered Stone's office just as he had arrived for work and was hanging his coat up. Waving the newspaper in his hand at Stone. Hillman asked him if he knew his niece had been murdered?

"Yes. I didn't have a chance to speak to you about it yet" replied Stone "Her body was found late last night by a guy walking his dog in Granada Hills. We think her body had been there for few days and was dumped there Sunday morning. An autopsy has been scheduled for tomorrow. It's already apparent she was viciously raped before being murdered."

"How did they know it was her?" asked Hillman.

"Detectives Howell and McShane attended the crime scene. McShane recognized her. He'd seen her when she and your sister visited you here a few weeks ago" replied Stone.

"Who gave her name to the newspapers?" asked Hillman.

"I don't know. But there were reporters there at the crime scene. Perhaps someone overheard McShane or Howell talking with the paramedics. I'm speculating though. You know what reporters are like. They always have their ear to the ground" responded Stone.

"Did you let my sister know or is she finding out through the newspapers like me?" asked Police Chief Hillman still very angry.

"McShane and Howell visited her late last night and she is coming in to identify the body" replied Stone.

"I'm not happy about the way I found out about my niece's murder but there's not much I can do about it. Let's talk later" said Hillman. As he was getting up to leave a police officer put his head in the door and told him his sister was here.

After consoling his sister he asked her if she had the number for her daughter's boyfriend. She was surprised by the request but provided the number before going to identify her daughter's body.

Before calling her boyfriend Police Chief Hillman was thinking *that over the years at family gatherings he had noticed that his sister's daughter, his niece Sandy, was quite rebellious.*

He felt her bleached hair, tattoos and body piercings were a sign of this. Even though his sister told him it was just a normal part of growing up these days.

The last time he had seen Sandy she had looked awful and very skinny. Her bloodshot eyes standing out from her pale complexion was very likely a sign of drug abuse.

She never said much but instead just hung onto her spikey haired, heavily tattooed, boyfriend. He looked even worse than her and said even less.

The Police Chief phoned Sandy's boyfriend Chris Dean. He asked him if he'd heard about Sandy's murder. He said he had.

Hillman asked him if he was with her last Saturday night and he said he was.

Apparently it was late and they'd had an argument and he'd gone for a drive to cool off. Leaving Sandy on her own.

"Where did you leave her?" Hillman asked.

"At a Desperado Club downtown" replied Dean.

"Did you go back there?" asked Hillman.

"Yes I did. Just as it was closing. She wasn't there so I figured she'd taken a cab home and I left" replied Dean.

"How often do you see Sandy?" asked Hillman.

"Sometimes on weekends" replied Dean.

"So you didn't know she had been missing until you read about her murder in the newspaper today?" asked Hillman.

"Yes. That's when I found out about her" replied Dean.

"Thanks for the information" said Hillman and hung-up.

What her boyfriend didn't realize was that as soon as he left her on her own she turned into a sitting duck. It hadn't taken long for Jimmy the Fixer to be informed of her whereabouts. No one had been selected yet on that Saturday night so she immediately became the chosen one

When the murder team got there the usual drinks were bought even though it was clear she'd already had too much to drink. She indicated to the two good looking guys sitting either side of her that her boyfriend would be coming back soon. But they knew he wouldn't because if he did he would be grabbed by the other members of the murder team waiting outside.

Inevitably the club began to close up for the night and Sandy was offered a ride home and before she knew what was happening she was bundled into the back of their van.

The Police Chief wasn't sure what to do. He decided to make an impromptu visit to Martin Nelson's place. He wanted to know if he knew anything about his niece's murder. It had been rumoured that he was behind the murders of the young women.

Nelson denied any involvement and like he always did said the Police Chief would be the first to know if he heard anything. Following his brief meeting with the Police Chief. Nelson figured he was in trouble and should head for Big Fish II.

He called Osvaldo into his office and asked him to make preparations for them to go and stay in St Tropez. He asked him to tell Sam to make the arrangements for a crew and to arrange airline tickets for tomorrow. He also asked him to get in contact with Jimmy the Fixer and ask him to come and visit him as soon as possible.

Nelson figured the Police Chief and the other city officials would be ambivalent as to what to do because they relied on his dirty money to augment their lavish lifestyles.

Jimmy arrived and met Nelson out by his pool. Jimmy had his thick black hair slicked back. He was wearing a Polo golf shirt, white pants and white patent leather shoes.

When Nelson began to talk Jimmy took his sunglasses off and leaned forward to listen.

"You know two weeks in a row now I would say your guys have definitely selected the wrong young woman. Johnny Rossini's daughter in law and last Saturday the Los Angeles Police Chief's niece" said Nelson.

"Yes. From now on I plan to go and check out the victim myself before I give the go ahead. I realize killing these two women has caused you big problems and I'm sorry. I think if I personally attend the scene this will ensure we don't murder the wrong woman again. But I don't want it to be too obvious as to what is going on" said Jimmy.

"Okay. You should know I'm going on vacation for a few weeks so please work with Brian while I'm away. Thank you Jimmy" said Nelson.

Jimmy got up and headed for the parking lot.

* * * *

While flying back from Las Vegas I overheard someone talking about the murder of the Los Angeles Police Chief's niece. As soon as I got into the terminal building as I passed a gift shop I glanced at today's newspapers. Sure enough there on the front pages were headlines about the murder.

I immediately began to think *this was perhaps my opportunity to link Nelson to the murder of the Police Chief's niece. Along with the other young women who he'd had murdered since the start of the year.*

Obviously, it would be better if I could find Shelley. Even though I wasn't sure where the Police Chief's allegiances lay. She had told me he was on Nelson's payroll since being elected two and half years ago.

But I figured that right now he would be torn between continuing to take Nelson's dirty money or going after him for his niece's murder.

Shelley had also mentioned that she and the Police Chief were acquainted. This apparently as a result of varying sexual favours she had provided while working for Nelson. He was not the only city dignitary she had catered to either.

I knew from the time I had been kidnapped that my editor Simmons was friends with the Mayor. So I phoned him.

Simmons was surprised to hear from me saying "I thought you were taking some time off?"

I said "I have been. I just got back from Las Vegas. I wondered if you could phone the Mayor on my behalf. I have a backpack full of things I've found at various crime scenes of murdered young women. I am willing to hand them over to the Police Chief in the hope it might assist him to find out who murdered his niece.

"I'll see what I can do" Simmons said.

*   *   *   *

Detectives Howell and McShane became aware that a white cube van had recently been impounded. It had been found illegally parked in an alley downtown last Saturday evening. They hoped it might be connected to the young women murders.

They had just got forensic results indicating human head hairs had been found. It had been dusted for fingerprints but very few had been found. Forensics figured those using the van must have worn gloves. Because the case against Nelson was closed this as far as the Forensics investigation had gone.

Although Detectives Howell and McShane had a hunch the van was likely involved in the murders they couldn't officially do much.

The Petrescu brothers had eventually talked and it turned out that they did spend the night with a young woman. She hadn't been murdered and had been tracked down.

It was also determined that the Petrescu's did occasionally provide muscle for Joe Salvatore but were not members of any of his murder teams.

*　*　*　*

Although Nelson had never wanted a steady love relationship, Brian on the other hand always had. He'd had several over the last few years and had recently got engaged to get married to a beauty from a well to do west Hollywood family.

For some reason Nelson had become obsessed with the idea of sleeping with Brian's new fiancée.

Perhaps part of his makeup of always getting whatever he wanted. He should have. But hadn't given a thought to what this would do to his friendship and working relationship with Brian.

He was running out of time to have his way with the gorgeous Anne Wilson before leaving for St Tropez tomorrow.

Several weeks ago he had offered to host a hen party for Brian's fiancée and her friends out on his yacht. At the very same time Brian would be having his stag party at the Beverly Hilton.

Nelson planned to attend both events. Brian's stag then the hen party. The latter being where he would hopefully make his conquest of Anne Wilson.

Midway through the evening at the stag party when it became obvious Brian was too far gone and would soon need to be helped to his room. Nelson quietly left the party.

Anne was quite drunk by the time Nelson and Lenny arrived on Big Fish following a speedboat ride from Marina Del Rey. As with Brian the constant peer pressure was forcing Anne to drink more shooters than she normally would. However, this was her night and this was the first luxury yacht she and her friends had ever been on.

Nelson immediately picked her out of the crowd. He asked her if she and her friends were enjoying the party. She responded that they were. He asked her if she would like to take a tour of the boat.

Below decks feeling a little woozy. She sat down on the bed in Nelson's suite. Slurring her words she told him how impressed she was with everything.

The situation was nothing like he'd had in mind when he thought of having his way with her. He had imagined intimacy between the two of them leading to mutual agreement on how far they went.

He realized under these circumstances it would essentially be rape. He continued anyway. He sat down on the bed next to her and started to kiss her. Although she tried to push him away she was too far gone to fight him off for very long.

He quickly undressed her while kissing and fondling her. Before she knew it. He was ravishing her and had soon penetrated her. Not long after he was overcome with a feeling of ecstasy.

After getting up off the bed he saw that she had fallen asleep. He picked her up and took her into one of the guest cabins.

Once back up on deck when asked where Anne was he said she'd fallen asleep.

"Two or three shooters too many I guess.

We only managed to get halfway through the tour. Now if you will excuse me" he said moving towards the bar to speak to Osvaldo, who was hosting the hen party.

"So what's the plan?" Nelson asked.

"Any of them that can get into the speedboat will be dropped off at their homes. Taxi's will be waiting at the marina. Those who can't. Will need to flop in an empty cabin or on a pool lounger" replied Osvaldo.

"Okay. The head hen has already crashed for the night. So I suggest in about another hour you break things up and take care of everyone as you just mentioned" said Nelson.

Nelson didn't stay on the boat.

He and Lenny left almost immediately taking the speedboat back to the marina.

FRI AUG 11

Friday morning I was sitting opposite Police Chief Hillman in the Los Angeles Police Department headquarters building. He was very cordial offering me a coffee or tea as I sat down.

I asked for a black coffee. He made a phone call and a woman in uniform soon appeared with it.

He said he'd heard I had some information about the 'downtown' murders as he called them.

"I know who has been orchestrating them. Someone I think you know by the name of Martin Nelson" I said.

"Yes. I know him. In fact I was speaking to him just yesterday. He told me he knew nothing about my niece's murder" replied the Police Chief.

"Well he's lying. I think you might also know he is involved in organized crime and in his case 'very' organized crime" I remarked.

"Yes. I know what you mean" replied the Police Chief.

I unravelled a large chart across his desk facing him so he could easily read it. It showed the month and day where the bodies of the murdered young women had been found. Normally on a Sunday morning far from downtown. Cindy Samuels and three others being the only exception. Along with the Police Chief's niece who had been discovered yesterday several days after her murder.

I also told the Police Chief I had collected a number of things from different crime scenes. Which I'd brought with me."

After briefly studying the chart. Police Chief Hillman said "I think you should show your chart and the things you've brought with you to Detective Sergeant Stone. He has been looking into these murders up until recently. I believe you know him."

"Yes. Do you want me to go and see him now?" I asked as I rolled up my chart and picked up my backpack.

"Yes. I guess there's no time like the present. You'll find him just down the hall" responded the Police Chief "Take your coffee with you."

"Thanks" I said getting up to leave.

"By the way" said the Police Chief "I know Nelson kidnapped you."

If I'd told the Police Chief anything new or uncomfortable he certainly hadn't shown or acknowledged it. He'd just listened.

I soon found Detective Sergeant Stone and told him the Chief had suggested I show him my chart and the stuff I'd collected.

Detective Sergeant Stone said "I don't know if you know Harry but I've closed Nelson's case due to a lack of conclusive evidence.

Nelson himself refuses to cooperate in anyway and we don't even have a statement from your friend Shelley but I'll take a look at what you've got."

"Okay" I said as I unfurled the same large chart I had just shown the Police Chief across his desk facing him.

I said "I have twenty-three young women murders listed here. As you probably know all the murders, except Cindy Samuels and three others, all took place on a Saturday night.

It shows that there were three murders each month during the first six months of the year, then four in July and the Police Chief's niece so far in August.

I have detailed where each victim was found and any distinguishing features such as hair colour, tattoos, birth marks or signs of child birth by caesarean section."

"Yes. I'm interested but before you go on let me tell you what we have" responded Detective Sergeant Stone.

"We have statements from medical examiners which indicate the young women were all found naked with no jewelry or personal effects.

Like me you probably know those doing the murders certainly haven't made it easy for us.

Most of the women had some shade of blonde hair, bleached, dirty, strawberry, light or natural. It seems like they have been selecting women with blonde hair of some kind or it is just purely a coincidence.

As you mentioned some of them had tattoos. They had different colour eyes and were different heights.

We've checked their fingerprints against the criminal database. Only seven of them don't have criminal records for prostitution at one time or another.

The bodies were found in five different locations. Six beside the Chatsworth Reservoir and four in Granada Hills. These are both north-west of downtown.

Five close to the Morris Reservoir, four in Bailey Canyon and four in Monrovia. These are all north-east of downtown" said Detective Sergeant Stone.

I interjected "You know from what Shelley told me. Nelson has four murder teams so maybe each has their own favourite dumping ground. I'm not sure why there are five?"

"By the way what happened to Shelley. Are you still in contact with her?" asked Detective Sergeant Stone.

"I don't know where she is. I can't find her. But as soon as I do we'll be here to see you" I replied.

Detective Sergeant Stone responded saying "You know her statement and testimony could be of great help."

Detective Sergeant Stone continued "As you know each of these young women were violently sexually assaulted multiple times. In all cases including Cindy they were suffocated to death."

"From what you've just told me it seems our records pretty much match. Now would you like to see what I've collected at different crime scenes?" I asked.

"Okay. Go ahead" replied Detective Sergeant Stone.

I rolled up the chart and emptied my backpack onto Stone's desk.

I said "I found this employee name tag for someone called Courtney Adams. I think the killers must have thrown it out of their truck as they were fleeing. It was quite a distance from the crime scene. The forensics people obviously hadn't searched that far out.

By the way each of the things I've got here is marked to show where it was found."

Picking up another item I said "There is a credit card inside this wallet with the name Charles B. Harrison on it. I found this on the field side of a hedgerow. I'm not sure how it got their unless one of the killers threw it over the hedge.

The killers obviously didn't want to leave any evidence in their van and it seems sometimes panicked and just threw stuff away."

Pointing to Stone's desk I said "I found this gold chain, a scarf and some loose beads. I found these outside where the crime scene tape had been. These things might even have been picked up and moved by birds perhaps seagulls who are known for this. I also found this nondescript ring in a ditch not far from a crime scene."

"I'll have them put into evidence bags. Tagged and added to the evidence items Forensics already have" replied Detective Sergeant Stone.

"That's about it" I said.

"Thanks. If you find Shelley please bring her in. I'd like to hear what she has to say. I'll get someone to see you out" replied Detective Sergeant Stone.

Soon after I was escorted out of the police headquarters building.

*   *   *   *

The day after his stag party Brian found out that Nelson had raped his fiancée Anne Wilson. He knew he had no choice but to kill him.

Anne knew nothing about the businesses he and Nelson were involved in and he didn't want her to ever know.

His wedding was coming up in just over a week. He didn't think it would be possible to kill Nelson before then. So it would have to wait until afterwards. He had no idea how he would do it. But just knew he had to.

*   *   *   *

I found out following my meeting with the Police Chief. He had directed Detective Sergeant Stone to put the wheels in motion to go after Nelson full bore given it had now affected his own family.

He had apparently asked Detective Sergeant Stone to assign as many detectives as he needed regardless of what they were currently working on.

So the case against Nelson was definitely no longer on ice.

I later heard that my name had come up on a number of occasions as a potential source of additional information.

Detective Sergeant Stone told Detectives Howell and McShane to assemble all the murdered young women evidence boxes in one location. And involve as many other homicide detectives as they needed to sift through them to try and identify their killers.

*   *   *   *

Nelson figured he'd lie low for awhile on the French Riviera.

He really enjoyed staying in that part of the world. The best times he'd had were when it was just him and a lady friend on his yacht. He found when there was a crowd he didn't enjoy it as much perhaps because he liked to be in control at all times.

That Friday all the arrangements had been finalized for himself, Osvaldo and the required support staff to make their way to St Tropez arriving by mid-day on Saturday. The local crew should already be on-board.

Nelson and Osvaldo flew first class on a non-stop Air France flight to Nice. The support staff were on the same flight at the back of the plane.

Nelson had left Brian in charge.

SAT AUG 12

After my meetings with Police Chief Hillman and Detective Sergeant Stone I felt energized when I awoke on Saturday morning. I was thinking *I should try and seek out Detectives Howell and McShane to compare notes with them.*

Detective Sergeant Stone had asked me to show my chart to them and had given me their phone numbers. I got through to Detective Howell and setup a meeting with him and Detective McShane at Jules.

I was already there when they arrived that evening. We quickly got down to business.

Between them they had several notebooks full of information that they had gleaned from the online case files.

I rolled out my chart and we compared their notes with it. Essentially confirming that our information matched. It was a most productive exercise. If nothing else. As recap for us.

Detective Howell told me they'd met with Carol Bromley and the guy in the office at the Marina Hotel. He said they had both confirmed they had met with me under the guise of Mr. John Reynolds.

Detective McShane told me about the Petrescu brothers and the white cube van they'd impounded. He said now the case was open again. Forensics were checking to see if they could be match what they'd found in the van to any of the murdered young women.

Both detectives said they were very impressed with my chart. Because they said it captured everything on a single page and asked if they could get a copy.

I told them they could take it as I really didn't have any further use for it. I told them it looked like it would be of more use to them, now Nelson's case was open again.

I told them that based on the conversations I'd had with Shelley there was no doubt Nelson is behind the murders but the question is still how do we prove it.

They said they would see if they could connect the van to him.

With that they got up and said their goodbyes. I went over to the bar and got into conversation with Bert. He asked me what I was doing talking to a couple of Dicks?

I told him we were comparing notes and left it at that.

* * * *

Saturday evening after he'd finished unpacking. Nelson went ashore to have dinner with a glamorous up and coming French actress. He enjoyed her company whenever he was staying in St Tropez. A date with her also allowed him to practice speaking French.

Osvaldo had gone ashore earlier and was waiting on the dockside in a luxury limousine. He had already picked up Nelson's date and she was waiting for him inside the car. It wasn't far to the old town and they soon arrived at the hotel where Nelson would be having dinner and staying overnight.

Sheri Lapointe had met Nelson at the Cannes Film Festival a few years back. He occasionally went there and liked to mingle with Hollywood A Listers if even only from a distance.

After an enjoyable dinner. Sampling some of the finest French cuisine. Nelson and Sheri had adjourned to the hotel's famous champagne bar.

While having a quiet drink they were suddenly interrupted and surrounded by three very attractive women. They were holding fancy trophies talking excitedly about winning them.

This did not sit well with Nelson. He asked them politely if they wouldn't mind celebrating elsewhere. He hated having his space invaded.

One of the stunningly good looking women looked him directly in the face and said we hear you own the largest yacht in St Tropez and we'd love to visit it.

"I'm sorry to disappoint you ladies but I'm staying here at the hotel tonight. Perhaps some other time. Now would you please move along. Thank you" Nelson responded.

The women were persistent and another one told him they would still be there in the morning.

He was thinking *to himself that these jet setters have no concept of time. It is just a continuum to them.*

He couldn't help noticing their slim, well-endowered figures and assumed they rarely ate. When they did it was probably through a straw placed in some formulated concoction.

They obviously didn't have regular meals or bed times. Theirs seemed to be a keep going until you drop lifestyle.

The loud attractive women did move on to continue their celebrations. Nelson and his date enjoyed the rest of the night and he never gave the three women another thought.

Nelson and Sheri talked the night away. He really enjoyed her company. She always seemed to relax him. Sheri knew it was only a dinner date nothing more. That is all she'd ever had with Nelson unless he was planning to surprise her at the end of the night.

He didn't. After signing the bill Nelson escorted Sheri through the majestic hotel. He handed her over to Osvaldo who helped her into the limousine.

After seeing Sheri safely off. He went over to the elevators. While waiting he couldn't help noticing several well dressed men, standing looking into space, which he thought was a bit strange.

He took the elevator up to his luxury suite on the top floor of the hotel which overlooked the lights along the St Tropez shoreline.

Just as he was dropping off to sleep he heard Osvaldo returning after dropping Sheri off.

Osvaldo was staying in the adjoining suite.

SUN AUG 13

In the middle of the night there was a soft knock on the door to Nelson's suite and being a light sleeper it woke him up. Bleary eyed he made his way over to the door wearing only his underpants and peered out through the peephole.

Outside to his surprise he could see the three attractive starlets who had been bothering him and Sheri earlier in the evening.

He quickly assessed the situation. Lust getting the better of him. Very much out of character he unlocked the door opening it as far as the chain safety lock would allow.

The stunning dark haired woman looked through the crack and whispered "We wondered if you'd like some company?"

Nelson thought about it and couldn't resist and removed the chain. He let the three captivating women into his suite. It had been awhile since he'd been with more than one woman. He quickly put a robe on and sat on the end of the bed. He became quite nervous when they surrounded him.

Osvaldo was awakened by women's voices coming from Nelson's suite. He went over to the adjoining doors and listened to what was being said.

Even during his adult film and escort days he'd had very little desire to have sex with any of the women even though it had been on a plate. This wasn't really his thing. He'd never even had a ménage à trois.

He'd never really got a great deal of pleasure from having sex. He didn't really know why except perhaps it was because of his very strict upbringing, limiting any spontaneity. He had never gone on a hunt for women or associated with anyone who had.

As he sat facing the three vixens he'd thought *of something*. He told them he'd asked them into his suite to apologize for being so rude to them earlier in the evening. Even though he didn't know who they were or know anything about them.

He asked them if they'd like a drink.

"No thank you" replied the dark haired one with an American accent who looked more Italian than French. The other two women also declined the drink.

He realized he may have made a big mistake letting these women into his suite thinking *they might be here to hurt him or worse.*

St Tropez is a lot closer to the Italian mafia and wondered if Rossini's influence reached this far.

Before he knew it one of the women had slipped off one of her high heeled stilettos and was raising it above her head in a threatening way.

At the same time the dark-haired beauty pulled a midnight special out of her impressive cleavage.

"Hey what's going on?" shouted Nelson raising a hand to defend himself.

"Please stay calm Mr. Nelson" said the brunette waving the tiny gun at him.

"You know I thought we were about to have a foursome?" he laughed trying to act unflustered.

Nelson was thinking *the so-called awards were perhaps just props.*

"Let me introduce myself" said the Italian looking brunette "I am Valentina Rossini and to keep this simple my father has asked me to find you and kill you for murdering my brother's wife."

Hearing this admission was Osvaldo's que.

He quietly opened the adjoining room door, flung it open and pointing his gun shouted at the woman holding the midnight special to drop it.

The two other stiletto women took a step back and Rossini's daughter still looking defiant threw the small gun onto the bed next to Nelson.

"Are you alright Mr. Nelson?" asked Osvaldo.

"I am now" he responded "No need for any bloodshed right ladies?"

Osvaldo pointing his gun at the three women started to usher them out of the suite.

"Hold on Osvaldo. The dark-haired one stays" said Nelson "Let the other two out."

Osvaldo continued to usher the other two women out into the corridor and made sure they got into the elevator. Coming back into the Osvaldo asked if there was anything else he could do.

Nelson was pointing Valentina's discarded gun at her where she was standing.

"Yes. Tie her up. I don't trust her" said Nelson tossing Osvaldo the belt from his robe saying "I guess I need to be more careful who I let into my room next time?"

Valentina was tied to a chair facing Nelson who was still sitting on the end of the bed.

"Thanks Osvaldo. I'll call you if I need you. Right now Miss Rossini and I are going to have a little chat" said Nelson.

"Here take her gun" he said handing Osvaldo the small gun.

Osvaldo took the gun and headed through the door to the adjoining suite.

"So Valentina. You're a long way from home. Tell me why you are here in St Tropez?" enquired Nelson.

"What we told you about the awards is true.

Myself and my friends are over here to receive international film awards. Cannes is not the only film festival in the world you know. There are many other smaller ones including here in St Tropez" responded Valentina.

"So what about killing me while you are here?" he asked.

"My father is still extremely mad with you. He knows you are behind the murder of my brother's wife and that you had almost every bottle in his expensive wine collection destroyed.

Anytime anyone visited from the old country they brought vintage wine with them as a present for him. You have devastated his life in at least two ways so why wouldn't he be hopping mad with you and still want revenge?" replied Valentina.

"So I guess me kidnapping you will be number three. You know he has tried to kill or hurt me on three occasions the third being you and your friends tonight. So I think we're even." Nelson suggested.

"Not really. You haven't lost anything precious to you. My father has. What have you lost? Nothing right?" replied Valentina.

"Your sister-in-law Dahlia's death was an accident. She just happened to be in the wrong place at the wrong time.

As for his wine collection I didn't appreciate almost being killed in my own backyard and in fact I am still in pain from a wound he inflicted on me.

He also sent someone to assault me at my golf club. Do you know about that?

As for you. You just tried to kill me. Does there need to be anymore killing?" Nelson asked.

Valentina said "For your information my father got wounded too."

"I didn't know that" replied Nelson.

Valentina just stared at him saying nothing.

Nelson got up and went over and knocked on the adjoining door and shouted "Osvaldo let's get the hell out of here. She's coming with us."

Nelson had decided to take Valentina back to his yacht until he could figure out how to best use her as a bargaining chip with Rossini.

Nelson quickly packed. Untied Valentina and they headed down in the elevator. They exited the hotel through a back door. Osvaldo had told Nelson he'd bring the limousine around to the back of the hotel.

They skirted the hotel pool in the dark. Valentina was in her fancy evening gown and heels. Nelson was carrying his suitcase. Osvaldo was waiting for them.

On the way to the harbour. Osvaldo woke the captain up and asked him to send a boat to come and pick them up. He then phoned the limousine company to tell them where to come and pick it up.

Bringing Valentina on-board had it's complications. Although being anchored off shore the chances of her jumping overboard were unlikely.

Unless she had some crime reporter blood in her thought Nelson.

Once on-board Nelson and Valentina grabbed a few hours sleep. After waking up Valentina began to explore the ship. She found the bar that Sunday lunchtime and was talking with Osvaldo who made her a fancy cocktail.

Nelson joined Valentina at the bar jokingly asking her what he should do with her? Right now she seemed to be really enjoying herself.

She suggested that perhaps he could come to some mutual agreement with her father. Something like if he promises not to try and kill you again you will set me free.

"By the way" she asked "How do you communicate with the rest of the world when you're out here on the water? How would I communicate with my father for instance?"

"Don't worry we have satellite phones and Wi-fi on-board. You could even e-mail him" Nelson replied.

"Are you kidding he doesn't use e-mail. I could try and phone him even though the conversations I have with him are usually face to face. He doesn't like communicating any other way" replied Valentina.

"Well let's try and phone him if you have his number. He doesn't need to worry. The conversation will be encrypted" said Nelson.

"Its probably better if I phone someone close to him and ask him to get him on the phone" replied Valentina.

"Okay. I have a phone in my office when do you want to call him?" Nelson asked.

"What time is it on the west coast?" she asked.

"They're nine hours behind us. So given it's two-thirty in the afternoon here now it will be five-thirty in the morning there. A little to early I would think?" Nelson commented.

"I guess seven this evening our time would be ten in the morning for him. Can we do it then?" asked Valentina.

"Yes. Provided you take it easy on the cocktails" quipped Nelson.

"No problem. After this one I'll go for a nap. Please wake me before seven. Thanks" she replied.

Nelson was thinking *he wouldn't mind having a nap with her himself.*

She looked absolutely gorgeous wearing only the white dress shirt she had found in Nelson's suite.

Nelson said he needed to check on a few things and excused himself and went below.

He was only able to find Ron on the phone and asked him if the Police Chief had been looking for him.

Ron told him as far as he knew everything had been quiet at his house. He said no one from the Los Angeles Police Department had been trying to contact him.

Back up on deck Valentina asked Osvaldo if he would give her one more drink. Something to knock her out so she'd sleep.

"How about a Harvey Wallbanger?" suggested Osvaldo.

"That sounds perfect" replied Valentina.

"Coming right up" responded Osvaldo mixing up the vodka, Galliano and orange juice drink.

After polishing it off. Valentina jumped off her stool. Said goodbye to Osvaldo and went down to her guest cabin. Once inside. She threw off the dress shirt she'd been wearing, got into bed naked and fell asleep almost immediately.

She was woken by soft knocking on her cabin door. Osvaldo quietly let her know it was time to get up and that Mr. Nelson was waiting for her in his office.

After reviving herself and putting the dress shirt back on she found his office.

"Oh Hi" Nelson said as if he was surprised to see her.

"So what shall I tell my Dad?" asked Valentina.

"Tell him you are currently my guest and have been thoroughly enjoying your stay on my yacht on the French Riviera.

Let him take on-board, no pun intended, what you've just told him and when he's calmed down tell him what the proposal is.

That if he agrees to never try and kill me again you will be free to leave whenever you like. Is that okay?" Nelson asked.

"Yes" said Valentina.

"Good. Have you got the number?" Nelson asked.

"Yes" she said "Try this number."

Nelson dialed the number and handed her the phone as soon as someone answered.

"Hi Vito. It's Valentina. Can I speak to my father?" There was a pause "Hi Daddy. I'm fine. No I'm fine. I want to speak with you about something" said Valentina.

"Yes. It is a secure line" she said before repeating what Nelson had suggested.

The cursing on the other end of the line stopped and she turned to Nelson and told him her father agrees and is on-board with the arrangement.

How do you like that 'on-board'? asked Valentina.

Nelson laughed telling her he wanted her father's agreement in writing and gave her an e-mail address where he could send it.

Valentina told Nelson her Dad had gone but Vito says he will make sure it gets sent with my Dad's concurrence.

She gave Vito the e-mail address and passed the phone back to Nelson who hung it up.

"Why don't we have a celebratory drink to both of our freedoms?" suggested Valentina.

"Sounds good to me. Let's go and visit Osvaldo. I'm sure he's got some Dom Perignon on ice" Nelson said following her out of his office and down the hall.

After having drunk several glasses of champagne Valentina jumped off her bar stool. She gave Nelson a big hug and a kiss on the lips and asked him where had he been hiding all her life?

She'd obviously had a little too much to drink and was definitely in a very happy mood.

Although he would love to make love to her she was in her mid-twenties. He was twenty years older even though he was in great physical shape.

Regardless, feeling this was his golden opportunity to bed this dream girl. He suggested he give her a tour of the yacht. She agreed and when they got to Nelson's suite he asked her if she would like a drink to which surprisingly she said "Sure. Could I have a Harvey Wallbanger?"

Nelson knowing she'd already had too much to drink decided on a variation and began to kiss her passionately while removing the dress shirt he'd given her.

He quickly stripped off his own clothes and they lied down on the bed. Her naked body felt wonderful against his. He was primed and ready even though she was asking him if they should be doing this.

He didn't answer knowing he couldn't help himself and penetrated her hot body. She immediately submitted to him and joined in energetically holding him tightly, kissing him and thrusting her body at him.

He wasn't able to hold on for long and was soon gasping for air thinking *he wasn't as young as he used to be but felt extremely satisfied.*

Valentina fell asleep.

He got off the bed praying she wouldn't remember what he had just done.

Thinking *if her father found out about this the war would be on again for sure. Agreement or not.*

Nelson's recent conquests of Anne Wilson and now Valentina Rossini was of concern to him and was a worry because they were so out of character. It seemed he suddenly had an appetite for impromptu sex which was very unusual and unlike him.

He was thinking that he might have been on power trips to prove to himself he can get whatever he wants, whenever he wants.

* * * *

Following the murder of his daughter-in-law. It seemed Johnny Rossini was unknowingly helping the crime families back east by trying to take Nelson out.

They had been keeping up to date on Rossini's failed attempts and although they were disappointed, they weren't ready to give up on him yet.

They liked his inventiveness, even though he had failed so far. They had especially liked the last attempt to kill Nelson. They heard it had almost succeeded and was masterminded by Rossini's daughter Valentina.

*   *   *   *

It was nearly lunchtime when I awoke. I figured I'd have a lazy day. I was due to go back to work tomorrow. I figured I'd enjoy the last day of my vacation which had been uneventful, even though it had included a few days in Las Vegas.

So far today there hadn't been any reports of a body being found on the outskirts of the city. Perhaps the murder of the Police Chief's niece was going to be the last one.

I didn't know Nelson was currently in the south of France on his other luxury yacht.

I was beginning to think about what I would write when I got back to work tomorrow.

Whether I'd carry on writing about the murders or go back and cover the multitude of other crimes that were undoubtably continuing to happen in the City of Angels.

I figured I would need to discuss it with Simmons.

My thoughts turned to Shelley and what could have happened to her. I hoped the pig farm wasn't a possibility, but knowing how ruthless Nelson was, nothing could be discounted especially the way Shelley had suddenly disappeared.

I tried to remember the last time I'd seen her.

Looking at the Calendar on my laptop I was pretty sure the first time we met was late on Sunday July 23rd when she was waiting outside my building to speak with me.

We went to Jules and talked through the early hours of Monday the 24th. We met again that night or early the next morning Tuesday the 25th.

After Nelson let me go I saw Shelley that night Monday July 31st. This was the third time I'd seen her. That same night we both briefly met with Detective Sergeant Stone of the Los Angeles Police Department ending up with us going to Jules and back to the place she was staying.

This was the last time I'd seen Shelley.

Then I tried to figure out when I checked on her the first time and remembered it was the night I got released from jail which would have been Wednesday August 2nd.

That was when I found out she'd disappeared.

It was now Sunday August 13th and I thought to myself *maybe I should see if I could find her again?*

I decided that this evening on my way to Jules I would check out the place where she'd been staying. Then a thought came to me. *Perhaps she'd moved back to her own place in west Hollywood but I didn't know where that was.*

Just then I was surprised by a knock on my door. When I opened it there was a woman standing outside. She asked if she could clean my room. I asked her to give me a couple of minutes.

During those few minutes I decided I was hungry. I drove to a place I'd seen close by called Frank's Diner. I had a burger and fries. Something I hadn't had for awhile.

As I headed back to the motel I was assuming I would find a nice clean room. But instead found the room had been ransacked. Stuff was strewn all over the floor, including the mattresses and bed clothes.

Here we go again I thought. All I could think of *was whoever had turned the room upside down might be looking for Shelley's whereabouts too.*

Feeling like I had been violated. I tidied up as best I could and for the rest of the afternoon watched TV before setting out for Jules.

I parked in my usual spot. Under my building and headed over to where Shelley had been staying. When I came out of the ancient elevator I surprised a dark haired woman, wearing glasses sitting watching TV.

Looking over at me somewhat startled she said "Oh Hello."

"Hi, I'm a friend of Shelley's" I said.

"Oh. I see. Yes. She sometimes stays here when I'm away?" she replied.

"Yes. She gave me the code to the freight elevator if you're wondering. Do you have any idea where Shelley is?" I asked.

"No. Actually I don't. I've only been back for a few days" she replied.

"Could she be back at her own place?" I asked.

"Yes. Maybe" she responded.

"Do you know her address there?" I asked.

"Yes" she said checking her phone "It's 1862 North Wilson Boulevard, Apartment 823."

"Do you have a phone number for her too?" I asked.

"Yes. 844 368 2781" she replied.

I wrote the information down in my notepad and thanked the woman. She said her name was Linda. I told her my name and who I was and went straight to Jules.

Once I had a beer in front of me I asked Bert if he'd seen Shelley. He replied he hadn't.

Being a Sunday night it was very quiet so Bert and I had a good old chin wag. Me telling him about the few days I'd spent in Las Vegas and him making jokes about my unrecognizable tan.

When I got back to where I was staying. Although it was quite late. I phoned the number Shelley's friend had given me but got no answer. Not even a voice mail.

I thought *that perhaps Shelley didn't want to disclose or advertise that this was her phone number.*

I had my last smoke of the day and climbed into bed in my still somewhat dishevelled motel room.

MON AUG 14

Police Chief Hillman knowing the last time he'd visited Nelson he hadn't been home. This was quite unusual so he had asked the surveillance team leader to come and meet with him.

When the surveillance team leader Officer Bruce Cummings arrived the Police Chief asked him if he had anything to report.

He said since Detective Sergeant Stone had put the surveillance in place several weeks ago his team had accumulated a significant amount of video footage.

Cummings said they had documented vehicles coming and going and occasional visitors to the property.

He said "Mondays are by far the busiest day of the week with Tuesday being the second busiest. Every Monday between 8 and 9 am about ten vehicles arrive and men and women meet in a big tent in the back garden.

On Tuesdays, vehicles, sometimes taxi's, arrive approximately every hour or so and either a man or woman is greeted at the front door usually by the occupant himself.

Apart from this. Two guys frequently visit. They have been identified as a Mr. Brian James and a Mr. Ronald Wells, a well known lawyer.

"So really we haven't got very much we could use as evidence of any wrong doing? Is that correct?" asked the Police Chief.

"Well there have been one or two specific incidents. Like when a well dressed big guy showed up on a Sunday afternoon a week or so ago and we never saw him again. There was also a guy who showed up half naked one day and left the next.

There was also the day when a lot of shots were fired on the property after a delivery truck veered off the driveway into the gardens. I heard that police officers investigated the incident. I haven't heard anything more about it since. There is also another thing that happens every Monday.

Many of the people who arrive are dragging a suitcase behind them as they enter the tent in the back" said Cummings.

"That's interesting" responded the Police Chief.

"Apart from this we really don't have much else" said Cummings.

"Okay. Thanks for coming in" said the Police Chief getting up and walking Cummings to his office door.

*   *   *   *

Brian chaired the Monday meeting and told everyone it was going to be a very short meeting.

He asked the Heads if they had any revenue issues. He said he knew Hustle had and was planning to speak with him after the meeting so as not to hold anyone up.

None of the Heads said they had any issues so Brian continued. Sam chipped in that the issue down on the border had been resolved and said the boss knows about it.

Brian asked Jimmy the Fixer to tell his murder teams to stand down and lie low for the time being.

He told everyone Nelson was instituting a new rule for new prostitutes. From now on they would need to be at least twenty-five and be smart enough to understand the importance of always keeping their mouths shut.

"Except when they're working of course" chuckled Hustle.

If any of you don't already know the boss is currently on vacation over in Europe.

"That's it for today. Let's all meet over at the garages in a few minutes" said Brian.

* * * *

Although Nelson had been in the south of France for a few days he was anxious to know how things were going back home. He was also most interested to know if Anne Wilson had said anything about their encounter and if there had been any fall out as a result of it?

Nelson hadn't had a chance to spend anytime with Brian before he left and more than anything wanted to know how he was doing following the Anne Wilson incident.

He asked Osvaldo to get in touch with Brian and ask him to take the overnight Air France flight to Nice where he told Osvaldo he should pick him up.

Brian knowing what Nelson had done to Anne immediately jumped at the opportunity to come over and meet with him.

* * * *

Early that morning I phoned the number Shelley's friend had given me. It rang a number of times but no one answered. So on my way into work later in the day. I drove out to her west Hollywood address.

It looked like Shelley lived in an upscale neighbourhood. *Amazing what dirty money can pay for* I thought. She lived in a clean looking white apartment complex. After I managed to get into the building no one answered the door when I knocked.

So Shelley's whereabouts continued to remain a mystery.

TUES AUG 15

Brian arrived in St Tropez on Tuesday evening looking remarkably fresh considering he'd been travelling for almost twenty-four hours. As he sat down Osvaldo came over and asked him if he would like a drink?

This was funny Brian thought *because Osvaldo had just driven him all the way from Nice and now he was asking him if he wanted drink?*

Brian asked for a skinny Manhattan.

"Did you have a good trip?" asked Nelson as he joined Brian where he was sitting.

"First class on Air France is phenomenal. I sampled some of the finest French cuisine and managed to get a few hours sleep" replied Brian.

"So bring me up to date please" requested Nelson.

"Not much has happened since you left last Friday. Revenues remain steady across the board with the exception of prostitution which you already know about. I met with Hustle who told me with you away his recruitment is on hold. I mentioned to everyone that you were going to recruit more mature prostitutes" said Brian.

"Okay. I guess Hustle's correct. Me being over here is certainly not helping his recruitment drive. So when you get back whenever you get any spare time please take over the interviewing.

Also knowing bringing new women in is a top priority please try and interview them whenever you can. It doesn't have to be just on Tuesday's anymore. Hopefully, this will help Hustle" said Nelson.

Brian continued "Sam said the matter down on the border has been resolved. He said you know about it and should be pleased."

"Do you know what he meant by this? Is the guy that got arrested dead?" asked Nelson.

"I don't know. That's all he told me" replied Brian.

Brian continued "After the meeting yesterday Jimmy the Fixer told me that one of his cube vans has been impounded. He said he's pretty sure the police won't find anything.

The Police Chief came to visit you on Sunday and was told you weren't there. When he asked where you were he was told no one knew. This apparently really upset him from what I heard."

"I don't like the fact one of our vans has been seized by the police. There's not much I can do about the ungrateful Police Chief. Let's talk again in the morning. Please take your usual cabin" said Nelson getting up and walking away.

Osvaldo brought Brian's skinny Manhattan over, which contained half the alcohol of a normal one.

As Brian began to sip it a scantily dressed extremely attractive woman approached him.

"Hi! Who are you?" Valentina asked.

Brian responded "I could ask you the same question. I'm Brian pleased to"

Before Brian could finish the sentence Valentina said "I know who you are. You were with Martin when my Dad tried to kill him. You're Brian."

Brian was already thinking *she must be Rossini's daughter. She seemed full of herself and was already using first names.*

"I get who you are" responded Brian "But what are you doing here?"

As Valentina sat down she shouted over to Osvaldo to get her a Harvey Wallbanger.

"You know this is my new favourite drink" she said.

Osvaldo came over with Valentina's drink and she jumped up and hugged him thanking him.

Brian was amazed with the story Valentina told him about last Saturday night at the famous Maison Blanche hotel in St Tropez. But didn't let on.

Brian and Valentina sat and talked for quite awhile until Brian said he was beginning to feel tired and needed to go to his cabin.

* * * *

As Brian lay in his cabin he couldn't stop thinking about the events of the last few days and Nelson himself.

Anne Wilson had broken off the engagement the day after she'd been raped by Nelson. Asking Brian what did he think she was? A common slut that could be shared around with his friends.

Anne had been the love of Brian's life and now Nelson had to pay for what he had done. He thought back to when he'd first met him.

He was the one who had made him what he was today.

He was the one who had grown up out here who had introduced him to the key people running the city and even the pig farmer.

Although he himself had no reason to enter the criminal world he had done it as a friend. Eventually getting in too deep to get out.

*　*　*　*

I was back in the office trying to get back into the swing of things. As per Simmons request I was no longer reporting on the murders of young women. I was however still occasionally answering questions put to me by Detectives Howell or McShane.

They were still trying to build a case against Nelson. Their first question was always. Had I found Shelley yet?

I told them I had been trying to find her but hadn't had any luck yet. I knew this always disappointed them.

It hadn't been a good start to the week.

I felt as if I was being pushed aside. I had been putting a story together about a drive-by shooting in south-central Los Angeles. Killing one person and injuring several others.

The police were treating it as just another gangland homicide. Adding to the toll of young men who had been killed or maimed during the ongoing turf wars.

Before the murders of the young women had begun I'd been reporting on these kinds of shootings. It seemed to be a constant theme and part of everyday life in the City of Angels.

Most people who live here. Although they aren't happy with the situation. They are resigned to it happening. They just hope it doesn't affect their lives.

WED AUG 16

As the sun was slowly rising over the French Riviera, a French Gendarmerie Maritime police vessel was maneuvering it's way through the small boats surrounding Nelson's yacht in St Tropez harbour.

As soon as it was close enough a uniformed police officer using a megaphone indicated that the police were planning to board the yacht.

Brian, Osvaldo and others up on deck heard the announcement and shortly after two uniformed police officers came aboard and announced they had an arrest warrant for a Mr. Martin Nelson.

No one said anything.

"Alright. We will have to see if we can find him" said one of the officers in broken English.

Valentina arrived on deck. Her hair was wrapped in a towel around her head. She looked resplendent in one of Nelson's white towel bathrobes.

Brian and Osvaldo just looked at each other.

Valentina asked "What was going on?"

Seeing her the other officer who spoke better English said "We are looking for Mr. Martin Nelson."

Valentina clammed up saying nothing.

The police knew Nelson was on-board. The yacht had been under surveillance since last Saturday when he'd arrived.

When Nelson had gone ashore Saturday evening. The police authorities on shore had been notified. Plain clothes detectives had watched his every move until he returned to his yacht early Sunday morning.

Sitting in his office Nelson had heard the megaphone announcement. So he knew the police were looking to arrest him. However, he had a way to hide from them.

Back when he'd had both yachts built. He'd included a false cabin in their design for just this eventuality. Thinking *he may have to hide from rival crime bosses, other unknown enemies or even as in this case, the police.*

He reached down under his desk. Pressed a button and immediately the bookcase on the adjacent wall opened outwards.

He entered the hiding place and closed the bookcase. There was just enough room for him to stand in the hidden space.

He stood and waited.

Several minutes later he could hear someone moving around in his office.

After not finding Nelson. The lead police officer told those up on deck that they would be coming back with a search warrant. This would allow them to search the boat more thoroughly. He said in the meantime it will be under twenty-four hour surveillance and no one should leave.

Osvaldo came down into Nelson's office and whispered into the bookcase that the police had gone.

"That was quick" commented Nelson after he came out of hiding.

"They said they'd be coming back with a search warrant. This would allow them to search the boat more thoroughly next time. Until then they said it will be under continuous surveillance" said Osvaldo.

"Did they say when they'd be coming back?" Nelson asked.

"No" responded Osvaldo.

"So how are we going to get me off the boat without them seeing me?" Nelson asked.

"I don't know boss. Do you want me to get Brian?" asked Osvaldo.

"Yes. Please ask him to come and see me right away" Nelson replied.

Brian appeared almost immediately and Nelson asked him the same question he'd just asked Osvaldo about getting him off the boat.

Knowing what Nelson had done to his fiancé. Brian wasn't in the mood to get creative and told him it was a difficult situation. This wasn't what Nelson wanted to hear but said he'd come up with an idea of his own.

Nelson said "I'll just swim to the shore tonight. Just like the crime reporter did when he jumped off Big Fish. Hopefully, it won't take me two or three days like it did him. We will need a diversion of some kind to keep the police busy.

So Brian please arrange to get a rowing boat. Osvaldo and you can be rowing in the other direction. Out to sea. At the very same time I'm swimming for the shore.

Please arrange it as soon as you can."

Brian figured Nelson would soon be arrested one way or another but at that moment didn't really care how. He just wanted him to get caught.

He figured Nelson getting arrested was the best outcome because he wasn't sure he had the guts to kill him.

Nelson knew there was a change in Brian's attitude towards him and obviously knew why and wished what had happened hadn't.

But it had, so there wasn't anything he could do about it and actually at this time, he needed Brian more than ever. What he'd done was selfish and thoughtless not like him at all. But it couldn't be undone.

As Brian was leaving his office Nelson said "Can you ask Ron to fly over as soon as he can. I might need him depending on how things go tonight. Thanks."

"Okay" responded Brian.

Under the cover of darkness. In the early hours of the morning. Nelson slipped into the oily harbour water and began to swim towards the lights along the St Tropez shoreline.

He figured doing the breaststroke would create less splashes compared to other more strenuous strokes. His yacht wasn't anchored that far from the shore so he thought it should be fairly easy for him to swim to the beach.

Meanwhile Osvaldo and Brian had just climbed into the small rowing boat Brian had acquired and were slowly rowing out to sea away from the yacht and the St Tropez shoreline.

The large police vessel in the harbour had been constantly watching the yacht for just this eventuality. Within minutes of the appearance of the rowing boat a powerful searchlight was switched on pointing directly at it.

Within minutes a police launch was rapidly approaching Brian and Osvaldo in the small rowing boat. Someone on a megaphone was telling them to stop rowing and remain in place.

As Nelson was swimming the short distance to the shore he was thinking *that it was that damn crime reporter who was responsible for his current predicament.*

Before leaving for St Tropez. Nelson had heard that the reporter had hooked up with Shelley Green. This was bad news and would need to be addressed.

He wasn't aware Walsh had also met the girl whose murder had gone wrong that had cost him a murder team and a Head.

He couldn't think of any other reason why the French police had moved in on him so quickly after his arrival in St Tropez.

It had to be the crime reporter.

Nelson was making good progress as he swam towards the shoreline.

He was wearing a black wet suit and had a small waterproof backpack strapped to his back. It contained a tee shirt, shorts, a pair of flip-flops, cash in US dollars and a camera.

It didn't take him long to reach some of the smaller boats anchored close to the shore.

He scrambled into one of them. Detached it from the back of a bigger boat and rowed it to a jetty where he jumped out.

It was dark apart from the lights shining out of the buildings in close proximity to the shoreline. He quickly got changed, dumping his backpack and wetsuit into a nearby garbage barrel.

The weather was warm and the sun would soon be coming up. Nelson already had a plan. He would look and act like a tourist with the camera around his neck.

Until he found a taxi driver willing to take him further up the coast.

Long before Nelson had reached the shore. Brian and Osvaldo had been unceremoniously pulled out of the rowing boat up into the police launch and shuttled to the larger police vessel.

Once on-board they were interrogated separately and asked why they had been rowing out to sea?

Osvaldo said nothing.

Brian wanting to make sure Nelson got arrested. Told the police they were rowing out to sea to take the attention away from Martin Nelson. While he was swimming for the shore. He said he and Osvaldo were a decoy if they knew what that was.

The police authorities on shore were immediately notified and a manhunt began. It started in the cobblestone streets leading up from the harbour.

Nelson walking in the old fishing quarter began to see an increased police presence. Walking the streets at dawn wearing his bright clothes he stood out like a sore thumb. Tourist or not.

So to try and stand out less and get off the street he began to try the doors of shops but found without exception they were all locked.

Instead Nelson hid in a dark doorway until he was discovered by a police officer. The officer was shining a flashlight on him while at the same time speaking French into a walkie-talkie.

The police officer asked Nelson in French what he was doing out this early in the morning? Nelson understood what he said but knew if he replied he would give himself away. So he acted like he didn't understand saying "Huh?"

While Nelson continued to stoop in the doorway. Other police officers started arriving. They were excitedly speaking to each other in French. Nelson understood what they were saying but didn't let on.

A newly arrived police officer had a copy of the arrest warrant. It had Nelson's photo on it. He excitedly shouted "It's him. Look" in French. Which Nelson also understood.

Nelson thought about resisting but there was at least six or seven of them and more arriving all the time. He was wearing flip-flops. Trying to out run them would be futile. So he didn't resist. He was handcuffed, frisked and read his rights in French, then in broken English.

Nelson asked what he was being arrested for and one of the officers started reading off the arrest warrant. Murder, racketeering …

"Alright that's enough" said Nelson in English.

By now several police cars and vans with Police Nationale emblazoned across their sides had shown up.

Nelson was pushed into the back of one of the vans and as he sat on the backseat he was thinking. *So much for his plan.*

It hadn't worked out too well. He'd probably only been free for a few hours more than Brian and Osvaldo. Perhaps he should have stayed on the boat and hidden on-board in his secret hideaway.

After being fingerprinted. Photos taken and swabbed for a DNA sample. As he sat in his cell he was thinking *he probably should have quit while he was ahead.*

He had often thought about giving it all up and buying a beach house in Malibu. Close to the ocean. Where he could enjoy the rest of his life.

He hadn't done it because he was so committed to his organization. Even now it wasn't running as smoothly as he would have liked. He was still dealing with too many problems every day.

He couldn't understand why smart people couldn't follow simple rules. He had always felt it was a reflection on him because he obviously hadn't made the instructions clear or simple enough.

He had always tried to recruit smart people. But quite a number of them seemed unable to carry out basic instructions no matter how straightforward they were. He still needed to understand why so many things were always going wrong.

It wasn't that in the scheme of things he wasn't making giant profits. It was just that it should be almost problem free after two decades.

He himself followed simple principles. Putting in a good day's work, drinking only occasionally and always confronting problems as they arose. Never procrastinating.

He had enough money to last him several lifetimes. Brian and Ron didn't need the money either. They were both wealthy in their own right.

It was obviously the murders that had drawn attention to him. This was completely the opposite of what he was trying to accomplish with them. Thinking they would draw attention away from him.

Brian and Ron had warned him against them on numerous occasions and he didn't know why he hadn't listened.

He thought back to the last twenty years. Starting with the adult movie and escort businesses. Acquiring the fourteen clubs and for the last few years making almost half a billion dollars in profit.

He was thinking to himself he could have been successful at anything he'd put his mind to.

He had meticulous work habits and superior leadership skills. But it was illegal money making activities that had excited and challenged him the most.

As he sat and looked at the graffiti on the wall in his small concrete cell he thought to himself. *Is this it?*

THURS AUG 17

Around noon I got a phone call from Detective McShane. He told me early this morning the police had arrested Nelson over in France.

He said Detective Sergeant Stone figure's with Shelley's statement and the evidence from each crime scene, your kidnapping, threats to Shelley's and your life and the forensics from the van there may be a chance Nelson could go to trial.

I must say this surprised me.

I still didn't know where Shelley was but Detective McShane was confident she would be found soon.

Detective McShane seemed to think that once Shelley identified the key people in Nelson's organization and pressure was applied to them. More evidence would come to light and everything would come down like a house of cards.

* * * *

After being held in a custody cell all day Nelson couldn't wait to speak to Ron and was amazed he was still allowed to represent him, given he was a key member of his organization.

Nelson hoped to speak to Ron in private to impart his ideas on how to hide what was going on in his businesses. The cocaine business being of prime concern. If the State Police got involved he wanted to make sure they wouldn't find any cocaine in his warehouses.

Nelson's thinking *was cocaine had to be dealt with first. Everything else could wait until later.*

He was going to suggest to Ron that he ask Sam to acquire sufficient tractor-trailers to temporarily store the cocaine. Parking them somewhere the State police authorities wouldn't find them or even if they did it would be difficult to connect them to him.

Unfortunately when Ron Wells arrived that evening Detectives Howell and McShane were accompanying him as he entered the interview room.

Before the two Detectives could ask Nelson anything Wells asked them why his client had been arrested and what he was being charged with?

"Good question" said Detective Howell.

"The murders of Courtney Adams, Chelsea Harrison, Dahlia Rossini and Sandy Palmer and nineteen other women. In addition to the murder charges Racketeering, Drug Trafficking, Illegal Gambling, Provision of Sexual Services and Tax Evasion."

Detective Sergeant Stone had formulated these charges in anticipation of having a statement from Shelley soon and using her testimony later in court which he would rely heavily on.

"Now if it's alright we'd like to ask Mr. Nelson some questions?" asked Detective McShane.

Wells responded saying "Just so you know my client will be responding with 'No Comment' to every question you ask him based on my learned council."

Detective Howell responded saying "If this is the case there is not much point in continuing with the interview. I suggest we move on to explain the international extradition process to Mr. Nelson."

"I can take care of that? offered Wells.

"Okay. Do you have any questions Mr. Nelson?" asked Detective Howell.

"No. I just need to speak to my lawyer in private" he replied.

"Five minutes. We'll be outside" said Detective McShane leaving the interview room with Detective Howell.

Once he was on his own with Wells. Nelson said "I want you to remove all the cocaine from our warehouses. Perhaps storing it in tractor-trailers."

Wells responded "Look Marty, although these guys think they have you in a box with a ribbon neatly tied around it. They are mistaken.

Although they think an American State Department's federal international arrest warrant is sufficient to bring you back to the United States, because we have an extradition treaty with France.

It is not.

You still have rights as a United States citizen, wherever you happen to be residing in the world.

If you choose to the fight the extradition. The United States government will have to make their case to a judge here in a French court. He is the one who will decide whether or not you will be extradited to the United States to face the criminal justice system there. Rather than here in France.

Usually the country being asked to extradite someone. In this case France. Will want to make sure they get a fair trial and will not be subjected to the death penalty in the other country.

However based on the charges we were just read it is unlikely you'll get bail. So you'll be spending a lot of time in custody here in a French prison while everything goes through the French courts.

You will need to come to terms with this."

"I understand" Nelson responded still upbeat "Surely I have been sufficiently insulated from being directly connected to any of these charges. As you know I didn't murder any of these women or sell drugs myself?"

"It all depends on what evidence they have linking you to the murders and the other charges" replied Wells. "You will need to clean up any loose ends especially potential prosecution witnesses. Do you think that crime reporter has anything that could be used against you?"

"It's hard to tell but he certainly didn't get my signature on anything. I guess it depends on what kind of story he spins about his kidnapping and whether they have any proof that it actually happened. Surely he must be facing impersonation charges himself?" said Nelson.

"I heard they were dropped last week when we wouldn't cooperate" replied Wells.

"Listen Marty. I need to tell you something else. Given what has happened to you and the likelihood of you being behind bars for quite a while. Brian and I are planning to close the organization down and require your Power of Attorney in order to do it. Are you willing to give it to us?" asked Wells.

"No way! It's too early to do that until we know if any of these charges are going to stick" Nelson replied.

"Okay then. You will need to find someone else to run things because as of right now Brian and I are out. Also, I will not be representing you anymore but will do my best to find you a top notch defence lawyer to takeover from me" replied Wells.

Brian and Ron certainly didn't want to carry on Nelson's illegal businesses knowing they themselves would now need to tread very carefully so as not to face the same fate as him. Neither Brian nor Ron needed the money and they knew they would both be lucky to escape unscathed.

After Ron had left and Nelson was back in his cell he was thinking *how the last few days had been the worst of his life.*

Why was this happening to him when he was at the top and supposed to be untouchable? Was it being done for show or was he actually going to be put on trial in a court of law?

If it was for show he was not amused. If it was for real then it was all down to that crime reporter.

The fact that Ron and Brian had bailed upset him no end. This indicated he could assume his arrest was definitely for real. Why would they want to distance themselves from him unless they saw pending doom. They obviously didn't think it was for show.

FRI AUG 18

Nelson decided almost immediately not to fight his extradition back to the United States. He was able to let his new lawyer Bill Saunders know. He told him he would rather be back in Los Angeles to face the music. Nelson said he didn't want to be in some French prison, listening to inmates and guards talking French all day long.

Anyway he was convinced he wouldn't be in jail very long once he got home. Because the minimal evidence he figured the Los Angeles Police Department had wouldn't stand up in court. Especially if there weren't any witnesses to testify in person.

Nelson and Detectives McShane and Howell took an Air France flight from Toulon, where the French Gendarmerie Maritime police headquarters are, on to

Paris where they took a direct American Airlines flight to Los Angeles.

It had been a number of years since Nelson had flown economy and found being wedged between Detectives Howell and McShane most uncomfortable.

He was thinking *he'd been successfully involved in illegal money making schemes for almost twenty years without incident. It was his need to murder young down and out women that might potentially put him away for the rest of his life. That is if he managed to escape the chair.*

He was once again trying to figure out why he'd felt it so necessary and had insisted on carrying out these murders. He had often discussed it with Brian and Ron who had been vehemently against them. Telling him he was completely misguided and they were unnecessary and very dangerous.

His sister would be devastated if she found out what was happening to him and thank God his parents were dead because their reputations would likely be ruined.

Police Chief Hillman was waiting to welcome Nelson back as he was brought in through the back door of the Los Angeles County jail that Friday evening.

The murder of the Police Chief's niece had upset him very much. He had spent much of the week consoling his sister, ensuring her that those responsible would be brought to justice.

He really didn't have anything to say to Nelson. He just wanted to see him in person. To know he was back in Los Angeles and in custody.

He told Nelson he would speak to him in the morning.

*   *   *   *

I called Detective Sergeant Stone to see if he could tell me what was going on with Nelson. This was something Simmons might let me write about. He said he'd been flown back here to Los Angeles and asked me if I'd located Shelley yet?

I told him I hadn't but I was really happy to hear that Nelson was under arrest.

SAT AUG 19

At the Los Angeles County jail early on Saturday morning. Police Chief Hillman was face to face with Nelson and didn't beat about the bush. He immediately confronted him with regard to the murder of his niece.

"Martin. I know you are responsible for ordering the murders of at least twenty young women including my niece. We have evidence and witnesses to prove it. Do you have anything to say?"

Nelson said he had nothing to say. He said he still wouldn't when his new lawyer was present and it was his right under the law.

"Well, I guess I'll see you in court" replied Police Chief Hillman.

*   *   *   *

I called Detective Sergeant Stone again on Saturday and he told me nothing had changed. Nelson was still in custody awaiting a bail hearing.

He told me because Nelson's racketeering activities had only taken place in California, the State police were getting involved. He said they were currently getting search warrants to allow them to search Nelson's clubs. They assumed illegal activities were continuing despite his arrest.

He said if we're lucky this might provide additional evidence.

SUN AUG 20

I had been at work writing about Nelson's arrest after getting Simmons blessing.

It was almost midnight by the time I got to Jules. To my great surprise Shelley was sitting at the end of the bar in conversation with Bert.

"Well Hi there" I shouted as I began to almost skip over to where she was sitting saying "So?"

Bert pushed a cold Michelob my way.

"Nice to see you too! If you must know I've been staying with my mother in Santa Barbara. I didn't contact anybody while I was there. I was essentially in hiding" Shelley replied.

"Well believe it or not I am relieved and happy to see you. What happened?" I asked.

"Nelson's guys caught up with me again. This time at my friend's place where as you know I'd been staying.

Looking down into the street I saw a white cube van parked across the street. There were several guys standing around it talking. I figured it was likely one of Nelson's murder teams. So I quickly grabbed my things and slipped out the back" she replied.

"How did you get to Santa Barbara?" I asked.

"It was easy. As you know I don't have a car. So I flagged down the first cab that came by and it took me to the bus station. From there I took the first bus to my Mom's place" she replied.

"So now you're back?" I commented.

"Yep. Just got back yesterday. I'm staying at my friend's place again" she responded "She's out of town."

"If you're concerned they may show up again? Why don't you come out to the motel where I've been staying? I haven't seen any sign of Nelson's guys since I've been out there. By the way Nelson has been arrested and is in the Los Angeles County jail" I said.

It had slipped my mind that my motel room had recently been ransacked!

"I'd like that. I've really missed our early morning get togethers if you know what I mean?" chuckled Shelley.

I said "I was worried about you and you know you still need to go and speak with Detective Sergeant Stone and make a statement. It could really help the case."

"We could go and speak to him tomorrow. Is that okay?" Shelley asked.

"Yes" I responded "You know these have been the craziest weeks of my life. I've almost been murdered, met a girl who later got murdered, met you, almost drowned and have been on a luxury yacht." I was also thinking *I'd had the best lay of my life* but didn't mention this.

"Surely there's more?" Shelley commented.

"Well yes. I guess I tried my hand at marathon swimming, got kidnapped, became known by those running the city, cleaned out a pig pen, spent time in jail and tried to bring a crime boss down" I replied.

"Yes. You've certainly been living dangerously" she responded "So are you ready to come and help me get my stuff?"

I paid the bill and we said goodnight to Bert. He was surprised we were leaving so soon. Arm in arm we left Jules and went to pick up Shelley's stuff.

MON AUG 21

We picked Shelley's stuff up in the early hours of Monday morning and made our way to where I was staying. We quickly got reacquainted, so to speak. Until the sun began to shine in through the cracks in the curtains.

*   *   *   *

That morning Nelson had his bail hearing and was on live video from the jail.

The Los Angeles County and State of California public prosecutors explained to the judge the crimes Mr. Nelson was charged with were much too serious for him to be granted bail. Also if found guilty he could face the States death penalty.

They said they also considered the accused, Mr. Nelson, to be a potential flight risk. They said as it was he had already been arrested in France where he had a luxury yacht in St Tropez on the French Riviera.

They said there were no guarantees he wouldn't leave the city, state, or country again. They also said he had part ownership of a private jet and helicopter.

There wasn't much Nelson's defence lawyer could refute in the prosecution's submission. Except to say if his client was returned into custody they would be appealing to a higher court on his behalf. Not much of a threat or bluff given the serious charges against Nelson.

Nelson's bail application was denied.

* * * *

Monday lunchtime Shelley said she was going to get some ice and just as she stepped out the door a volley of gunshots rang out.

The door to the room was half open and the gunshots had been very loud. I peered out from behind the curtain and saw Shelley's body lying in a pool of blood out on the porch.

As I was getting over the shock my immediate thought was *there goes the case against Nelson because it relied heavily on Shelley's testimony.*

It was amazing how quickly Shelley had been murdered once she'd come out of hiding.

I was scared to leave the motel room in case the shooter was still outside and began to hear police sirens off in the distance. The fact I was so scared upset me no end after all I'm a crime reporter and someone I knew had been murdered right outside my door.

Within a matter of minutes the police had arrived and cordoned off the area around where Shelley was lying. Based on the fact her body had been covered with a dark plastic sheet it must mean no vital signs had been found.

I closed and locked my door knowing it wouldn't be long until a knock came. I had little time to figure out what to do or say. Surely I needed to tell the truth that Shelley was staying with me but then why hadn't I approached the police as soon as they'd arrived?

I decided it wasn't too late. I unlocked and opened the motel room door. I could see a policewoman standing nearby and went over and began to speak to her. She acted like she didn't want to hear what I had to say.

"I know the woman who was killed. She was staying with me" I said.

"Oh! Just stay here please" she said as she headed off towards a group of police officers. Almost immediately an older looking cop turned and began to head in my direction.

When he reached me he said "Hi, I'm Sergeant Paul Williams. Do you have any identification?"

Here we go again I thought. I reached into my back pocket to get my wallet. I took out my drivers license and handed it to him. He jotted down some details in his notebook and handed it back to me saying "Thank you Mr. Walsh."

"I understand you knew the deceased?" asked the Sergeant.

Oh know I thought *he's talking in past tense so she must be dead.*

"Yes. I knew her. She has been staying with me since early this morning" I replied.

"So you can help us identify her?" asked the Sergeant.

"Yes. Her name is Shelley" I replied.

"Last name?" asked the Sergeant.

I responded that unfortunately right at this moment I can't remember.

"So what kind of a lady friend was she if you only know her first name? "asked the Sergeant.

"It's not like that" I said "I just can't remember it right now. I'm still shaken up and not thinking too straight."

"Okay. Her name is Shelley. Do you have an address for her?" asked the Sergeant.

I said "She lived in west Hollywood. I have her address and phone number written down somewhere. She has been staying at a friend's place downtown near where I work at the Los Angeles Times."

This didn't register with the Sergeant who asked me "Do you know anyone who would want to kill Shelley?"

I couldn't help myself and burst out laughing.

"Did I say something funny" asked the Sergeant looking somewhat perturbed.

"Where do I start. Have you heard of someone called Martin Nelson?" I asked.

"No" responded the Sergeant.

"Well this is going to take a while then. Do you think we could continue talking about this in my room? It's this one here" I said pointing to the open door.

"This is so you can tell me who might have wanted to kill her?" asked the Sergeant.

"Yes. But I need to explain what has been going on with her and me and tell you who is very likely responsible for her death" I replied.

"Give me a minute" said the Sergeant as he started to head over to where the other police officers were still huddled waiting for Forensics and the Coroner to arrive.

He returned almost immediately with a young officer who he introduced as Officer De Santos and said he would like him to sit in on our conversation. The two police officers got comfortable sitting at a small table while I perched on the end of one of the beds.

I began "Shelley used to work for this guy Nelson who your associates downtown are very familiar with. Detectives Howell and McShane, Detective Sergeant Stone and even Police Chief Hillman know all about him."

"Hold on a moment" said the Sergeant writing their names down."

I said "Nelson is currently in police custody in the Los Angeles County jail. By the way I remember Shelley's last name it's Green.

Nelson is the owner of the Desperado Gentlemen's Clubs downtown if you've heard of them?"

"I have" responded Officer De Santos.

I continued "He has on occasion tried to have me killed and for your information I'm Harry Walsh the Los Angeles Times crime reporter."

It didn't register with either of them. They obviously didn't read the Los Angeles Times.

"He has also been trying to kill Shelley who until this weekend had been in hiding. It was me who suggested she come and stay here with me" I said.

"We get the idea. You were both scared that this guy was going to kill you. Well it looks like he got to Shelley first. Do you have anything else to add?" asked Sergeant Williams.

"Not really but you understand what's been going on" I said.

"Yes. Thank you for this information" replied Sergeant Williams.

"Please just make sure you speak to the detectives downtown they know all about this guy" I said as the Sergeant and Officer De Santo were leaving my room.

Not trusting these cops to do what I suggested. I immediately called Detective Sergeant Stone to tell him that Shelley had been murdered. He immediately let out a "Oh No" knowing like me that she was needed in his attempt to get Nelson convicted.

I told him I had made a statement to the attending officers at the crime scene. He didn't seem to be very interested in this knowing his case had just been blown right out of the water. He thanked me for the information and said he would get back to me but I got the feeling he never would.

The bad news soon reached the District Attorney who was of the same opinion as myself and Detective Sergeant Stone that without Shelley they didn't have much of a case.

After being notified about the news. The District Attorney notified the Mayor who said "Who?" playing dumb. The Mayor told the District Attorney to let the Police Chief know because the name might me something to him and hung up.

With Shelley having been murdered. I figured Nelson would be coming after me next even though she would have been the better witness. I should have known when I began to pursue him that I was playing with fire and might get burned.

If the Los Angeles Police Department had been reluctant to go after Nelson where did that leave me? One thing I knew for sure was I needed to find somewhere else to stay.

I looked out of the window and could see that the police and Forensics people were surrounding Shelley's body.

I quickly gathered up what little stuff I had and put it in my backpack. I took Shelley's unopened suitcase and put it in my trunk. I went to the motel office and paid my bill. I then got into my trusty old Buick and drove off to find the southbound on ramp onto the Pacific Coast Highway.

I obviously needed to keep a low profile but wasn't sure where to go. I thought perhaps I could find a motel midway between Los Angeles and San Diego. After driving for almost an hour, south of Mission Viejo, California I found a Motel 6 and checked in.

I left Shelley's suitcase in the trunk thinking *I'd get it to her mother somehow.* All I wanted to do right now was to get what had just happened out of my mind.

The first thing I did was phone Simmons to let him know where I was and to tell him I would be working remotely for the foreseeable future.

He said he understood the situation now that Shelley had been murdered.

I was thinking *people like Simmons are always in the know no matter what's going on.*

I had decided to leave Los Angeles for sure now after what had just happened to Shelley. With her murder I realized Nelson was playing for keeps and there was no doubt his guy's would be gunning for me next. For sure I'd stuck my nose in where it wasn't wanted.

The next thing I did was phone my old boss at the Chicago Tribune but was told he no longer worked there.

I still had a few friends there so phoned and got through to an old buddy who gave me the name of the person who had taken over from my old boss. A woman who I didn't know.

*   *   *   *

Everyone in the Los Angeles County jail already knew Nelson was in there. They knew what he was capable of so were treating him extremely well, especially those working there.

When Osvaldo visited Nelson he got word of the successful hit on Shelley Green and immediately knew the District Attorney's case against him had been shot to pieces.

When he thought about it. *It was a good way to put it.* His chances of walking free were now almost assured.

Nelson said "I think the time has come to eliminate that reporter too. My life has been hell recently because of him. He needs to be found and killed."

Osvaldo replied "Leave it to me boss. I'll take care of it."

"Good. I will leave it to you. Make sure you let Lenny know so he can cover for you. You know I could ask Jimmy the Fixer to get one of his murder teams to get rid of him?" said Nelson.

"No boss, two murder teams already failed to kill him. Let me take care of it" replied an adamant Osvaldo.

"Okay. Okay. You do it" responded Nelson somewhat agitated.

As he was leaving Osvaldo mentioned what had happened to him and Brian the morning Nelson had swam ashore.

He said he and Brian had been released the next day because they hadn't been charged with anything. They were picked up in Toulon and taken back to the yacht where they found Ron making arrangements to disperse the crew. Once back on-board Brian arranged everyone's flight back home.

All the systems on the yacht were shutdown. Everyone boarded a tender and were taken ashore. This included Valentina wearing her evening gown and high heels. Once ashore she got into the first taxi that came along and disappeared.

The local crew were either picked up by their wives or friends once ashore and the rest of us including Ron and Brian were driven to the Nice airport in a minibus and flown home via Paris.

Brian told me to continue to maintain your house with the full staff until it is known what is going to happen to you.

"That's great" said Nelson "That's just what I want."

"I haven't seen Brian since we got back and Ron hasn't come around either" commented Osvaldo.

"That's okay. I think they are both scared that they will be charged as accessories to my alleged crimes and are staying away for now. I'm confident you can keep things ticking over until I'm released. Have the police been around?" Nelson asked.

"No and there was no Monday meeting today although everyone showed up and found out what had happened to you" offered Osvaldo.

"The Monday meetings need to continue. Tell Estelle that I said she should chair the meetings from now on until I get back" Nelson said.

"Yes. Is there anything else boss?" asked Osvaldo.

"No. That's all. Just keep the ship afloat until I get back. Thanks" Nelson replied.

Sitting in his cell Nelson's thoughts drifted back to the time when he had joined an American crew when they sailed Big Fish II over to the Mediterranean.

At the time he had hired the best crew money could buy and insisted he come along too.

But even this most experienced crew it turned out were more than challenged by the North Atlantic that summer. Everyone Nelson had talked to before he set sail had said it was a piece of cake to cross the Atlantic during the summer months. They said the sea would be as calm as the surface of his own pool on a hot day.

The Atlantic that July turned out to be just the opposite. From what he had learned later. A hurricane that had started off the west coast of Africa had come further north than any other hurricane over the last two decades or even longer. It had come north skirting the island of Bermuda. The warm waters at that time of the year further fuelling it's fury.

Without a doubt it had been the most frightening experience of his life. At the time he thought he was going to die. Although both of his luxury yachts had been certified ocean worthy. A hurricane does not respect a piece of paper.

They had left Marina Del Rey and headed south down the west coast of the United States to the Panama Canal. He was really excited to be going through the Panama Canal and surprised to see how narrow it was in some places. Especially for the huge multi-story cruise ships ahead of them who only seemed to have a few feet on either side.

After getting through the Panama Canal he figured it would be plain sailing but as they got north-east of Bermuda they encountered the ferocious storm which they later found out was a hurricane. The swells and waves were monumental.

Once the storm or hurricane had passed the sea became calm and they continued to enjoy the rest of the voyage.

Once across the Atlantic they made their way into the Mediterranean Sea past Gibraltar. Along the coast of Spain past Barcelona. Onto Marseille in France before reaching their destination in St Tropez.

TUES AUG 22

That Tuesday morning Osvaldo and Gordo, one of his most trusted bodyguards, started the hunt for me. They had begun by staking out the Los Angeles Times building where I worked.

They didn't know I'd told Simmons that I wouldn't be in the office and that I was working out of a motel in Mission Viejo.

*   *   *   *

I was somewhat worried about the company Simmons sometimes kept. The power brokers at the highest level of Los Angeles society. I was beginning to think *that they perhaps wanted me gone as much as Nelson did.*

*   *   *   *

After Osvaldo had seen no sign of me he decided to phone my office. Once he was put through from the main switchboard all he got was my voicemail which didn't give anything away.

Next he asked to be put through to my supervisor. When Simmons answered in a deep authoritarian voice and asked who was calling Osvaldo panicked and hung-up.

After his experience on the phone Osvaldo told Gordo he was going to go into the building to see what he could find out about my whereabouts.

Once inside the building Osvaldo went to the security counter and was told to take a seat while the security officer tried to locate me.

After several minutes Osvaldo was informed I couldn't be found. Osvaldo got up and went over to the counter and asked one of the security guys if they kept records of who was in the building?

One of them responded saying "We only track visitors, not employees so this doesn't help"

Osvaldo thanked him and made his way out of the building. He walked back to the car empty handed and after getting in asked Gordo if he had any ideas?

"It looks like we're not going to find him where he works any time soon" responded Gordo "I think you should let the boss know. He might have some ideas."

"I can't do that. I told him I'd take care of it. If I ask for help he'll ask Jimmy the Fixer to find him and kill him. No. We need to find him ourselves" said Osvaldo angrily.

"Okay" replied Gordo.

"I think later we should check out the bar I've heard he goes to late at night after he gets off work but right now let's go and get some sleep" suggested Osvaldo.

* * * *

After getting search warrants. California State police officers visited some of Nelson's Desperado Clubs. They interviewed the managers and some of the staff, taking down any information they could glean.

They were amazed at how much cash there was in the clubs.

*   *   *   *

Just before midnight Osvaldo and Gordo parked around the corner from a bar called Jules. When they went in they found it to be almost empty.

There were a few people sitting at the long bar watching television and a guy sitting in a booth reading a newspaper.

I wasn't there.

Osvaldo and Gordo went over to the bar and Osvaldo asked the barman if he'd seen the reporter from the Los Angeles Times. He said he had heard he was often in here.

Bert said he hadn't and asked Osvaldo if he and his buddy wanted a drink?

Osvaldo said "No" and asked him if he knew where he could find me.

Bert suggested he should try the Los Angeles Times where I worked. Osvaldo thanked him and he and Gordo left and headed back to Pacific Palisades.

Osvaldo knew Nelson would soon be asking him how the hit on the reporter was going so he needed to locate him sooner rather than later.

WED AUG 23

Early Wednesday morning Police Chief Hillman and Detective Sergeant Stone were sitting in District Attorney Greg Hanley's office. They were discussing if there was any way forward with the case against Nelson. Especially now Shelley Green had been murdered.

Hanley asked "Let me understand what evidence you have against Nelson?"

"We have the statement from the Los Angeles Times crime reporter Harry Walsh which has been corroborated by a Miss Carol Bromley and a guy working at the Marina Hotel" said Stone.

Hanley said "Yes. You know I'm still trying to get my head around what this was all about. Maybe one of you can help me?

Firstly. How did Walsh. Posing as someone else. Come to be on Nelson's yacht?

Secondly. Why did he jump overboard?

Thirdly. Why was he kidnapped as such and do we have any proof of this?"

"I'll have ago at answering the questions" replied Stone.

"Your first question. From what I understand. Walsh had been told by Shelley Green that Martin Nelson was behind the murders of young women. She also told him Nelson was responsible for other illegal activities here in Los Angeles.

Walsh had met Cindy Samuels after she had almost been abducted. A few days later when he found out she'd been murdered. He was so mad he decided he would try and get some evidence that could be used against Nelson to try and bring him down.

In order to do this I understand Walsh setup a meeting with him. Nelson suggested it be on his yacht. I don't know what was discussed but this is why Walsh was on his yacht. Why Walsh was posing as someone else I don't know but this is not really about Walsh. It's about Nelson.

Second question. I guess jumping off Nelson's yacht was perhaps the only way Walsh could escape after his plan had obviously gone wrong. Why it went wrong I don't know because I don't even know what the plan was.

Thirdly. We have surveillance video of Walsh arriving and twenty-four hours later leaving Nelson's house. Whether he was being held there against his will. Is his word against Nelson's." said Stone.

Hanley replied "The way I see it. Walsh's story provides a whole lot of nothing. Certainly, there is no evidence we can use against Nelson. I don't think any of this could even be considered as circumstantial. What else do you have?"

Stone said "We have Walsh's statement about following one of Nelson's murder teams out to where the body of a young woman was dumped near the Chatsworth Reservoir."

"From what I understand you weren't able to trace this back to Nelson in anyway. In fact you were never able to find the van that was involved unless it is the one you recently impounded" replied Hanley.

Stone said "We have some forensics evidence from the van that was impounded but nothing we can trace back to Nelson.

We also have evidence collected at each crime scene which we are still trying to connect to Nelson.

I'm not sure where the State police are with their investigation. I've heard they have been to a number of Nelson's Desperado clubs."

"I understand so far no one is talking at any of them" replied Hanley.

"Gentlemen. If this is all we have right now we have no choice but to drop the charges against Nelson and release him" said Hanley.

"Are you sure?" asked the Police Chief.

"Yes. It seems you and the State police haven't been able to turn anybody or directly link Nelson to any of the murders or illegal activities. I hate to tell you this. But the defence lawyer I hear Nelson has hired. Bill Saunders. He will just chew up what we have so far and spit it back at us. Sorry" replied Hanley "Good day gentlemen."

*　　*　　*　　*

Osvaldo and Gordo were back sitting outside the Los Angeles Times building in the hope that I might show up. But I hadn't.

Osvaldo knew he didn't have much more time before Nelson would expect the job to be done. So as a last resort Osvaldo decided he would go and meet with the person I worked for. Because surely he or she would know where I was.

Osvaldo told Gordo he was going back to the building and while he was gone he wanted him to sit tight and keep watching out for the reporter.

Upon entering the building he told a lone building security guard, who he hadn't seen before, that he had been urgently trying to get in contact with a reporter called Harry Walsh since yesterday.

He said he hadn't had any luck and wanted to speak to his supervisor.

"Give me a minute" the security guard said and he made a phone call.

While on the phone he asked Osvaldo what it was concerning?

Osvaldo said "He contacted me looking for information for a story he was working on."

The guard relayed the information to Simmons who was in two minds about how to respond.

He was aware of Walsh's tenuous situation but on the other hand was always looking for something to print that might sell copies of the newspaper.

So when he got off the phone he asked his assistant to go down and bring the guy up and when he was ushered into his office and he saw Osvaldo he became immediately concerned.

He was a big muscular brown skinned man, almost brutish looking.

"Hi I'm Mike Simmons. Please take a seat. I here you are looking for a reporter?" he asked.

"Yes for Harry Walsh. Do you know where I can find him?" asked Osvaldo.

"Can I ask why you want to speak to him?" Simmons asked.

"He wants some information from me" growled Osvaldo.

"Well Harry is off on leave at present" he replied "You can give me the information if you like?"

Osvaldo got up and shut Simmons office door. As he turned around Simmons could see he had a gun in his hand.

Osvaldo looking very agitated said "I need to know where he is? You must be in contact with him because his column is still being printed sometimes."

"You know these strong arm tactics aren't going to work with me. If you kill me you will never find him because I think I'm the only one who knows where he is.

Why don't you stop playing games and tell me why you are really looking for him. Could it have something to do with your boss Martin Nelson?" asked Simmons in a defiant voice.

This left Osvaldo with nowhere to go and he put the gun away.

Simmons said "I know you want to find him to kill him like you killed Shelley Green. But I'm not going to give him up."

"That maybe. But right now we're going to go for a ride. So get up" demanded Osvaldo.

"I'm not going anywhere with you" replied Simmons.

Osvaldo was at a loss about what to do when his mobile phone rang.

By now Nelson was wondering how he was doing and had phoned him to ask him to come and see him.

When he ended the call Osvaldo told Simmons that was his boss on the phone asking me if I'd found your reporter yet.

Seeing Simmons office door had been closed for quite a while his assistant came over and knocked on the door and Simmons shouted "Come in." His assistant entered and asked if she could get him or his guest anything?

Simmons said no they didn't need anything and asked her to ask Neil Collins Head of Security to come and see him and his assistant quickly left.

Osvaldo was most uncomfortable knowing security were on their way and didn't know what to do knowing Simmons was his only hope of finding Walsh.

Neil Collins soon arrived and Simmons said "Hi Neil. Would you please escort this gentleman off the premises. Thank you."

Osvaldo stepped forward and said to Simmons "We'll need to meet again very soon to discuss this matter."

Osvaldo was ushered out of Simmons office and escorted to the elevator and out of the building.

He was most upset and wondered if it had been a mistake to tell Nelson he would take care of the reporter. But he wasn't going to give up.

He went back to the car and asked Gordo if he had any ideas and predictably he said he didn't.

"Okay. I've got an idea" said Osvaldo.

* * * *

After Lenny picked Nelson up from the Los Angeles County jail. Upon arriving home he found his support staff lined up waiting for him outside his front door. Brian and Ron weren't there.

Miraculously he had only been in police custody for eight days in St Tropez and Los Angeles.

Rossini had been informed of Nelson's release but given their agreement wasn't planning to go after him again especially now Valentina was home safe.

Others were most unhappy about Nelson's release, especially Brian. He felt the criminal justice system had failed miserably and figured he would now have to take his own revenge.

The Police Chief was upset too but would have to accept District Attorney Hanley's decision.

I fully understood the lack of evidence problem. I had failed to get any against Nelson myself and knew Shelley's murder had ended any hope of convicting him of anything.

The State police hadn't found any official paperwork in their searches of Nelson's clubs. Instead just a few hand scribbled notes and codes and dollar values on odd sheets of paper.

THURS AUG 24

I'd decided to leave the motel in Mission Viejo early on Thursday morning. As I was putting my backpack in the trunk next to Shelley's suitcase, I heard gunshots ring out and felt the wind as a bullet whistled past my left ear.

I'd obviously tried to make my getaway too late. It looked like they were on to me. I looked around and could see someone peering out from behind a curtain and prayed they'd call 911.

As I crouched behind the rear wheel of my car I could see two men hiding behind a dark Lincoln town car parked close by.

As it turned out Fred the motel owner had called 911 as soon as he heard the gunshots and I began to hear police sirens getting closer all the time. Osvaldo knew he and Gordo had lost the advantage of surprise so climbed into their car and drove off.

Within seconds a police cruiser had arrived and two police officers had rushed into the motel office with their guns drawn.

This was my que. I closed the trunk. Backed up and quickly drove off hoping the town car wasn't waiting for me just up the road. It was nowhere in sight. I headed for Interstate 15. This was it. I was on my way to Chicago. My time in Los Angeles was over.

I noticed I needed to gas up and drove around until I found a gas station that was open twenty four hours. While I was standing at the gas pump a dark Lincoln town car pulled up beside me.

As the drivers side window was rolled down I could see the familiar face of Osvaldo.

He quietly whispered "I hope you are leaving Los Angeles so I can tell my boss I killed you? If not you're a dead man right here and now!"

"I'm leaving for sure. Don't worry" I said. Guaranteed!"

"We'll follow you just to make sure" mumbled Osvaldo.

I finished gassing up, paid and drove off to join the Interstate.

I took the on ramp and the town car continued along the service road that ran parallel with the Interstate until it came to an end.

Although going after Nelson had perhaps been crazy. I still felt I had tried to do the right thing. Trying to at least do something to help get justice for Cindy.

I saw a sign for Las Vegas, settled into my seat and lit up a cigarette. I figured I'd let Simmons know where I was when I reached Chicago. My motel bill was not a problem because I'd paid a month in advance.

I still had Shelley's suitcase in the trunk so now would have to courier it to her mother whenever I got her address. Detective Sergeant Stone probably had it by now given she was the next of kin.

I began to think about how Osvaldo had found me but still couldn't figure it out.

*　　*　　*　　*

When I called Simmons about a week later.

He told me that Nelson's men had been waiting for him when he left the Los Angeles Times building late the night before he heard I'd left. They told him he was going for the ride he had been promised.

Simmons said they bundled him into the back of their car and after reaching their destination, an old deserted factory, his arms were stretched around a pillar and his hands handcuffed.

His captors. The big guy and his friend immediately started asking questions about your whereabouts.

Simmons said he held out as long as he could, taking many body blows until he couldn't take it anymore.

He had hoped he'd be able to tip me off before they got to me. But as it turned out they left him handcuffed to the pillar and he wasn't found until two days later.

*　　*　　*　　*

The morning after his release Nelson was back doing laps in his pool when he heard voices and swam over to the edge and could see Brian and Ron walking towards where he was.

As they got closer he could see Brian was pointing a gun at him.

"What the hell is this? What are you doing?" asked Nelson, squinting up to where Brian and Ron were standing.

"We're going for a ride" said Brian continuing to point the gun at Nelson.

"What are you talking about?" asked Nelson looking up from the edge of the pool.

"We realize what we've been doing all these years has been exhilarating and challenging but it has been wrong, very wrong" said Brian.

"Especially this year with all the senseless murders" calmly offered Ron "That's why I told you we're out. What you did to Brian is unforgivable. I can't even imagine the hate he must have inside for you."

"So what's with the gun? Are you planning to shoot me? Murder me?" asked Nelson as he started to climb out of the pool.

"Don't get out. Stay in there" said Brian waving the gun at him.

"Let's talk for awhile" said Brian standing above him "You know when we first met you had just become an investor in a struggling start-up adult movie company which not long after collapsed. Then I suggested the escort business to you.

I know it was you who ran it and made it into something, but it was me who convinced the women to try it and who got you most of your clients. Then we come to the drug business.

Once again it was me who connected you with the dealers I knew and now you're a billionaire and what thanks do I get? You rape the woman I'm in love with and was about to marry!

I was hoping the criminal justice system would take care of you. But it didn't so now what Ron and I have in mind is probably an even better outcome."

"What are you talking about?" asked Nelson.

"Lenny!" Nelson shouted as loud as he could.

"He's not here. We arranged a day off for him and cancelled this morning's bodyguard shift too. So it's just the three of us, apart from the guys on the gates" said Brian.

"Just us? Me in a swimsuit and you holding a gun. So what happens next?" Nelson asked.

"We're going to go for that ride. Ron's going to drive and you're going to be in the trunk.

So get out of the pool and make your way to where Ron's car is parked" said Brian.

"Can I get toweled off and put a robe on?" Nelson asked.

"No. You are fine just the way you are. Now get moving" Brian said poking him in the back with the gun.

In bare feet dripping wet Nelson made his way to Ron's car. Ron opened the trunk and Nelson climbed in. Brian closed it leaving him in almost complete darkness.

Nelson knew he should never have slept with Brian's fiancé but felt he shouldn't be murdered for it.

The pig farmer had just got up and was in the kitchen making coffee when he heard a car pull up out the front.

He made his way through to the front room and peeked out through the curtain and could see a shiny new Cadillac.

As he kept watching. Two men, one he recognized, got out of the car and opened the trunk. His almost naked benefactor, who he knew only as Marty, got out.

This was it.

He quickly ran and grabbed his shotgun and made his way out onto the back porch and waited. He was holding the double barreled shotgun across his belly his finger on the trigger.

As the three men rounded the corner of the farmhouse, the one he recognized, started to shout something but the pig farmer didn't hesitate and let the two men pushing Marty ahead of them, have it with both barrels.

Blood, flesh and bits of bone flew everywhere. Still in one piece Nelson lay flat on the ground his arms covering his head.

Although it didn't matter now. Brian and Ron lying dead didn't know Lenny had brought him to visit the pig farmer a few weeks ago to put an agreement in place.

That if he was ever brought there under duress or in a compromising position, the pig farmer was to kill whoever was bringing him there. No matter who it was.

When Nelson had put the agreement in place he had conjectured it would likely be his bodyguards who had turned against him. He never contemplated it might be Brian or Ron or both of them.

The pig farmer had done exactly what he was being generously paid to do and by now was helping the person who he knew only as Marty to get to his feet asking him if he was alright?

There was carnage all around and quite a lot of blood had splattered on Nelson himself.

"Can you get me a towel or something" demanded Nelson.

The pig farmer disappeared into the house and emerged with a multi-coloured beach towel and a dark blue robe.

While the pig farmer had been gone. Nelson had grabbed the keys to Ron's Cadillac out of what was left of his jacket pocket.

After being handed the towel Nelson wiped the blood spatters off his face and body and put the robe on.

"Great job! You sure made a mess of them. I'm sure the pigs will enjoy what's left. Rather them than me. Anyway I've got to skedaddle" said Nelson.

"Don't worry I'll clean up the mess" replied the pig farmer.

"Thanks" Nelson replied as he disappeared around the corner of the farmhouse.

THE END